"I have a new favorite
Close Your Eyes, H
wish I'd been sma
a masterpiece of narrative voice."
—Jodi Picoult

"Chris Bohjalian is a master. . . .
Emily Shepard is his greatest
accomplishment."
—*Los Angeles Times*

"A chilling and heartbreaking
suspense novel."
—*USA Today*

"Enthralling and indelible." —*People*

"Intelligent, rich in detail, filled
with full-blooded characters. . . .
Bohjalian at his finest."
—*The Seattle Times*

"A 'must read' book." —*St. Louis Post-Dispatch*

"Haunting and resonant."
—*The Miami Herald*

Praise for Chris Bohjalian's
Close Your Eyes, Hold Hands

"Emily's character is written so well and her story so absorbing (this is very much a read-in-one-or-two-sittings type of book) that it is easy to forget you're actually reading. . . . *Close Your Eyes, Hold Hands* reminds us of our innate need for connection." —*Pittsburgh Post-Gazette*

"A masterful storyteller. . . . Bohjalian hits every note. His characters have depth, his story sings."
—*The Advocate* (Baton Rouge, LA)

"Bohjalian delivers a thoroughly engrossing and poignant coming-of-age story set against a nightmarish backdrop as real as yesterday's headlines from Fukushima and Chernobyl. And in Emily he's created a remarkable and complicated teenager . . . [with] a wry, honest voice as distinctive as Holden Caulfield's." —Associated Press

"Dazzling. . . . A novel for the ages. . . . This is pure beauty in book form."
—*The Free-Lance Star* (Fredericksburg, VA)

"A potent story of loss, hope, and the overpowering yearning for home." —*The Armenian Weekly*

"Rings with poetry and truth." —*Library Journal*

"A dystopian nightmare entwined with a wrenching personal crisis. . . . The notion of 'just a life I left' grows more intense for somebody like Emily Shepard who can't return and is unsure about how to go forward."

—*Burlington Free Press*

"[A] brave saga." —*Booklist*

"Impressive. . . . [Emily's] admiration for kindred spirit Emily Dickinson serves to humanize her plight, as does an epiphany in the book's bittersweet conclusion."

—*Publishers Weekly*

"Bohjalian once again reveals an uncanny talent for crafting a young female protagonist who is fatally flawed, but nevertheless immensely likable. . . . Resonates with a message of hope, truth and the fragility of life." —*BookPage*

"Emily's voice is a compelling one . . . and hers is a journey readers will avidly follow." —*Kirkus Reviews*

Chris Bohjalian

Close Your Eyes, Hold Hands

Chris Bohjalian is the author of seventeen books, including the *New York Times* bestsellers *The Light in the Ruins*, *The Sandcastle Girls*, *The Double Bind*, and *Skeletons at the Feast*. His novel *Midwives* was a number one *New York Times* bestseller and a selection of Oprah's Book Club. His work has been translated into more than twenty-five languages and three of his books have become movies (*Secrets of Eden*, *Midwives*, and *Past the Bleachers*). His novels have been chosen as Best Books of the Year by *The Washington Post*, *The Hartford Courant*, the *St. Louis Post-Dispatch*, *Publishers Weekly*, *Library Journal*, *Kirkus Reviews*, *BookPage*, and *Salon*. He lives in Vermont with his wife and daughter.

www.chrisbohjalian.com

BOOKS BY
CHRIS BOHJALIAN

Novels

The Light in the Ruins
The Sandcastle Girls
The Night Strangers
Secrets of Eden
Skeletons at the Feast
The Double Bind
Before You Know Kindness
The Buffalo Soldier
Trans-Sister Radio
The Law of Similars
Midwives
Water Witches
Past the Bleachers
Hangman
A Killing in the Real World

Essay Collections

Idyll Banter

Close Your Eyes, Hold Hands

Close Your Eyes, Hold Hands

A NOVEL   ※   ※   ※

Chris Bohjalian

VINTAGE CONTEMPORARIES
Vintage Books
A Division of Penguin Random House LLC
New York

FIRST VINTAGE CONTEMPORARIES EDITION, MAY 2015

Copyright © 2014 by Chris Bohjalian

The Library of Congress has cataloged the Doubleday edition as follows:
Bohjalian, Chris.
Close your eyes, hold hands : a novel / Chris Bohjalian.—First edition.
pages cm
1. Teenage girls—Fiction. 2. Runaways—Fiction. I. Title.
PS3552.O495C58 2014
813'.6—dc23   2013034613

Vintage Books Trade Paperback ISBN: 978-0-307-74393-0
eBook ISBN: 978-0-385-53484-0

Book design by Maria Carella

www.vintagebooks.com

Printed in the United States of America
10   9   8   7   6   5   4   3   2

For Jenny Jackson
and
Khatchig Mouradian:
Godparents.

For Grace Experience:
Voice.

If I can stop one heart from breaking,
I shall not live in vain;

EMILY DICKINSON

Tell all the Truth but tell it slant—

EMILY DICKINSON

Close Your Eyes, Hold Hands

PROLOGUE

I built an igloo against the cold out of black plastic trash bags filled with wet leaves. It wasn't perfect. The winds were coming across the lake, and the outside wall that faced the water was flat—not like the igloos I had seen on TV somewhere or I guess in a book. It looked like the wall on the inside of a cave: flat and kind of scaly. But the outside wall that faced the city looked round like a melon. I couldn't stand all the way up inside it, but in the middle I could crouch like a hunchback. It was big enough for three people to lie down if you curled up, and one night we had to squeeze in four. But most of the time it was just Cameron and me. I really had to trust the fuck out of someone before I would let them anywhere near Cameron in the night. But, the truth is, people came and went. You know how it is. Especially in the winter. But the igloo kept me warm. Warmer, anyway. I mean, it's not like I got frostbite. I knew kids and grown-ups who did. I knew one kid who got gangrene. They say the doctors had to cut off both of his feet, but I don't know that for a fact because I never saw him again.

I'm going to try and tell you only the things that I know for a fact are true. When I'm guessing, I'll be honest and tell you I'm guessing.

You build the igloos in the day when the leaves are soaked but the ice has melted from the sun, and then they freeze at night inside the bags. So does the water on the outside of the bags; that's why the bags stick together like glue.

....

Some people said I left the shelter because someone must have tried to rape me. No one tried to rape me. I left for a couple of reasons. I mean, I did feel kind of hounded—by the other girls, one especially, but not by the people who ran the place. The "staff." Whatever. One of the girls was starting to suspect who I was, and I knew that once my secret was out, she'd turn me in. I thought she'd want no part of me. And you know what? I wouldn't have blamed her. A lot of days I wanted no part of me.

Also, I knew the staff wanted me gone. Or, at least, they wanted to figure out who I really was. They were getting pretty frustrated because they couldn't find my parents. My story was starting to unravel. So, I just left.

Given that I was always kind of—and here's a pretty awesome little euphemism—a troubled teen, it's a miracle that the counselors who ran the shelter didn't send me packing a lot sooner. It wouldn't have surprised a lot of people who knew me if I really had managed to get myself thrown out on my ass. But I didn't. That's not what happened. I was already plenty scared, and so I tried playing by the rules. I tried to behave. But it didn't work. And so it would be the last time I'd try for a while.

This was back in the days when the city was still trying to figure out what to do with the walkers. Technically, I was a walker, even though I didn't walk. I stole a bike and rode to the city from the Northeast Kingdom. I don't know how many miles that is, but it took me two full days, because I hadn't ridden a bike since I was in, like, fourth or fifth grade. The worst was going up and over the mountains. I just walked the bike up the eastern slopes. That took an entire afternoon right there. One time a guy in a bread truck gave me a lift, but he only took me about twenty miles. Still, a lot of those miles were uphill, so I was grateful. Lots of people—most people—had families or friends in the city or the suburbs around Lake Champlain who could take them in. And people were taking in total strangers. Vermonters are like that. I guess decent people anywhere are like that. But there were still a lot of walkers just pitching tents in City Hall Park or sleeping in their cars or pick-ups or out in the cold, or building their igloos down by the water. Squatters. Refugees.

I guess it would have been a lot worse if Reactor Number Two had exploded, as well. You know, gone totally Chernobyl. But it didn't. It was only Reactor Number One that melted down and blew up.

. . . .

When I was a little kid, I used to take my American Girl dolls and play orphanage. The make-believe stories were always based on *A Little Princess*. The movie and the book. Whatever. One of my dolls would be a beautiful rich girl who suddenly winds up poor and in an orphanage. No mom or dad, no aunts or uncles. Some of the other girls hate her, but some love her. The woman I had run-ning the place was always a total whack-job bully. Think of that lunatic in the musical *Annie*. She was the model. So, I guess, *Annie* was an inspiration, too. When I got bored, I'd simply have the girl rescued. Her dad or her mom and dad would just show up at the orphanage. Boom. Game over.

Sometimes I tried playing the game with Barbies, but that never worked. The Barbies looked pretty hot. If they were going to be trapped somewhere, it sure wasn't going to be in an orphanage. It was going to be someplace way more awful. I know that now, too.

. . . .

My family had a beautiful woodstove. Not one of those black boxes that look like they do nothing but pollute the crap out of the air. It was made of gray soapstone that was almost the color of my mom's favorite piece of jewelry: an antique necklace that was made of moonstones. I think it had once belonged to my grandmother.

It was Danish. Anyway, the woodstove had a window in the front
that was shaped like the window in a castle or a palace. I'm sure
there's a word for that shape, and I will look it up.

My dad or mom would build a fire in the woodstove when we
were all home on the weekend and hanging around in the den.
The den was next to the kitchen, and the woodstove would heat
the den and the kitchen and even the TV room on the other side
of the kitchen. The rooms had baseboards and LP gas heat, too,
of course. The whole house did. It was pretty new. I know now
that a lot of people called our kind of house a meadow mansion
or a McMansion behind our backs, but we didn't build it. We just
moved there from a suburb of New York City when I was a little
kid.

There was a thermostat stuck through a pipe-cleaner-sized
hole in the stovepipe about a foot and a half above the soapstone
box. When we had a fire going, my dad wanted it to be around
four hundred to six hundred degrees. When it got above six hundred, one of us would close up the flue and the temperature would
go down. If it got above eight hundred, you were in danger of a
chimney fire. The thermostat was kind of like a car's speedometer:
the numbers went a lot higher than you were ever going to need.
It went up to seventeen hundred, and you were totally fucked if it
ever got that high. We're talking chimney fire for sure.

My parents' running joke when the woodstove thermostat
climbed above six or seven hundred? It was "Chernobyling"—or
about to melt down. I can still hear my mom's voice when she
would say that to my dad when he would come home from skiing
late on a Saturday afternoon: "Honey, be sure and watch the stove
when you add a log tonight. The damn thing nearly Chernobyled
this afternoon." You wouldn't know it from the things people
write or say about my dad these days, but he could be very funny.
My mom, too. They could both be very funny.

I guess that's why I use "Chernobyl" like a verb.

I don't use Fukushima or Fukushima Daiichi like verbs.

But I could. After all, Fukushima had a pretty fucked-up end, too. And it even sounds a bit like a swear.

. . . .

I don't know why I began my story with the igloo. The igloo was really the beginning of the end—or, maybe, the end of the beginning. Here's a sentence I read about me in one of the hospital staff's case management notes: "Every kinship had fallen away." Well, yeah. Duh. Even Maggie—my dog—was gone.

By the time I was building my igloo, the worst of the shit-storm was over. At least it was for most of Vermont. It wasn't for me, of course. It wasn't for a lot of us from up in that corner of the Kingdom. But it was for most everyone else. By the time I was building my igloo, I was just another one of the homeless kids who freaked out the middle-aged people at the Banana Republic or Williams-Sonoma when they saw me on the street or in the mall in Burlington.

So, maybe I shouldn't begin with the igloo. Maybe I should begin with the posse and the SSI apartment where we crashed. That was a home, too, if a home is a place where you can say you lived for a while. Or I could begin with the Oxies—the OxyContin. Or the robbery. Or Andrea Simonetti, who for a few months was like a sister to me, but now I have no idea where she is and I worry. Or I could begin with Poacher or the johns or the tents with the squatters. Or the shelter—with the girls in the shelter. Or the people who tried to help me. (Yeah, there were sometimes people who wanted to help me.) Or I could begin with Cameron.

Or maybe I should just begin at the beginning. With Reactor Number One.

B.C.

※

Chapter 1

It was the middle of June, and we only had two days of school left. We had one more day of exams and then one day when most of us would either not show up or, if we did, the teachers were pretty chill and didn't mind what we did so long as we didn't get stoned in their face or do something ridiculous that would make them look bad or get ourselves killed. I was in eleventh grade. It was midmorning, and I had just taken my physics final. I did okay, I think, but who knows? Doesn't matter now and, to be honest, I really didn't care that much even then. Besides, I was going to be a poet and a novelist, if only because I figured poet and novelist was a career choice that meant little or no human interaction. I kind of understood at a young age that I didn't play well with most other kids in the sandbox. (Not all, of course. I mean, I had friends. Not many, but a few.) Anyway, I really believed I was going to write great books. I honestly thought like that. I was going to go to Amherst—the town, not the college, because there was no way I was getting into the college—and find out who Emily Dickinson actually was. You know, get the real dish. Discover things about her that no one else knew. Friends. Lovers. A secret society. Not kidding. I thought like that. We had the same first name, and her poems were as short as mine. Hers, of course, were better. But you see my point. There wasn't a lot of logic to the connection. Still, she wasn't hugely social, and we had that in common, too.

Dare you see a soul at the white heat?
Then crouch within the door.
Red is the fire's common tint;
But when the vivid ore

Has sated flame's conditions,
Its quivering substance plays
Without a color but the light
Of unanointed blaze.

Obviously this poem wasn't about a nuclear core. But it could be, right, if you didn't know it had been written in the 1860s? Also, Emily's pure hell on a computer's spell check—and this poem isn't anywhere near the grammatical nightmare that some of her other work is. I used to love that, too.

That day a bunch of kids in the tenth and eleventh grades were just hanging out on the side of the cafeteria with all the windows that looked out on the courtyard, watching it rain, when we heard the sirens from the fire station. The courtyard had a couple of concrete tables and benches where mostly seniors went, especially the smokers, but it had been raining for days—weeks, actually, since Memorial Day weekend—and so nobody was out there now. There were mushrooms growing up between the tiles outside, that's how wet it was. But the windows were open, and so even with the sound of the rain we could hear the sirens. Most of the seniors had peaced out by then because they were done with high school and knew what they were doing in September. A lot of us usually got out, you know. People outside the Kingdom think we're all dumb shits up here, and a lot of us are; but a lot of us aren't. I went to Reddington Academy, which is named after the town, and was built and funded years and years ago by a guy named James Howard Haverford. He fought in the Civil War and then made a fortune making sewing machines. Every kid in Newport and Reddington and Barton and Lowell goes to the Academy for free, like it's a public school, but it's also a pretty expensive boarding school and students from something like seventeen states and a couple of countries come here every year. There are about four hundred locals and about two hundred boarders. Or there were. The school is still closed and will be pretty much forever.

It was ten o'clock in the morning, so they weren't serving lunch yet. I was sitting on the table and kind of flirting with a boy named Ethan Gale, who was sitting on the bench. I was wearing pretty tight jeans and I had kicked off my sneakers, so I was barefoot. I don't know why, but being barefoot always made me feel very sexy. Think poet. We were talking about a couple of local girls who worked after school at this nearby fitness club and, looking back, being kind of snarky. But the two of them sort of didn't know what they were doing and just sat behind the front desk where gym members were supposed to sign in. If someone dropped a boatload of weights on his chest or something, he was completely screwed, because those girls sure as hell wouldn't have known what to do. I mean, they were perfectly nice, but what the hell they were doing working at a gym was completely beyond Ethan and me.

Ethan was a junior and, like me, he was a local. His dad was the Eye on the Sky—the meteorologist for Vermont Public Radio—which meant that Ethan was kind of a celebrity because his dad's voice was super well known. But it also meant that we gave Ethan cascades of shit because even a very good weatherman is wrong, like, half the time.

My dad sometimes joked about that. "What a great job," he would say. "Imagine if pilots only had to be right half the time. Or doctors. Or architects. But the guys who try and forecast the weather? We sure cut them a lot of slack. And no matter how many times they're wrong, we still tune in." See what I mean about my dad? We used to have some very impressive fights—not nearly the shouting matches I used to have with my mom, but still pretty gnarly—but he really was kind of funny.

And, of course, he was very smart. I agree with him about the weather. With all the satellites and stuff we have orbiting the earth, I have no idea how you could ever get the weather wrong. Really,

I don't. And doesn't the weather usually just move from west to east? Frankly, I'd think you could just call some town a few hours away in New York or Ontario and ask what the hell was going on outside the window. But technology is what it is. It doesn't always work. Exhibit A? A nuclear reactor, apparently.

I always figured Ethan was going places. Maybe he still is. Maybe, like me, he kind of gave up. I should make a note to see if he's anywhere on Facebook. I should make a note to see if lots of people are anywhere on Facebook. I haven't been super social the last year—even less than before the meltdown, if that's possible. I know Ethan's dad is no longer on the radio; they have a new Eye on the Sky. But that might only be because VPR doesn't broadcast from the Fairbanks Museum in St. Johnsbury anymore. St. J. isn't in the Exclusion Zone, but it's close. Lots of people left, most of the town, they tell me.

Anyway, I knew instantly what the sirens were, but I figured it was just a drill. We'd had one a couple of years earlier. A pretend evacuation. Still, even those "this was just a drill" moments on the radio that the FCC requires could always make the hairs on the back of my neck stand up. I remember Ethan looked in the general direction of the firehouse and then in the direction of the plant.

"What do you think that's about?" he asked.

The sirens were loud, but not so loud that we had to raise our voices or anything. We could still hear three serious overachievers from out of state freaking out about physics, and a couple of drama geeks making a very big deal about some summer musical in Stowe one of them was in. Everyone stopped talking for maybe a second or two when the sirens started and looked around, and then went right on with their conversations.

It was only when Mr. Pettitt, a history teacher, came into the cafeteria and clapped his hands to get our attention that we shut up. Most kids liked Mr. Pettitt, and a lot of them even called him Brandon—his first name. I wouldn't. I wouldn't call him anything. He kind of rubbed me the wrong way. I thought he was totally bogus. He was in his early thirties, and he had a cute wife and twin baby boys. He had curly blond hair, and I know there were girls who had a crush on him, but obviously I wasn't one of them. Two things happened at almost the same time when he clapped. First, everyone looked at him, and then, once he said there might be a problem at the nuclear power plant, everyone looked at me. Second, Ethan handed me my sneakers.

"You better put them on," he said.

"You think?"

"Yeah," he said. "I think."

By then, of course, the crisis at the plant had been going on for roughly two and a half hours. I'm sure someone caught some serious shit for waiting so long to sound the alarm.

. . . .

The Northeast Kingdom got its name a long time ago from a Vermont governor. It was, I think, a way to promote tourism. It's the northeast corner of the state and, even by the standards of Vermont, crazy rural. But there are a couple of ski resorts and Lake Memphremagog, which is nowhere near as big as Lake Champlain. Not long after one Vermont governor nicknamed this part of the state the Northeast Kingdom, another one convinced the state legislature that Memphremagog was the perfect spot for a nuclear power plant, especially if it was built beside one of the rivers that fed the lake. Some people had been talking about constructing a plant on Lake Champlain, about ten miles south of Burlington. Can you imagine what kind of cluster-fuck disaster this would have been if the plant had been built there and had the same accident? God. People actually live in Burlington. Hundreds of thousands of people must live in Chittenden County and around Lake Champlain. Fortunately—there's a weird word for me to use— they chose Memphremagog instead. It was just big enough, and the river current was just powerful enough for a nuclear power plant, especially after they built a special dam.

And you know what? None of us really cared that we had a

nuclear power plant. I mean, there were some folks who made a little noise after Fukushima. A few politicians and a few do-gooders with nothing better to do asked for a study of the evacuation plan and an investigation into the state of the reactors because they were pretty old. (How old? The plant was designed in the 1960s with slide rules—yup, slide rules—and built in the early 1970s.) But it was really no big deal. And it sure wasn't our *local* politicians or our *local* do-gooders. I mean this: *None of us cared.*

The plant existed along a spit of land covered with pine trees called Cape Abenaki (that was, as a matter of fact, the official name of the plant), where the Coburn River met the lake. The plant was a quarter mile downstream from the dam. You couldn't even see it from Newport or Reddington, unless you were out in the middle of the lake or almost over onto the Canadian side of the water. And then, when you did see it, it was just a part of the shoreline. People used to ice-fish within maybe three hundred yards of the two long lines of cooling towers. People used to kayak within a stone's throw of the two big rectangular blocks that housed the reactors themselves. I swear, no one thought about it until the meltdown. It was like the prison. We didn't think about that either. They both gave people jobs. So, we boated and swam and fished in the lake, sometimes noticing the plant and sometimes not. We figured it was perfectly safe.

Or, if it wasn't perfectly safe, it was safe enough.

. . . .

My mom, who had always been in public relations, thought the name of the plant was really pretty and really exploitive. "It speaks to the proud heritage of the Native Americans in the United States and Canada," she would say publicly, and then add (but only in private), "and the way we screwed them in every way possible." That's because nuclear power might be clean (except for when it's spewing radioactivity like a Roman candle), but uranium mining is seriously toxic. I don't know precisely how it poisons the water, but it does. One night I saw my mom looking at an article on the computer in the den about the way the uranium mines have fucked the Crow, the Odawa, the Algonquin, and the Sioux.

"What's that?" I asked her.

"Propaganda."

"Oh."

"But it's really not."

I waited.

"It's our bargain with Mephistopheles. Unfortunately, radioactivity lasts as long as the soul." I really didn't know what she was talking about until I shared this memory with one of the doctors here, and he told me the story of Faust.

. . . .

A couple of months after the meltdown, when I was living in Burlington, I almost told Poacher who I was. He just thought I was one of the walkers who had streamed into the city. I think I wanted to see what he'd do if I told him. Would he freak out the way I always suspected the girls in the shelter would have, or would he be chill? Instead, at the last second, I told him that my dad was Ethan's dad. You know, just lied. I said my dad had once been the Eye on the Sky.

"Abby," he murmured, flat on his back on the mattress on the floor, "you are a revelation." Poacher was long and lean with thick dark hair he combed straight back off his forehead. His eyes were a little narrow, but otherwise he could have been an over-the-hill movie star—one of those dudes who was a leading man once but had managed to drink and party himself into early retirement and now only got work on TV shows like *Celebrity Apprentice.* He had sideburns that somehow didn't look ridiculous and a goatee and mustache that were just this side of creepy. He had a tattoo on each biceps: barbed wire on his left arm and a marijuana leaf on his right. He had a leather vest that he was very—and I mean *very*—fond of.

He was staring up at the ceiling when he said I was a revelation, stoned off his ass, and he thought I was stoned, too. I wasn't. But he sure did use that word a lot. *Revelation.* It was one of about half a dozen words that peppered his vocabulary and seemed unexpected until you got to know him and realized what a total loser he was and why he used them. "Why are you not more fucked up?" he asked me. He meant generally—not why wasn't I as baked as he was right that moment.

"I think I am pretty fucked up," I said. *Really, if you only knew,* I thought.

He must have been forty-five, which meant he was about the age my parents had been. That also meant he was more than twice as old as the rest of us—three times as old as some of us—and some nights he had nine or ten of us crammed into his apartment. It was pretty squalid, because there was only one bathroom and one bedroom and no beds at all. There was hardly any furniture at all. He said he was a war veteran on disability, which was where he got the money for the apartment. He said he had liberated Kuwait and he said it like he had done it single-handedly. Yeah, right.

"No," he reassured me. "You are not fucked up at all. You have a future. I will see to that."

"You will, will you?" I was, as my mom would have said, dubious.

There were two other girls who were, more or less, passed out on another mattress in the Pink pajamas we'd lifted that afternoon from the Victoria's Secret in the mall. One was Andrea, and she'd been a cutter even before all hell broke loose in Vermont. Still was, of course. A nuclear meltdown changes people—and I don't mean radiation sickness or *Twilight Zone* kinds of mutations in babies— but it sure as hell doesn't make a cutter *stop* cutting. Especially a cutter who's now doing OxyContin and Percocet. God, the whole world becomes fucking anxious when there's a meltdown. Anyway, Andrea was eighteen, two years older than I was back then. One of her eyes was closed, and the other was open just a slit. She had just done a little of that hillbilly heroin and was really content.

"Do your dad again," Poacher said, his eyes closed. When I had told him my dad was the Eye on the Sky, I had mimicked the voice we all knew on the radio.

"It's not that good an imitation," I said.

"Oh, it is. It is. It is . . . awesome." He put his hand on my knee and tried to run it up toward my thigh, but I put my fingers on his like I wanted to hold his hand and stopped him. Then I pretended to be the Eye on the Sky and made up a weather report. I made up one from the days before the accident, when it just rained and rained and eventually—and here is some of the nuke-speak the plant experts and engineers like my dad just loved—there was a LOOP: a loss of off-site power. There was an SBO: a station black-out. In plain English, there was a flood. It was one of those once-every-five-hundred-years kinds of floods, someone said. Then lots of people said that. Then it was the once-in-a-millennium flood, because that sounds way more epic. It sounds downright biblical, doesn't it? But it's not subtle. It's not poetic.

> But no man moved me till the tide
> Went past my simple shoe,
> And past my apron and my belt.
> And past my bodice too.

See what I mean? That's what you do with high water.

On the day of the Memphremagog flood, the waters poured over the Coburn River Dam and climbed up and over the sides of the brooks and rose from the marshes. It wasn't a tsunami, but people who were there said it sure felt like one. Officially, the dam was breached at 7:31 in the morning. The lake and river water flooded the rooms where the diesel generators were kept and so the diesel generators failed. The water swamped and short-circuited the power lines that led to the plant, which cut the electricity to the pumps that must always—and I mean always—circulate coolant water through the reactors. That meant Cape Abenaki had maybe four hours of life left: the length of time the batteries would last.

My father and the engineers who worked for him had that much time to restore power and get the pumps back online. They didn't make it. The reactors began to overheat.

By then it had been raining for two solid weeks, of course, but that dawn it was raining something like four inches an hour, especially between five and seven a.m. If my dad was concerned, he'd never said anything around me in the days before the disaster. I don't remember my mom saying anything either until that very morning. My dad had already left for the plant when I came down for breakfast that day. My mom said he had left sometime in the middle of the night. And I could see as I ate my Cheerios that she was worried. (Cheerios. What a weirdly happy memory Cheerios have become for me. Eating them once upon a time had just seemed so normal.)

The last time I ever saw my dad had been the night before. The last time I ever saw my mom? That morning. She actually went to work, though I'll never know if she went knowing the dam had been breached. But I think she did. I think she went knowing that she was doing something that was either very stupid or very brave. I opened the back door and let Maggie, a shelter dog that looked a lot like a black Lab but was really a mutt, run into the woods way behind our house to poop, and watched for a moment as she wrestled with a piece of birch bark that was at the edge of our lawn. She didn't play with it long because she never much liked the rain. She was nine and very, very sweet. In the winter she slept in a dog bed we kept near the woodstove, but in the summer she slept on the window seat in my bedroom.

After I let her back inside, I went to school, took my physics final, and went to the cafeteria. Then I watched the world—at least the corner where I had lived since I was a little girl—go completely to shit.

Chapter 2

It would be months before I would meet Cameron. Or, I guess, before I would find Cameron.

Here's the weirdest part: I had always completely sucked as a babysitter. I just wasn't into it. I really wasn't into kids. When I was in sixth grade, I took a babysitter's course at the library in Reddington. It was my mom's idea, not mine. (Yeah, we fought about that, too. But I went.) It met once a week after school for six weeks, and it taught us things like what to put in a babysitter's bag. The woman teaching it, who was kind of like the social workers I'd meet when I was older but was also seriously New Age, said we should put a flashlight and first-aid stuff in a special bag we would always bring with us when we had a job. (And by "first-aid stuff," she meant Bactine and Band-Aids, not iodide pills.) She also said we should include things to entertain little kids. So, while mine did have a couple of Band-Aids, mostly I wedged picture books and little paperbacks like *Junie B. Jones* and *Bunnicula* into it. I stuffed paper dolls and Barbie dolls (lots of Barbie dolls) and Magic Markers into it. It was kind of retro. I also put in a lot of my dress-up feather boas. I don't know why. My dad said it was so I could tie the kids up when they misbehaved. Nope. As you can see, I was a lot more comfortable babysitting little girls than little boys. As I recall, I didn't have the slightest idea how to entertain little boys. The few times I babysat a boy it was always Michael Dinnan, and I just plopped him in front of his Xbox and let him go to town killing things and blowing shit up.

My favorite moment from that babysitting class was when one of the other girls taking the course with me asked the teacher, "What happens if you die?" My second favorite was when another sixth grader told us, "My mom says to stay out of the high school band closet. You can get pregnant in there." When I told my mom and dad that at dinner that night, my dad nodded and said, "Well, then: under no circumstances will you ever be babysitting in the high school band closet." It gave us all a pretty big laugh. (I guess I could tell you the names of those two girls, but they're probably both still alive, even though one lived in a house that was pretty close to the plant. So I won't.)

Looking back, it seems totally crazy that it wound up Cameron and me against the world. I mean, it's not like I had an Xbox to sit him in front of while I figured out what the hell we were going to eat or how we were going to stay warm.

. . . .

So, the sirens. I put on my sneakers, and Ethan and I were herded with everyone else from the cafeteria. We started toward the lockers to get our backpacks, but we weren't allowed. They said there wasn't time. Mr. Pettitt and Ms. Francis, who was one of the guidance counselors—she was always talking to me about my "potential" and how I wasn't living up to it—instead ordered all of us outside into the parking lot in the front of the school. Other kids were already there, and I could see a long line was climbing onto the first of seven school buses. I remember I was kind of pissed because I had my period, and of course my tampons were in my backpack. I asked Ms. Francis if there was any chance I could run back inside to get it, but she was pretty freaking tense and ignored me. She shoved me ahead into the lines with the other kids, and even though it was pouring, most of us didn't have our raincoats or hoodies or anything. We were all soaked and—for reasons I didn't understand at the time—that was causing a few of the teachers outside with us to seriously wig out. And whenever any of us would try to find our own school bus, one of the adults would just scream at us, telling us we were wasting time, it didn't matter, we were just to get on the next bus in line.

It was right about then I noticed that it wasn't even our regular drivers behind the wheels of the buses. The bus in front of Ethan and me, which we just missed getting on, had some young guy driving who Ethan said was a volunteer firefighter from Newport a few years older than us. The volunteer looked pretty stoked, like driving this school bus was the most important thing he had ever done with his life. And the bus we got on had a middle-aged guy in a National Guard uniform behind the wheel.

Meanwhile, the sirens just kept screeching. And, of course, it wasn't just the one at the Reddington firehouse. It was every firehouse in the county. It was the sirens at the plant.

Even before we got on the buses and saw it wasn't our regular drivers, the rumors were insane. Some people were saying there had been terrorist attacks in Boston and Montreal, and one boy was telling everyone that a plane had crashed into Cape Abenaki, just like the planes that had crashed into the World Trade Center years ago. And some kids were still saying—hoping, really, you know, whistling past the graveyard in the dark—that it was just a practice evacuation. Especially the other kids whose moms or dads worked at the plant. (Looking back, I find it interesting that my parents weren't friends with most of the families who worked at the plant—and so neither was I. Obviously they hung around with a few of the other employees, but the only close pal my dad had among the other engineers and managers was a guy named Eric Cunningham. Hours after the meltdown, late that afternoon, Mr. Cunningham would kill himself.)

But we had our phones so we were all checking the news, and pretty soon it was the news itself that was firing the rumors. By the time Ethan and I found seats in the middle of one of the buses, we knew that something seriously awful was happening at the plant. Some girls started crying and asking me what was going on, like I'd actually have a clue, and whether the worst reports we were reading or watching on our phones were the accurate ones. But how could I know? I called my mom to see what was going on, but she never picked up. I sent her a text and never heard back. Same with my dad, but I never really expected to hear from him. I figured he was up to his ass in whatever nightmare was going on.

Still, not hearing from my mom was what started to freak me out inside. I tried to keep it together, because I didn't want to get as dramatic as those other girls, but it was hard. Supposedly, there was a flood at the plant and the power was off. Some people thought that meant there was nothing at all to worry about, while others were already talking meltdown. One boy whose dad worked at the plant was debating with one of our science teachers the difference between a meltdown and a melt-through, like this was just a regular, everyday physics class.

But, in fact, none of us really knew anything. And us kids? We didn't even know where we were going.

....

I'm an only child of only children. It's not as weird or as rare as you might think. My parents always said that they had loved being only children and, until Cape Abenaki, I don't think it had any effect on me one way or another. (I mean, yes, I had what one therapist called "behavioral issues," but they had nothing to do with being an only child. If they had to do with anything, they had to do with the hardwiring inside my head and the fact my parents hated Vermont, drank too much, and sometimes fought like fisher cats.) As a matter of fact, being an only child might have worked for me even after the reactor blew up. Who knows? Yeah, I was seriously alone afterward. But those first months when all hell was breaking loose? I was in no condition to take care of a younger sister or brother. If I'd found Cameron back then, in the early days? It wouldn't have been pretty. I don't know, maybe it would have been nice to have had an older brother or an older sister at the time. Or a twin. Sometimes I wondered what it would be like to have a twin.

But aunts or uncles or cousins were what I needed, I guess. I had two grandparents still alive. My mom's mom and my dad's dad. But my grandma was deep into the shadows of Alzheimer's by then. The last time I had seen her had been about three months before the explosion. She lived in a place for people with Alzheimer's in Hanover, New Hampshire, and she couldn't even find her way out of the bathroom by the time I was in eleventh grade. And my grandpa lived in Phoenix, Arizona. That's where my dad grew up. My grandpa had had a colostomy the year before and wasn't coping real well with it. He was also in an assisted living place.

Still, on some level I was also really angry in those months after the meltdown. Really pissed. Way more pissed than usual. That's pretty clear. The truth was, I felt deserted. I felt unbelievably alone, but not in a playful "I'm nobody! Who are you?" sort of way. I just knew I had no one. Not a soul. Even my Maggie was gone. It didn't matter that my parents hadn't made a conscious decision to peace out on me. It's not like they were at some spa in Montreal or Venice or someplace.

And, of course, I was terrified. It was like the end of the world.

About a month after the explosion, when things were starting to settle down for most of New England, I was watching TV at this bar on Main Street in Burlington. I wasn't actually in the bar because I knew I smelled awful and I looked pretty sketchy. I was outside on the curb. But this was July, remember, and so this big awning was open and I could stand there on the sidewalk and look in at the TV behind the bartender—a pretty handsome dude in his mid-twenties. He had red hair, and it was pulled back in a ponytail with a blue rubber band. A lot of guys can't make that look work, but he sure could.

On the TV screen was a map of something the newswoman was calling the "Exclusion Zone." She was explaining that nothing had been decided yet, but it looked like there was going to be an exclusion area around Cape Abenaki. It was more of an oval than a circle, because the wind had been blowing northeast, and the anchor said it might be as large as thirty square miles. There had been some sort of presidential decree, and the whole area was going to be under military control for a while. (Translation? Forever.) They said there were people's pets—dogs and cats—left behind and running wild inside the zone, and of course I thought of Maggie. The truth is, I thought about Maggie a lot. Maybe I thought of her as often as I thought of my mom and dad. Sometimes, when I'd imagine her trapped inside our house, slowly starving to death, I'd get a little sick and hope for a miracle: Maybe my mom had let her out before she left for the plant. Maybe my friend Lisa's mom had rescued her. Of course, even if Maggie was outside, that didn't mean she was going to be okay. She still might starve to death. She still might die of radiation. She still might get eaten herself by a coyote or a wolf. A couple of times I considered texting Lisa to see if she knew if Maggie was okay, but what if she wasn't? What, at that point, could anyone have done? Besides, I didn't want anyone to know where I was. I wanted to remain anonymous.

Anyway, as big as thirty square miles sounded, it really didn't look that huge on the map—and a part of it was Lake Memphremagog. Of course, it did include most of my world when I was a kid. All of Newport and Reddington were in the middle. The woman on TV said they were in the "black" zone. And Barton and Lowell were in something she was calling the red zone. But then there was the issue of the rivers. There were three of them, the Clyde, the Coburn, and the Black. In theory, they all flowed north into Lake Memphremagog. But it's impossible for people outside of the Kingdom to look at a map of Memphremagog and not assume that all that water is flowing south. And so when people were talking about the Exclusion Zone in the beginning, they often talked about the plume and the rivers. In the end, it was mostly the plume that mattered. Besides, no one was going to fish in those rivers again: everyone figured the trout would all have three and four eyes and glow in the dark.

As far as I know, the fish never did glow. But by the next spring there would be some super-scary, super-gross mutations. There were frogs with three legs. There were turtles with shells as soft as damp pastry dough. There were fish with strange, funky lumps. I saw the photos on the web and one day in a newspaper—which, you can bet your ass, I hid from Cameron.

. . . .

The word for the kind of window on my family's woodstove was "Palladian." I told you, I'd look it up.

. . . .

One night Andrea showed me her kit, and the first thing I thought was this was a really twisted version of my old babysitter's bag. I didn't watch her slice herself, at least not that night, but she showed me the cuts. I think she thought it would turn me on and then, maybe, I would cut myself, too. You know, join her or something. Which, I guess, I did.

We were sitting on the mattress we shared on the floor at Poacher's, and she was wearing nothing but her underwear and a T-shirt that said "War Is Over" and had one of the Beatles and his wife on it. She'd lifted it from the Urban Outfitters on Church Street the day before.

"This is what you do," she said, and she sounded like a very confident kindergarten teacher. *Children, this is the way you clean up your blocks. This is how you do it.* You know the tone of voice. She was sitting cross-legged, and she pointed to the insides of her thighs. It was like a cat had scratched her over and over, or maybe a much bigger animal with much bigger claws. Long, swollen red marks, some pretty new and some pretty well healed. There were some scars, too. Most were on her left leg because she was right-handed. One of the cuts was infected: it was straight like the others, but bloated and raw and there was a pretty gross discharge. Her kit had old-fashioned razor blades and an X-Acto knife and Band-Aids and a bottle of hydrogen peroxide. There was a roll of gauze. There was a tube of Bacitracin. There was a pair of scissors. She kept her tools in a very elegant Estée Lauder cosmetics bag she stole from Macy's. That was her kit.

I make it sound like we were always stealing stuff. I guess we were. Sometimes we stole things just because we wanted them, like that T-shirt with the Beatles guy on it, and sometimes we stole stuff because we had to. Either we hocked it for money for food or drugs or we hocked it for money for Poacher. Sometimes if we didn't feel up to fucking the guys he brought over, he wouldn't make us if we gave him roughly the same amount of cash. Then he'd have another girl do the john—you wouldn't think Vermont guys are gross because the state is so "peace, love, and tie-dye," but I'm telling you, they can be as gross here as anyplace else—and he'd have twice the money to feed us and get us whatever drugs we wanted.

Andrea's mother and father used to deal out of their apartment in the North End until they were both arrested and sent to jail. She told me that when her mother was badly strung out, her dad would make her do seriously creepy stuff before he would give her a fix. Once he made her do another drug mom while he watched—just for kicks, he did that. Another time he brought her out to some physical therapy place and had her fuck his cousin. (At least that was for money.) Andrea had left home by the time the two of them were busted. Like everyone else, she had no idea that my dad was one of the engineers at Cape Abenaki who the NRC blamed for fucking up and helping to cause the meltdown.

That night when she showed me her kit, I said to her something kind of ridiculous like, "Do you know how bad for you that is?" Obviously, she knew how bad for her it was. That's one of the main reasons why she did it. "Do you really want to go through life with all those scars?" I asked.

She tried to hand me a razor blade in its little cardboard folder, but I wouldn't take it. "Let me show you how," she said.

"No."

"Why? Because it will hurt?"

"Yeah, for starters," I told her. But she pulled the blade from its packet and dropped it into my hand. I thought the metal was very pretty in an engineered sort of way. I'd never held one like it before. All my razors were plastic and pink. They all sounded like sex toys. Venus Vibrance. Close Curves. Bikini Trimmer.

"It will only hurt for a second. And then you'll feel great. Besides . . ."

"Besides what?"

"Even the pain is, I don't know, cool. It's out-of-body. You'll get a rush, I promise."

"Not interested."

"Try it!"

The fact was, I had already tried a lot of shit and nothing really worked. So why not try this, too?

"Where?" I asked.

"Take off your pajamas."

"No, I'm not wearing underwear."

"Since when did you get all modest on me?"

I shrugged and pulled off my pajama pants. Maybe I was scuba diving for the bottom of the sea. Still, I scooted an extra foot away from her so I'd have a little privacy. I pressed the razor blade on the inside of my thigh, pretty high up—close to where my underpants would have been. I'd figured out that the point was to cut yourself where no one would see. But I only pushed it against my flesh, and I didn't quite break the skin. I couldn't bring myself to do it. So, Andrea did it for me. Before I could stop her, she took my wrist and the back of my hand and in one almost instantaneous motion yanked my fingers down toward the mattress. She moved so fast, I couldn't stop her. It stung—not a huge surprise, I know—and I yelped. I pushed her away, and then together we peered down at the pencil-thin line about two inches long. For a second I didn't understand why it had hurt so much because I didn't seem to be bleeding. Then, like a creek bed filling with water after a summer storm, the narrow little gash started to swell. As if we had never before seen a cut bleed, which of course we both had (though she a lot more often than me), we stared at it. We watched some blood trickle down my thigh onto the mattress. I wondered how long it would bleed if I did nothing. I wondered how big the stain would be on the mattress.

Andrea spoke first. "You won't need any hydrogen peroxide," she said. "That was a brand-new blade."

"Just a Band-Aid?"

"Yup." Before she gave me a Band-Aid, however, she took the scissors and cut off a square of gauze. She pressed it very tenderly against the cut, and I was so stunned that I had let her do this whole thing in the first place that I didn't stop her, despite how close she was to the edge of my pubic hair. After a minute she took her fingers away and handed me a Band-Aid. The pad wasn't as long as my cut, but it would do.

"Feel any better?" she asked.

"I don't know," I answered, which was the truth. I mean, I knew I felt ashamed. But that would pass. By then I did all kinds of crap that left me feeling ashamed. I just didn't know if I felt—to use her word—better. Maybe I did. Maybe I hated myself a little bit less.

When I was a little girl and we still lived just outside of New York City, my parents said I would punish myself. When I misbehaved as a toddler, they had a "time-out" chair for me. It was a little wooden ladder-back chair, meant for a two- or three-year-old. I guess it had once belonged to my grandfather—my mom's dad, not my dad's. We kept it in a corner of the dining room. But my parents said they almost never had to put me there. I would put myself there. Most of the time, they had no idea what I worried I had done wrong. I was a very well-behaved tyke. At least they thought I was. Apparently, I thought differently.

So who knows? Maybe all along I was ripe for cutting. Anyway, that was the first time.

....

Did you know that the little kids in Syria who have been fucked by the civil war only want to color with red crayons? They almost always draw people with some kind of bullet wound or stab wound or injury from a grenade or a mortar. I can't remember where I read that, but I'm pretty sure it's true.

Chapter 3

One time I keyed a boy's mother's car. I got in pretty serious trouble for that one, but I am going to plead extenuating circumstances. (My parents had a friend who was a public defender, and one time when she was at our house for dinner, she said that a lot of her clients' stories began, "It's a long story." She said nothing good ever comes from "a tale of woe"—her expression—that begins, "It's a long story.")

It was a Saturday evening and I was fifteen. I had just spent the day in New Hampshire at Story Land, which is sort of like Disneyland except it's a million times smaller and still in the 1950s. But it has a few cool rides, and it was always fun to watch the little kids who didn't care that Cinderella's pumpkin carriage had an engine as loud as a snowmobile and the paint on the metal horses was seriously chipped. I had gone there with a seventeen-year-old boy named Philip Christiansen, and it was kind of like a first date. His family was from New Jersey. It was the summer before his senior year and the summer before my junior year. His dad was like forty-five, but already retired. Not kidding. He had been some kind of hedge fund manager—I honestly have no idea what a hedge fund is, except that it's clear if you run one you wind up with more money than Jay Z, and supposedly Jay Z has crazy money—and the family had moved to northern Vermont so he could ski and ride his bike most of the time. Not all of the time. Sometimes he would fly to Tampa or Phoenix or New York to meet with people about "the fund." And they still had that house in New Jersey and an apartment in New York City. When they were deciding where to chill in New England, they chose Reddington because of the Academy.

Philip and I had had a pretty good time that day at Story Land. Definitely promising, I thought. But then I blew it.

The two of us parked his Prius in the driveway beside his mom's Beemer SUV and his dad's Mercedes. (That's what I mean about how loaded they were. They also had a pickup truck to bring their garbage and recycling to the transfer station and a tractor for who knows what.) Then we went inside for sodas because we were parched from the two-hour drive back to Reddington. His family's Vermont place was a farmhouse they had transformed into something that looked like a museum home with velvet ropes and signs that said a president had slept in one of the beds. His mom was in the kitchen when we got there, and she was bent out of shape. I don't know why, but she seemed pretty PO'ed at the world. So Philip whispered to me that we should just split. But his mom pulled me aside.

"Have you given my son the gas money?" she asked.

I had no idea what she was talking about. Gas money? I was all, what the fuck? Who does that? But I didn't say anything.

"Mom, I didn't even ask her," Philip said. Then he kind of shrunk a little and mumbled, "Yet."

Here they are with Gringotts Goblin Bank piles of money, and his mom is pressing me for a few bucks for gas. "It's a hundred miles from here to Story Land," she said. "I checked." And she was standing there with her arms folded across her chest, leaning against this stainless steel refrigerator big enough for a moose.

"I don't think I have any left," I mumbled. I had brought money, of course, but I'd spent it already. I had maybe a crumpled-up dollar bill on me somewhere. So, you can see how awkward this was. But I can deal with awkward. What I can't deal with is getting hissed at for being "inconsiderate" and trying "to take advantage" of her son. Her precious Philip. I was embarrassed and I didn't get why. And I was royally pissed—way more PO'ed by the time we left than Philip's mom.

Now, a normal girl would probably have just gotten in Philip's car and gone home. A normal girl would probably have just steered clear of that whole whack-job family. Not yours truly. As part of the celebration a few weeks earlier when I had gotten my learner's permit, my dad had made me a set of keys to our car. So, I had them on me. As we walked past his mom's robin's-egg blue Beemer SUV, I stopped and said to Philip, "I think I'm going to owe your mom for a little more than gas." Then, right there in their drive-way, I took my car key and keyed in the letters FU on the passenger door and scratched away as much of the paint as I could before Philip stopped me.

I think I'd made my point. But my parents took away my keys for a while and my phone for a week, and I was grounded for almost the rest of the summer. And Philip and I never went on a second date, and we totally avoided each other when school started again in September.

Still, see what I mean about extenuating circumstances? I was a jerk, but so was Philip's mom.

....

I knew the school buses were driving southwest. I knew we were on Route 100. I wondered how far away they were going to take us. Some of the kids were stunned and super quiet, and some of the kids were going on and on about what they were reading about the disaster on their phones. I was seated against a window, which was filthy because of the rain, and I was glad Ethan was on the aisle between me and the next kid. Still, I had a girl named Sara from my history class in the seat behind me, and she knew my dad worked at the plant. She knew my mom and my dad both worked at the plant. It was why we had moved to Reddington when I was four. And she kept pestering me, asking me questions, and was even getting a little hysterical.

"How bad is it?" she kept asking me. Or, "Did your dad say anything this morning?"

"I didn't see my dad this morning."

"Did he say anything last night?"

"No."

"Did—"

Finally Ethan turned around and asked her to chill.

I held my phone in my lap, but I didn't open the browser to check the news. I just kept waiting and waiting for a text or a call from my mom or dad, which, of course, never came.

....

They brought us to Johnson State College and put us in the school's dining hall. By then we all knew that the crisis was bad and getting worse, because we had been on the bus for, like, forty-five minutes. All the news reports about the power outage and the batteries couldn't be wrong. People kept saying to me, "They'll fix it before it melts down, right?" I tried not to lash out, but a few times I did. I mean, how was I supposed to know?

We also knew from our texting that kids from other schools had been evacuated, too, and had gone to places like St. Johnsbury and Hyde Park and Stowe. At the college dining hall with us were kids from an elementary school in Barton. Most of them, especially a lot of the kindergarteners and first and second graders, didn't know enough to be really scared, and it seemed to me that their teachers were doing a pretty good job of keeping them from freaking out. There were a few girls who were crying, but they were clearly drama queen ten-year-olds—like the sixteen-year-old drama queen I had riding on the seat behind me on the bus.

I have no idea how they decided which kids would go where and why they put a high school in Reddington with an elementary school from Barton. Like everything else in those first hours, the grown-ups had to make decisions on the fly about us, and sometimes they made good decisions and sometimes they just fucked up. But it was fine. I think the older kids kind of liked having all of those little kids around. I saw a ninth grader from the Academy meeting up with his younger sister and brother, who went to Barton Elementary School. It was really sweet.

....

I found a bench against a window and tried calling the main line for the power plant, but I got nothing but busy signals. I tried my mom and dad, but I only got their voice mail recordings. Finally I stopped leaving them messages. Outside the dining hall it continued to rain and some of the branches on the pine trees moved up and down in the wind like Oriental fans. Ethan sat with me for a few minutes, but then my friend Lisa Curran found me. Lisa was one of the few girls whose families would have been there for me if things hadn't started falling apart for us all so fucking fast. I didn't have a lot of friends, but I had Lisa. She wanted to become a country music singer and was actually a pretty good songwriter. She had a beautiful voice. Her dad was an airline pilot, and when he was gone for three and four days at a time, I used to hang out at her house a lot. Actually, I would hang out with her and her mom, who was a librarian. She was a friend, too, I guess. Their house, like my family's, is now in the middle of the blackest black in the Exclusion Zone. They probably won't ever see it again. Or, if they do, it won't be for a very long time, and when they go they'll be wearing those hazmat suits you can still see people wearing sometimes at the edge of the zone when there's a rainstorm. They stand out there with their Geiger counters measuring how radioactive the rain is.

Anyway, Lisa sat down next to me and so Ethan figured he could take a breather from watching out for the zombie whose parents worked at Cape Abenaki.

"It's probably not that bad," Lisa said.

I looked at her. "And you think that . . . why?"

She shrugged, but she wouldn't meet my eye. "They're just taking precautions."

"Any minute now, the reactors are going to start melting down," I said. "Or, for all we know, they already are." I realized after I spoke—actually verbalizing what most likely was happening—that I was on the verge of seriously losing it, of seriously falling apart. It would only take a little push to move me from catatonic to hysterical. And, of course, that push was coming.

"But probably no one's going to die," she murmured. Then she reminded me of something Mr. Brodard, our chemistry teacher, had talked about the year before in the environmental sciences part of our chemistry class. While people died all the time working in coal mines, it was rare for them to get killed at nuclear power plants. There had been Chernobyl, of course. But he insisted that no one had died at Fukushima Daiichi and no one had died at Three Mile Island.

But sometimes you just know things. You really do. I don't know if it's instinct or intuition or we're just connected in ways that science can't explain. But I knew in my heart that Lisa was wrong. This time, up at Cape Abenaki, people were going to die.

. . . .

I find myself making connections between words that are usually completely ridiculous—the connections, that is. I do this a lot with Emily Dickinson's poems.

> *I can wade grief,*
>   *Whole pools of it,—*

You'd think it would be grief that would be the link for me or "grief" would be the word I would fixate on. Nope. That would be way too normal. It's "pools." I associate it with the spent fuel pools at nuclear plants. That's where you have serious radioactivity.

And then I imagine the pools of water that must have been flooding Cape Abenaki, first in the hours before the explosion and then after. In the beginning, the water is just murky. One time, the Reddington Library, which is right on the banks of the Clyde River, flooded: the first floor must have had three feet of water in it. I was maybe five years old and hadn't lived in Vermont all that long, but I remember well how a lot of the children's books were ruined because they were on the lowest shelves. That's what I think of when I first think of the flood: all those picture books. The next day my mom and Lisa's mom were helping with the cleanup and I was with them. The books were brown and waterlogged and smelled like the bottom of the river. Most of them had to be taken to the transfer station in the back of pickup trucks. Lisa's mom was working hard to hold back her tears, but as I recall she was still crying a lot. It wasn't her library, but it didn't matter. She was devastated. We were all devastated. It was really sad to see all those ruined children's books. Especially the bunny books, which I had always loved when I was a little kid. *The Runaway Bunny. Pat the Bunny. The Velveteen Rabbit.* They were all covered in brown crap and smelled horrible. It was awful. When I think of the water that flooded parts of the plant, that's what I suspect it was like: just muddy and swamplike and annoying, but not dangerous.

But then I think of the water in the spent fuel pool when it started to boil. And *that* water is a million times worse than annoying. It's freaking terrifying. *That* water is whole pools of grief.

They tell me, in the end, the pool boiled dry.

....

Cameron wouldn't let me call him Cam. "Cam" sounded too much like "Pam," which of course is a girl's name. "Cameron" sounds very regal, but it's really not. It's Gaelic and means "crooked nose." I told him that once after I had looked it up, and he laughed. His nose was tiny and covered with freckles.

He was—and I promise you, I am not making this up—a kind

of amazing duct tape artist. On our first day together he showed me one of his most prized possessions.

"It's a robot," he mumbled when I didn't say anything right away. I think he was afraid I didn't like it. I did like it. I thought it was from a museum store in Montreal or Boston and someone had bought it for him or he'd lifted it. It was about the size of a Barbie doll, but bulkier. It was a beautifully sculpted piece of modern art: a creature that was a bit like a Transformer, but even more colorful, if that's possible, and it was made entirely of cut and wound duct tape. I had no idea that duct tape came in so many colors: we're talking flower garden crazy, including purple and orange and highlighter yellow. When I asked him where the robot came from, he got very defensive and told me that he made it. I was impressed, in part because I am a total loser when it comes to the visual arts. I mean, I practically failed pottery in tenth grade, and you had to have hooks for hands to fail the pottery class at Reddington. It was the gut of all guts.

"You made that?" I said. It wasn't really a question, but I was so awed it came out that way.

"I'm not lying!"

"I didn't say you were lying. I just think it's awesome."

Quickly he put it back in his bag. He had long fingers for a little boy, and his nails were so feverishly gnawed that they were almost nonexistent. Over the next few months, he'd show me more of his duct tape creations. And to pass the time, I'd lift rolls of tape from the hardware store and he'd make new things. There was one night in the igloo when he was killing time by decorating this plastic horse we found in the garbage—it only had three legs—and I loaned him one of the razor blades from my cutting kit. (By then I had one of my very own.) He was a little weirded out that I had a blade like that, and maybe handing one to a nine-year-old wasn't the most responsible move on my part, but my biggest worry was that he would wonder what the fuck I was doing with that kind of blade. Obviously, I never wanted him to know I was a cutter. But he was careful. And by the time he was done with the horse, it looked like the sort of psychedelic animal you're supposed to see when you're tripping. (I say "supposed to see" because I know I never saw anything like that.)

We also read a lot. Yup. Crafts and reading. That igloo was just like a home school, right?

I remember one time I stole a copy of *Anastasia Krupnik* from the library to read to him, but already he was a little too old for it. Also, he was a boy. He was definitely more of a *Johnny Tremain* or *Harry Potter* kind of kid. I took the first *Harry Potter* when I brought back *Anastasia Krupnik* (which I really did return), and I read it to him so many times that I had the plot totally memorized. Okay, maybe not totally memorized, but pretty close. One night after we lost the book, when we were in the igloo, I told him the whole story, scene by scene, and he repeated back to me some of Ron's or Hermione's best lines.

There was another week when I read to him nothing but Louis Sachar's *Sideways Stories from Wayside School*. They were crazy fun and Sacher wrote lots of them. Also, the books were these little paperbacks that were very easy to lift.

....

My mom was the communications director for the plant. (You'd think someone who was in charge of communications and her daughter, an aspiring writer, would be better at communicating. In hindsight, we both just sucked, which is too bad.)

That meant my parents were—and this was a pun that was used to describe them in an article in the *Burlington Free Press* years before the accident—"Vermont's power couple." The article was very nice. It didn't say anything snarky about nuclear power. A few months later, tritium was found in a groundwater monitoring well at a nuclear power plant in New Hampshire, which suggested there was a leak at that plant somewhere. The newspaper interviewed my mom again, and this time the paper wasn't so kind. My mom was annoyed that she even had to talk about it because the New Hampshire plant was three and a half hours away from Cape Abenaki and she had nothing to do with it. But it was the same kind of boiling water reactor as Abenaki and built about the same time, and so I guess it made sense to ask her about it.

Tritium is a radioactive isotope of hydrogen. That's probably more than you need to know. All you really need to know is that it's radioactive.

. . . .

Obviously I made some bad choices. I'm still here, however, so I made some okay ones, too. But leaving the dining hall at the college when I did? That was bad. I get it. Looking back, trying to get back to Reddington and find my parents and Maggie was the chain reaction that started everything. It's that whole butterfly effect. If I had just stayed where I was and waited like everybody else, I have to believe that social services would have found someplace for me. Or one of my friends' families who wasn't homeless would have taken me in. People blamed my dad but no one was going to blame me, right?

Yes and no. There were a lot of people who wanted nothing to do with me. I wasn't radioactive, but I might as well have been. Look at the way that girl at the shelter treated me when she began to figure out who I might be. Look at what I overheard at the staging area. Look at what happened at that convenience store on my way into Burlington.

But none of that matters now because I did leave the dining hall that day. Like I said, I was on the verge of hysteria all morning and early afternoon. What finally pushed me over the edge? Around one o'clock, one of the news sites said there had been an explosion at Cape Abenaki. Another said there had been two. Both reported that there were fatalities, perhaps as many as seventeen, which they said was an indication of the size of the explosion—or explosions—because no one had been killed when a reactor had blown up at Fukushima. And, of course, everyone was talking meltdown. Everyone—in the news and in the cafeteria—was talking about plumes of radioactive fallout and the rain and the direction of the wind. And so I realized there was a chance that my mom and dad were injured or possibly dead—and a lot of folks in the cafeteria probably knew this but hadn't figured out how to tell me. I mean, seriously? Was no teacher willing to man up and break the news? Were none of my friends—not even Ethan or Lisa—willing to drop the bomb? I get it, I really do. They were all worried that they were now homeless. Or at least a lot of them were. And they were all worried about their own loved ones. Their moms, their dads, their dogs. Who knew how bad it really was, despite what Mr. Brodard had said in chemistry? People panic.

And, just so you don't think that I'm some kind of whack-job paranoid, I don't believe there was a conspiracy not to tell me my parents might be dead. I think, to be honest, everyone figured someone else would tell me. I'm sure Ethan and Lisa figured that one of the teachers would tell me—one of the "people in authority." In my mind, I can almost see Mr. Adams, who worked with Ms. Francis in the guidance department, whispering with my English teacher, Ms. Gagne, beside the water fountain against the brick wall. I can almost hear Mr. Adams saying, "You know her best. I'll come with you. But you know her best." Ms. Gagne was only about ten or twelve years older than me and liked me to call her Cecile. She worried about my behavioral issues and my underachieving, but I think she figured I'd pull myself together and be fine in the end. Maybe she thought I was a good writer. Maybe not. Maybe she thought I was a good writer but eventually I'd just put my head in the oven and there was nothing she could do. Anyway, I think a lot about that moment in the cafeteria. Maybe, if they did speak, it was more like Ms. Gagne saying, "Yes, I'll tell her. Let me just take a minute to figure out how to break the news." Then one minute became ten, and then ten became an hour, and then I knew. I knew.

Here's how I found out. A girl named Dina Ramsey whose mom was a technician at the plant asked to borrow my phone. She said hers was out of power and her charger was in her backpack at school. So I handed her mine, even though I only had, like, 10 percent power left. (I had, as a matter of fact, gotten a warning that I was down to 10 percent power a few minutes before Dina came over to me. Power figures a lot in my story, doesn't it?) But then I saw her talking on her phone—not my phone. And I knew it was her phone because she had one of those cases with plastic studs that were silver and gold. My case was straight-up black. I watched her for a while, figuring at first that she must have had a little bit of juice left after all, and some call had come in and she'd taken it. Not a big deal. But it was one freaking long conversation. After she hung up, she said something to a kid named Katina and then made another call—on her phone. That's when it clicked that something was up. She'd been talking with a bunch of kids and Mr. Adams before she had come over to me to get my phone. Why did she need to walk over to me to get mine? There were like five other phones right there with her. And hers sure seemed to have beaucoup battery left.

So, I went over to her and asked if she was done with my phone. I said I wanted to try my parents again. She said she had one more call. But she knew something; she looked seriously stricken. (Yes, I learned that word from the Dickinson poem.) I stood there and waited like a totally passive-aggressive asshole for her to dial someone—anyone—and for, like, thirty seconds she just stood there, fighting back tears. The file cards behind her eyes were flipping as she tried to think of someone to call, but she couldn't. She just couldn't. She froze. And, meanwhile, I could feel everyone was watching me. Everyone.

That's how I knew.

And then Ms. Gagne started walking over to me.

So I grabbed my phone from Dina's hand, turned around, and ran like a madwoman out of the cafeteria, down the corridor, and then outside into the rain. I heard them yelling for me to stop, to come back, but I wouldn't. I didn't. I wanted my mom. I wanted my dad. I wanted my dog.

. . . .

I divide my life after the meltdown into two parts: B.C. and A.C. B.C. is "Before Cameron." A.C., obviously, is after.

That's totally simplifying things, of course. I mean, I had a whole life—sixteen years—before the meltdown at Cape Abenaki. And all of that, technically, was B.C.

But you get my point.

I guess right now I'm telling you the B.C. part of my story.

. . . .

One day in the fall after the meltdown, Andrea and I were chilling on a bench on Church Street in Burlington. The night before, we had taken the bus to the University Mall, because it's right by the highway and there are all these exits with gas stations and motels. It's where the truckers gas up. So we'd gone there and hooked up with these two really sketchy, kind of disgusting truckers from Montreal. They were in their forties, and they actually listened to that embarrassing *Playboy* porn on the Sirius in their truck. But it didn't take very long.

(God, here's a weird little news flash for you: I was a virgin when Reactor One exploded. True story. So, maybe we should file "Emily Shepard's First Time and Sexual Awakening" under Yet One More Grotesque Nuclear Mutation. I mean, it's probably true I wouldn't be a virgin by now anyway, but with any luck the first time I had sex it would have been with some boy my age whose biggest issue would be—and here is more therapist-speak—"learned behavior." By that I mean learned porn. If I've figured out anything the last few years, it's this: everything boys and young men know about sex, they got from Internet porn, which means they have seriously unrealistic expectations. And girls my age? Sometimes they do freaky shit because they're simply afraid to say no. They want to be cool. They want to be liked. Yup, for a girl who they say has, like, zero self-esteem, I know my stuff.)

Church Street is made of bricks, and it's an outdoor mall smack in the middle of the downtown. Pedestrians only—no cars. Burlington is so crunchy that the bricks have capitals and cities and countries carved into them, including places that were seriously communist when the mall was designed. It was a Wednesday, and it was an Indian summer kind of day. (I know "Indian summer" isn't perfectly PC, but it works. It's two words and they say exactly what I want.) We were both wearing these blue-and-yellow rugby shirts we'd lifted from PacSun. They weren't as nice as the ones at Abercrombie, but it's much more difficult to shoplift there. You'd think with the way Abercrombie blares their music it would be easy to steal from them, because the kids who work there must be deaf and stunned from the noise. Think lab rats, maybe. Also, it's much darker inside an Abercrombie than inside a PacSun. But Abercrombie always has a lot more staff and the people at PacSun are way more "whatever."

There were lots of leaf peepers strolling up and down the middle of the street, and most of them were somewhere between the age of seventy-five and embalmed. Everyone had said the tourists wouldn't come that autumn because of Cape Abenaki, and I imagine a lot did stay away. But mostly they just stayed away from the Northeast Kingdom. Plenty still came to Lake Champlain and the western slopes of the Green Mountains. I mean, Burlington must have been sixty or sixty-five miles from the edge of the Exclusion Zone. And southern Vermont was nowhere near it. By the fall, Burlington's biggest issue was dealing with the last of the walkers and the last of the refugee tent camps. But most were gone and most of the people in them had found homes somewhere. Most of us had settled in somewhere. So, by that Wednesday, I was just a regular old homeless kid who occasionally fucked truckers from Montreal.

(And to think grown-ups thought I had "a lack of impulse

control" before Reactor One blew up. I guess it was always going to be a crapshoot to see who or what melted down first.)

"My mom's getting out of jail," Andrea said to me out of the blue.

"No shit? Where did you hear that?"

"A friend of hers sent me a text."

"You need a new phone."

"Yeah. Clearly."

"What does she want?"

Andrea shrugged. "She wants to see me."

"That's too bad."

"I know, right?"

"What are you going to do?"

"I don't know. The problem is, she knows Poacher."

I knew that; it was how Andrea had found Poacher in the first place. But I didn't yet see where this was going. "So . . ."

"I didn't text back," she said.

"No?"

She shook her head. "I don't want my mom to find me. I mean it: I don't want to see her. I don't want to see her or my dad—not ever again. They're both total sleazebags. And my dad? He's not just a sleazebag, he's nasty. He's just garbage."

"But you think she'll find you through Poacher," I said.

"Uh-huh." She pulled a half-smoked cigarette from her pants pocket and lit it with a very pink Bic. "I think maybe I'll have to leave."

I didn't like the sound of that. Andrea was like a big sister to me. Already she had taught me so much. "And go where?"

"I don't know."

"Poacher gives us a roof," I said. "And some freedom. And we have a little money."

"We have chlamydia," she said.

"We do not! At least I don't."

"You know what I mean. It's just gross what we do. Our lives are just gross. Maybe we don't have chlamydia today, but we will tomorrow."

"Poacher would just find you."

"Maybe."

I motioned for her to give me a drag on her cigarette. "Think he'd track you down if you left? Would he hurt you?" I asked, after I'd exhaled.

"No. He's way too mellow. That's not Poacher."

"Maybe he'd keep your mom away from you. You know, protect you."

She seemed to think about this. "I guess he might."

"Tell him your mom is getting out and you don't want to see her. See what he does."

"Okay," she agreed. We watched an old couple detour away from us when they saw us. Then she said, "Want to get a tattoo?" This was not as random as it sounds. She had been talking about getting a tattoo all week—or, in her case, another tattoo. She already had a string of ivy tattooed around her left ankle.

"Nah. I don't want to spend the money."

"I know a guy who will do it for free for a pretty girl."

"If she fucks him, I suppose?"

"No, it's not like that. It's that young guy with the dreadlocks—at the tattoo place on North Winooski. It turns out he knows my cousin. He'd do me a favor, I think."

"So it wouldn't cost us anything?"

"Nope."

So I said, "Why not?" (See what I mean about me and impulse control?) And off we went. She got her second tattoo—an animal that looked like it was part lion, part snake, and part (I am not making this up) goat—and I got my first. It's on my shoulder blade and my back. It says, "Set bleeding feet to minuets," and the writing looks like calligraphy.

When I told the dude I wanted a line from one of Emily Dickinson's poems, he nodded and said, "Hope is the thing with feathers, right?" He wasn't trying to be a smart-ass, but I still felt it was kind of condescending. It seems a lot of girls use that line, even if they have almost no idea who Emily Dickinson was. He even had the words on a pattern, and it was designed to wrap around a bird's wing. After you pick the line, you pick the bird, and you can either have something as sweet as a bluebird or barn swallow, or some winged nightmare with talons that looks like it belongs in a super-violent adults-only video game.

But I surprised him with what I wanted. He didn't know the poem. The truth is, the only line from any of her poems he knew was the one on the pattern about hope. So, I kind of threw him for a loop.

"I have some beautiful ballet slippers that could fit with those words," he said, and Andrea thought the image was perfect. But I told him I wasn't a *So You Think You Can Dance* kind of girl. I never took ballet. I don't even know what ballet slippers feel like. So he got out this fat notebook filled with patterns and wanted me to flip through it, but after a moment I realized the guy was on to something with his birds. He really was. I didn't want wings, but I wanted a feather: a quill. A quill pen. That was, I think, how my mind worked.

The tattoo hurt a little, but not very much. And it took Andrea's mind off her mom for a while.

So, that was the day I got my tattoo. All the guy wanted for payment was for me to wear beaters and halter tops when the weather was right to show it off, and then tell people where I got it. But, of course, I wasn't supposed to tell anyone I got it for free.

So, you're the first.

. . . .

Sometimes when I reread what I've written, I find myself creeped out by what's between the lines. What I haven't written.

For instance, that memory of Andrea and me chilling on Church Street, all carefree and la-di-da the night after we'd each done a trucker in the cabs of their eighteen-wheelers is six weeks after the night I lost my virginity. You don't need to know the details. It began with fake cool and ended with real hysteria. Me— not him. But here's the *Reader's Digest* condensed version. I owe you that.

He was a friend of Poacher's who was also a vet and was paying Poacher to do me. I thought I could handle it. I was living on Poacher's food and Poacher's Oxies and sleeping under Poacher's roof. I was smoking Poacher's weed. And the other girls did it, right? So, why not? I agreed. I was, I guess, trying to earn my keep. To be as down with the routine as everyone else. But it all went wrong, and I was a mess. That little part of me that was still sixteen kicked in, and I had one of those out-of-body experiences: There I was looking down at me from overhead and I was beneath a guy three times my age and I was bleeding on this crappy mattress and it hurt and it was ugly and it was gross. He was gross. And I was so small. Physically. I was just so little compared to this dude. And suddenly I was out of control and beating him on his back (which at first he had thought meant—mistakenly—that I was seriously into it and seriously into him), and I was begging him to stop, to stop, to please just stop. Finally Poacher and Andrea heard me and realized the situation was tanking fast, and yanked him off of me.

And there I was, scrawny and naked, and I curled up in a ball and hid my face in my arms. This was nothing like what the first time was supposed to be. This was nothing like what a hundred rom-coms had led me to believe it would be. This was nothing like what my life was supposed to be. And the Oxies weren't helping. I felt like the lowest, most vile, most pathetic thing on the planet. And, trust me, it's no small trick to feel both vile and pathetic.

But, looking back, you know what's the saddest thing? How easy it is to get used to that feeling when you're hungry and scared and alone.

Chapter 4

I had a few serious screaming fights with my mom over the years. When I was fighting with my dad or with both my parents, the battles were a little more subtle—like I'd just sit there at the dining room table, seething. Then, of course, I'd ratchet up the stakes big-time and get up and slam a door or something. Once, I broke these two crystal wineglasses that had their wedding date on them: I just went outside and hurled them, one after the other, against this phony stone wall that was in our backyard. (The rocks were real, but no farmer had ever built it to section off a field or try and be a good neighbor. See? I've read Robert Frost, too. Okay, I won't show off like that anymore. But the wall always kind of appalled me because the people who built our meadow mansion had a stone-mason construct it so the house would look more like it belonged on the outskirts of Reddington. Maybe it helped a little, but not very much. It was still kind of like putting mud boots on a dairy cow.) So, why did I break the wineglasses? Because I was frustrated and angry that my parents were drunk. Again. Their marriage worked a lot better before we moved to Vermont. At least I think it did. They didn't start fighting until they got here—or if they did, they did a much better job of hiding it from me. I guess there were a lot of reasons why Vermont was so toxic for their marriage, but I think the biggest one was that they just didn't belong in a place so small. So rural. We moved there because my dad was excited by the job: a chief engineer at a nuclear power plant that had two reactors. And they probably convinced themselves that Reddington was close enough to Montreal or Boston when they needed a city fix. But it's really not that close at all. We hardly went either place. And it's not like there were a lot of other flatlanders in Reddington. (Just so you know, "flatlander" is a real word in Vermont. That's not some teen-speak I made up. And it says it all about what it means to be an outsider, doesn't it?) There were some, of course, like Philip Christiansen's family, but I'm really not sure my mom had any close friends in Reddington or Newport. It's kind of sad, when you think about it. She just never fit in. My dad grew up in Phoenix and my mom in Westchester County. My dad did a little better than my mom because he could talk sports and nuke-speak with the other engineers, but my mom pretty much worked alone in her office. And she just didn't have that much in common with most of the other moms in Reddington. Even when I was in the third and fourth grade and my mom would help chaperone the field trips, it was agony for me to watch her. There would always be three moms, and she'd be the odd mom out. Just sitting alone on the school bus or walking alone while the other moms dished about whatever and kept one eye on the kids to prevent us from accidentally killing ourselves.

I don't know, maybe if she had tried more. But maybe she did and she just didn't belong in Vermont. Who knows? Maybe she just didn't belong anywhere. There are people like that, right?

A couple of times my dad interviewed for other jobs at other plants, but one was in Nebraska and I'm not sure Nebraska would have solved the rural problem, and he didn't get the job at the plant near Boston. And then, after he had the drinking suspension in his personnel file, he wasn't going anywhere. No other plant was going to hire an engineer with that kind of black mark.

Looking back, I'm not sure we would have moved even if my dad had gotten that job closer to Boston, because I was about to start ninth grade and my parents were sort of under the spell of Reddington Academy: a really good prep school I could go to for free. And I don't think they wanted to uproot me—move a kid as she starts high school. I seemed to be difficult enough as it was.

So, they were unhappy and they drank. Not, I gather, a unique story. Shit happens and the grown-ups dive headfirst into the Scotch. At least some do.

Anyway, the wineglasses. It was a Saturday night—only around seven-thirty—and my parents were both so drunk that neither of them felt sober enough to drive me to Lisa's house, where I was supposed to be hanging out. I was thirteen. So they said I couldn't go because they couldn't drive. And they didn't want me to call Lisa and have her mom come and get me, because they didn't want people to know they were hammered. And so they started arguing over whose fault it was that I couldn't go—in other words, who was supposed to have taken me and should have stayed sober enough to drive a car when it was spitting snow. So, young bomb thrower that I was, I told them that the world would be a better place if they just got divorced, and then I broke their wineglasses. (Once, after Emily Dickinson's father gave her some grief for setting a chipped plate on the dinner table, she calmly carried it to their garden and smashed it. I didn't know this story when I was thirteen, but it sure hit home when I read about it a year later.)

In all fairness, it's kind of a gray area, right? I mean, I shouldn't have gone postal on their crystal, but it would have been nice if one of them had been able to drive their thirteen-year-old kid to a friend's house.

If I ever get married and have children, I promise you I won't ever get stupid, stinking drunk in front of them. And I will never, ever fight with my husband in front of the kids. And, finally, I promise that if my marriage sucks because of where we live, we'll move.

. . . .

Of course, I also learned a lot of good things about parenting from my mom and dad. That's a fact. I knew they loved me, even when—my opinion—they seriously screwed up.

So, I really was desperate to see them or hear from them those first hours after the meltdown, especially since I knew in my heart that they were screwed (which meant I was screwed, too, but that honestly wasn't what I was thinking at the time). Days and weeks later, when I saw the things people were saying about my dad in the news and online, I was devastated. People said crazy mean stuff about him. People said crazy mean stuff about both my parents. It wasn't fair. I mean, they were—and I know this word because I once wrote an English paper about the Emily Dickinson poem "It dropped so low in my regard"—reviled. They were hated. That's why I gave up on the Internet. That's why I gave up on Facebook and Tumblr.

I think I did a good job with Cameron—and that's thanks to my parents. And I don't care what anyone says about *that*.

. . . .

So, I ran from the college cafeteria into the woods. I didn't run on the paved roads or the sidewalks around the campus, because I thought it would be easier for them to catch me if I did. Instead I ran straight down this grassy hill toward a line of trees. I fell once because the grass was like a Slip 'N Slide, which must have been when I lost my phone. I didn't look back for a while because I figured people were following me. Nope. Not Lisa or Ethan or Ms. Gagne. When I finally allowed myself to catch my breath, I was hidden by a wall of scrubby brush and birch trees. I looked up at the buildings, including the modern brick one that housed the cafeteria, and I saw cars and buses coming and going, and police officers and guys who I think were campus security herding kids and families and old people inside. If anyone was going to come after me, they hadn't started yet. Honestly, my feelings were a little hurt, which in hindsight is just crazy. I mean, there was a fucking nuclear meltdown going on and it was pouring outside. We're talking monsoon, practically. All anyone could think about was radiation and fallout and the "plume." Who had time to worry about little old me? And, for all I know, they did come after me. It just took them a minute to rally or to decide, *Hmmm, I guess she isn't just drama-queening out there and we better go get her.*

But by then I was off and running.

My plan was to try and find my parents. I actually thought I was going to go back to Newport and Reddington. Remember, I was kind of hysterical and, as I've told you, I've always had weird brain chemistry issues, and back then I wasn't on any meds. (When I first got here, there was some talk about whether I should be taking antipsychotics. Seriously? One doctor brought up lithium. Yeah, not happening. I was on something for a few days, but I found I couldn't write. The doctors said it was just my imagination. Wrong. When I was that medicated, I *had* no imagination. *That* was the problem. So, I try and stick to the antidepressants, and I am on a way lower dosage than I was when I was living with Poacher and downing painkillers like M&M's.)

The woods weren't super thick, and it couldn't have been more than a quarter mile to get back to the main road, Route 100. I wanted to go north, but it was amazing what I saw: all traffic was going south. Route 100 is a main road in Vermont—it goes all the way from Canada to Massachusetts, I think—but this is still Vermont, so it's only two lanes. And both lanes were being used to move people south, away from Newport and Reddington. And the lanes were packed. It was cars and trucks moving at a crawl as far as I could see. The people who had motorcycles or bicycles were weaving in and out and along the shoulders and making much better time than the vehicles. There were these two poor volunteer firefighters who were trying to direct traffic, and they were so out of their league. They couldn't have been a whole lot older than me, and things had really gone to shit since our buses had arrived at the college a few hours earlier. People were screaming at the two guys, and some dudes were honking their horns (like that was going to make a difference). Between the wind and the rain and the occasional thunder and the horns and the drivers who were yelling out their windows, it was madness. Everyone was so scared they were batshit crazy. I saw that the back of one pickup truck was filled with little kids—some were toddlers!—and there were two women who must have been my mom's age watching them. They were trying to hold this blue tarp over the children, and some of the kids were just wailing. Who puts (what I guess was) some little preschool in the back of a pickup? People who are scared shitless and just not thinking straight, that's who. I saw one station wagon that had a wooden desk with the drawers held shut with duct tape hitched to the top, and another that had four cat boxes—with cats in them!—strapped to the bars of a roof rack. There was one SUV after another filled with so much stuff that you couldn't see inside. There were people trying to get away on tractors and on horseback, and I saw one Mini Cooper that looked like a clown car: I swear they must have wedged seven or eight people inside it. I suppose some of those people ended up among the walkers. Maybe they'd run out of gas eventually. That happened to lots of people, I understand.

So, I just started walking north against the traffic. And even on the side of the road, walking against the flow was really hard: think salmon. (And, yes, I was as wet as a fish. But I probably looked more like a wet cat.) I could tell that everyone thought I was a lunatic. People, usually moms and ladies who looked to me like grandmothers, would yell at me to stop, to turn around, to go the other way, and some folks even opened their car doors and asked me to get in. I ignored them all and finally started to run. I knew I couldn't run or walk all the way back to Reddington, but I figured eventually I would find someone going in that direction.

And eventually I did.

Not far from the college I saw a Johnson fire engine stopped at a gas station at an intersection. The driver was standing beside his door and talking on his cell phone. I could see someone else was sitting in the passenger seat. I stood just close enough to figure out that he was getting instructions: he was supposed to go to some staging point near Newport where he would be given more information on what to do, and someone was telling him what alternate road to take since he sure as hell wasn't going to be able to buck the tide on Route 100. When he climbed back into the truck and shut his door, I jumped onto the metal back step and held on to the side rails. I had the kind of lightning-bolt thought that is completely inappropriate: *I'm in a James Bond movie.* But the thought passed, and there was really nothing crazy dangerous about what I was doing. The fire engine was going about five or ten miles an hour most of the time, and in fact I sat down on the corner of the back step and curled up against the rain and waited to see where we would go. I used a column of those orange traffic cones as a cushion. I had a feeling this staging area would be pretty close to Cape Abenaki or the village, and soon enough I would find out what had happened to my parents and what had happened at the plant.

I was right about the proximity of the staging area to the power plant, but I was wrong about everything else.

....

The way the teen shelter worked was pretty simple: If you were under eighteen, you had to have your parents' permission to be there. Otherwise, the staff had to call family services, and you'd probably wind up in a foster home. So, I had been lying from the second I arrived. My name was Abby Bliss, I was eighteen, I was from Briarcliff, New York. When I showed up, I told them I'd lost my wallet with my driver's license the night before when I'd been mugged. Given what I'd experienced on my way in from the Kingdom and the things people were saying about my family, the last person I wanted to be was me.

In the morning, they kicked you out, usually by eight a.m. You couldn't hang out there during the day, because they wanted you going to school or getting a GED or volunteering someplace where you could get job skills. They wanted you meeting with your counselors. They wanted you doing something.

But they did have what they called the drop-in, which I don't think was supposed to be some snarky reference to the reality that all of us were dropouts. But you could just "drop in" and chill for a while. Sit on the couches, which were kind of grungy and smelled like feet, or make yourself a peanut butter and jelly sandwich. (My favorite place to crash was one of these two big easy chairs that were covered in plastic so they were easy to clean.) The drop-in was on the first floor of the building beside the shelter and only about a block from the northern end of Church Street. You can bet your ass the visiting leaf peepers gave that corner of Burlington a *very* wide berth.

There were rules to hanging out there, the main ones being no drugs and no alcohol. And there were classes, which were important because they paid us to go to them. I am not shitting you. They paid us. For showing up for a week of classes we would get a MasterCard with fifty dollars on it. The card wouldn't work if you tried to buy beer or cigarettes, but otherwise it was as good as cash. And the classes were on things like how to write a résumé or how to rent an apartment or how to open a bank account. The classes were about "life skills." They usually lasted an hour, and other than fucking Montreal truckers, there's not a whole lot a sixteen- or seventeen-year-old girl can do that pays that kind of scratch. So before I left the shelter, I went to them. Altogether, I went to five.

And that's where I met Andrea. She wasn't living in the shelter by then. She wasn't even welcome in the classes. The counselors had decided that she was kind of a lost cause. For a time she'd done okay. But by the time I met her she'd concluded that it was easier to sleep and do drugs and turn tricks than to stop and try something else. She had sort of given up on herself. She told me that once upon a time the shelter's plan was to give her a shot at moving into one of the organization's transitional living apartments. Make her quasi-independent. But that never happened. She relapsed, and I guess it was easier to stay "relapsed." At first the staff tried to get her back, but it didn't work. So finally they gave her bed at the shelter to another girl. You can't save everybody, right? Andrea was built for anti-anxiety meds, and she was built for addiction. But she was so sweet. She really was. I loved that girl.

Anyway, she showed up at the class that day to try and get a

MasterCard, but she was kind of strung out and the staff was so on to her by that point. Even I could see she was in serious need of something that afternoon. She was pretty much busted before she had even sat down and started to cry. The woman who was teaching the class—it was about how to dress for an interview and what to say and what not to say and how to behave—knew Andrea and I could see her heart was breaking. The staff person's name was Edith, which is a completely awful name, especially because the woman kind of had it going on: she was thirty with strawberry blond hair and blue eyes behind those nerd glasses that beautiful women can somehow pull off. She had us call her Edie, and she was, like me, tiny. My second day at the shelter, when I was still shell-shocked and thought this shelter thing might work, she suggested we check out a bunch of the petite clothes that some preppy store had just donated so that I would have some interview threads. It was a nice idea, but it never happened. I kind of let her down. (Obviously I kind of let a lot of people down. But I think often about letting down Edie because she was so frigging well intentioned.)

Andrea was tall and gangly, and her hair fell flat down the sides of her head like a greasy waterfall. It was naturally black, but it had streaks of purple and pink. She was wearing a beater T-shirt the white and brown of two-day-old snow by the side of the road, and blue jeans that were ripped everywhere. Knees. Thighs. Pockets. And she was pretty anxious. Back then I was so naïve I was thinking it was heroin. Nope. Just painkillers. Lots of painkillers. But she was needy and over time had probably violated every rule the shelter had. She was also pretty goth. Pierced nose. Pierced eyebrow. Lots of black mascara—which, as you'll see, months later would start one of those event cascades that are only bad news.

As I said, I wasn't giving people my real name; I'd learned my lesson. So, I was calling myself Abby Bliss, because that was the name of one of Emily Dickinson's friends (yes, she had friends) and it's pretty unforgettable. I came up with it on the spot in a bread truck, and I kind of liked it. In hindsight, unforgettable was a mistake. I should have chosen Susan Huntington, Emily's sister-in-law. Or I should have stuck with Abby, which was the name that first came to me, but used her last name before she got married: Wood. Abby Wood is a name that does not draw attention to itself.

After Edie told Andrea that she wasn't going to get the Master-Card, she sat down on the couch next to me. Actually, she sort of collapsed. Her big long body was like a marionette's after you snip the strings. It just goes limp. And that's when I wondered how old she really was. I guess because she was pierced and four or five inches taller than me, I'd pegged her for nineteen or twenty. But maybe she had been lying all along about her age, too. When she sat on the couch, she brought her knees up to her chest, and I saw the ivy tattoo on her ankle. She was wearing flip-flops, but the bottoms of her feet were so dirty it was like she'd stepped in a fireplace after the logs were nothing but ash. She was pretty jittery: her legs were almost vibrating, and she kept playing with her earrings and her earlobes.

"I'm Andrea," she said, and I answered with my made-up name. There were nine or ten other kids there, some actually interested in getting help with job interview skills and some just after the fifty-buck MasterCard. Me? I was probably somewhere in between. I mean, I was seriously stressed out. And I was living this lie, and not just about who my parents were or what my name was. If the counselors had known I was a walker from the Kingdom, they would have turned me in to the Red Cross or one of the groups that was trying to help with the refugees from that corner of the state. And I wanted to disappear.

> *I'm nobody! Who are you?*
> *Are you nobody, too?*
> *Then there's a pair of us—don't tell!*
> *They'd banish us, you know.*

Yeah, that would be me. I had to be a nobody so I wouldn't be banished. The counselors thought I was a runaway from the suburbs of New York City who'd wound up homeless. I picked Briarcliff because it was the town where I'd been a little kid: it was only a few miles from the nuclear power plant on the Hudson River where my dad had worked back then.

"Bliss? Really?" she asked. "Rhymes with kiss."

"I know."

"Can you sing?"

"Nope."

"Too bad. You've got a great name for a rock star."

I hadn't thought of that, because in my head I always saw Abby Bliss in a bonnet and check dress that fell to her ankles. "I guess," I agreed.

"You're staying here?" she asked, and she motioned with her head upstairs to where the bedrooms were. We each had a bedroom of our own. They were small, but the counselors had figured out we were territorial and we needed our privacy. (Amazing, isn't it? The boarders at Reddington Academy paid $45,000 a year to go there, and they lived in doubles and triples. Us? We were homeless, paid nothing, and each got a little room of our own.) There was a bed and a chest of drawers for each girl. The nights I was there, most of us needed no more than a drawer for our stuff. But not all of us. There were two girls at the shelter who were over-the-top hoarders. Wouldn't part with anything. One of them had stacks and stacks of Burlington's free weekly newspaper. (She liked reading the sexy personals in the back.) The other collected those elastic Livestrong and friendship bracelets. She must have had a thousand of them.

"Uh-huh," I said.

"I used to live here. But I needed more room. I needed more space."

"What do you do?"

She shrugged. "This and that. You know."

I didn't know. She pulled her phone from the back pocket of her jeans and checked a text. It made me miss my phone.

"Anything new from Cape Abenaki?" I asked.

"What a fucking nightmare that is," she said. "I just can't believe it, can you? All those animals that are going to die? They say no one will be able to live in the Kingdom for, like, ten thousand years. Ten thousand years! They say the radiation—"

"Is there anything new about the plant operators?"

"You mean that guy who they think was drunk? The engineer who screwed up those condenser thingies?"

"Yeah . . . that guy."

"I don't know. I wasn't looking at the news. I really don't look at the news. How old are you?"

"Eighteen," I lied. "You?"

"Eighteen." Then she said, "I like your hair." She reached over and pushed a lock behind my ears.

"It's kind of dirty," I said. I wanted to lie and say I liked her hair, too, but I didn't think I would sound convincing. I liked Edie's hair a lot more.

"If my hair was like yours, I wouldn't color it. I always wanted to be a blonde. My grandfather was an ad guy: 'Blondes have more fun.' He produced TV commercials. I think that was one of the slogans from one of his ads."

"Are you from New York?" I asked.

"No, but my grandparents were."

"Until I came here, I lived in Briarcliff," I said, which actually was only a lie if you interpreted the word "here" to mean the drop-in or Burlington.

"I've heard of it," she said, and then she leaned in close to me and whispered, "Look, everyone here is crazy righteous. Crazy. Righteous. We're talking super do-gooders. If you ever need someone to really talk to, call me."

"I don't have a phone."

Her eyes went a little wide. "You don't have a phone?"

I shook my head. "I lost it."

"Okay, I know someone who can fix that for you."

"How?"

"Leave that to me. In the meantime, if you need me, sometimes I hang out on Church Street. I like the benches by that statue of the kids playing leapfrog. And sometimes you can find me at Muddy Waters—the coffee place on Main Street."

It was right about then that Edie and another staffer, a young guy in his twenties named Bret, came over and stood over us. I thought Edie was going to cry when she looked at Andrea. But the dude? Way too tough. He looked more like a Marine than the sort of crunchy granola types who usually tried to help us. Practically a buzz cut and serious guns for arms. He was wearing a black T-shirt and it was almost a second skin.

"Hello, Andrea," Edie said.

"Hey," she murmured, and she looked down at her phone, instead of making eye contact with the social worker. She pretended to be very focused on a text.

"Why are you here?"

"Why do you think I'm here?" she answered. "Life skills. That's what it's all about, right?"

"Where are you living?" the guy with Edie asked.

"I have a place," she answered.

He folded his arms across his chest. "Where?"

"Girl's gotta have a little privacy," she mumbled.

"Are you clean?"

"Of course," she said. "Wouldn't be here if I weren't, right? Isn't that the rule?"

Edie leaned in to get a closer look at Andrea's face. I guess she wanted to scope out Andrea's pupils. But Andrea jumped up from the couch and swiped Edie out of her way, knocking the social worker off balance and sending her to her knees. Somehow, the girl also sent her phone flying onto the hard wooden floor of the drop-in. It slid like a hockey puck into the baseboard radiators. Edie and Bret froze, and everyone in the room just went silent— except Andrea.

"My phone!" she shrieked. "Goddamit, my phone!" She ran to the radiator and picked it up and immediately started checking to see if it still worked. Then she turned back to the two staffers and hissed at them, "You could have broken it. You know that, right? You could have broken it!"

I expected one of them to say something to her. Maybe point out to her the detail that they hadn't done anything. She was the one who had accidentally hurled her phone across the floor like a skipping stone. But Edie just got back on her feet and stood there next to Bret, taking it all in. Totally chill. I guess I shouldn't have been surprised when Andrea finally broke.

"I don't need your sympathy!" she said, and she started to cry. "Stop looking at me! I don't want your fucking help. I can take care of myself! Besides, you don't want to help me. You don't want to help anybody. You say you do, but you're like everybody else. So, fuck you! Fuck you all!" She was sobbing suddenly, the mascara running down her cheeks like raindrops on glass. "I need money and if you don't want to help me, then fuck you! Fuck you all!"

"Andrea—" Edie said.

"No, don't take that tone with me. I don't need your condescending bullshit! I just don't need it!"

One of the boys who was watching this train wreck unfold walked past me toward Andrea. I don't know what he had in mind, but Andrea put out her hand like a crossing guard signaling a kid to stop. So he did. Then Andrea kind of gathered herself. She turned toward the drop-in entrance to leave, but on her way out she said to me—and she said it really loud so everyone could hear—"Hey, Bliss, you remember where to find me, right? I'll get you that phone and whatever else you need, since these fuckers are no help whatsoever." Then she was out the door.

It would be three days before I'd leave the shelter myself. But when I did, she was the first person I thought of.

Chapter 5

The first time I saw Cameron, he was dragging a black plastic garbage bag that might have been as big as he was. I'm not kidding. He was like this Green Mountain Gavroche—you know, from that musical? The bag was filled with everything he owned, which wasn't much because most of the space in it was taken up with something he called his mummy bag. A mummy bag is basically just a sleeping bag. But I remember the way he insisted a mummy bag was a lot better than a sleeping bag, and that he would have frozen to death the night before in a plain old sleeping bag. The way he loved that bag, you would have thought it had magical powers. Frankly, I thought the term "mummy bag" was kind of creepy, but Cameron didn't think anything of it. What else was in there? A pair of those Heelys, those sneakers with wheels on the bottom, that he had tricked out with black and red duct tape so it looked like there were flames on the heels. A stuffed zebra. One of those zippered plastic bags the airlines give you when you're traveling in first class, with a sleep mask and ChapStick and a toothbrush. (When my family went to France so my dad could visit a couple of nuclear power plants, the energy company flew us there in something called Envoy class. It sure beat coach, let me tell you. My dad joked that I shouldn't get used to it. I didn't.) Cameron also kept his comb in the kit. He had a few rolls of duct tape and some of his art, including the robot I told you about. And he had some clothes in the bag, like his pajamas and a couple of shirts and some underwear. His socks. But a lot of his clothes he was wearing, because it was the end of December. He had just run away from what he said was his seventh foster home, which, he'd confess later, was an exaggeration. It was his fourth. But he was right to get out, that's for sure. He was nine, and so his favorite thing might have been his Red Sox hoodie, which he was wearing under this total piece-of-crap parka. His boots were crap, too. I'm amazed he wasn't one of the ones who wound up with gangrene.

He was dragging the bag along a dusting of snow just outside of this derelict coal plant down by the waterfront, and he looked wider and bigger than he would turn out to be because of all the clothes he was wearing. He was, in fact, pretty thin. I mean, he was a kid. His hair was crow black and, when he pulled off his knit cap, a mess.

The plant had been empty for decades, and while the police used to try and kick us out, we'd still sometimes find corners and crevices where we could escape the worst of the cold. And while an empty coal plant is pretty filthy, unlike an empty nuclear plant at least it's not radioactive. (I know, that's not fair. There are plenty of decommissioned nuclear plants that aren't radioactive. But you get my point.)

Cameron had been there the night before, but none of us had noticed him. There were four of us that I was aware of, maybe more, but I wasn't with the others. They were strangers. It was one of those nights where I really didn't sleep because I didn't know whether to trust them. The group was three adults, two women and one man. (If it had been two men and one woman or three men, you can bet your ass I wouldn't have stayed.) The police had scattered us the night before, and all of the people I knew hadn't come back yet.

I had seen homeless little kids before, but not one who was so clearly alone. Usually I saw them sleeping with their moms—in a car, at least a dozen times—or coming or going from the shelter for families.

I don't know why I stopped Cameron. It was only after I stopped him that I saw his black eye. I could have let him keep walking to wherever. But I did stop him. I guess I didn't think I should be a bystander. Or, maybe, I was just curious.

. . . .

I seem to be jumping around a lot. This is supposed to be the B.C. section of my story: Before Cameron.

I should probably try and organize my thoughts.

. . . .

What they were calling the staging area was a madhouse. It was the parking lot of the high school in Orleans, which made sense because the school was right off the interstate highway and only about ten miles from Newport. Plus, there were acres of asphalt. Still, the vehicles were spilling out onto the track and the football field, too. There were all kinds of trucks from the National Guard and fire engines from all over northern Vermont and New Hampshire and Canada. I saw a couple of ambulances, just waiting, I guess. I saw a lot of guys in FEMA windbreakers with walkie-talkies on their belts. There were two tractor-trailer trucks with women and men from the Guard handing out those bright yellow hazmat suits with the window masks and respirators. And there were lines of white cruisers for the sheriffs' departments and green ones for the Vermont State Police. Most people were inside the gymnasium—which had its big, gray double doors open to the parking lot—because no one wanted to get rained on: everyone was worried the rain was radioactive. It was, of course, but it wasn't as bad as we feared because the wind was blowing northeast and Orleans was south of Cape Abenaki.

I hopped off the back of the fire engine, and not a soul knew I had ever been on it. I ran into the gymnasium, and I have a feeling that anyone who noticed me assumed I was just some young, eager-beaver first responder. I saw a fair number of them, too:

adults in their twenties, wearing rain slickers and gloves—gloves, even though it was June, because they were worried about fall-out—and hats. A lot of them were wearing those little gauze masks my dad would wear when he was using an electric sander.

Immediately a woman who said she was a nurse asked me if I'd been given potassium iodide yet. I shook my head no, and so she plopped two tablets into my hand, telling me to take one right now and one tomorrow. Then she pointed at a long folding table with stacks of bottled water. "Do not use the water fountain," she warned me. "No one knows yet how much has seeped into the groundwater." The iodide wouldn't protect me from leukemia in five or ten or fifty years, but it might reduce the risk of thyroid cancer.

After I'd taken the pill, I looked around to see if there was anyone I recognized from the plant or the Academy or my village. I saw no familiar faces at all. Not a one. But I did pass by two men with their sleeves rolled up, poring over a huge diagram of Cape Abenaki—the power plant itself. There were the two lines of cooling towers, and there was the pair of massive concrete boxes with the reactors. I must have been standing there long enough that one of the men turned around and looked at me.

"Are you supposed to be somewhere?" he asked. He was—and here's a great SAT word—brusque.

"I was looking for my dad," I answered, which was a pretty lame answer. But I was. It was the whole reason I had ridden back to the Kingdom on the rear of a fire engine, for crying out loud. I was looking for my dad *and* my mom.

"Little girl," he began, and he was clearly going to tell me to run along; the world was falling apart, and he had much more important things to do than find some lost child's father or mother—which is true. He did. But in my defense, it's not like I'd asked for his help. He had, more or less, asked me what I was doing, and I'd answered. I didn't expect him to stop what he was doing. Anyway, the guy who was with him cut him off and asked me who my dad was. So I told him. And that was the first indication I got that my name might not be an asset.

"Your father is Bill Shepard?" he said, and his jaw hung a little slack.

I nodded.

The first guy, the one who called me a little girl, turned away and I heard him mutter, "Jesus fucking Christ." Then he yelled across the gymnasium to a woman whose name was Libby and who did something with FEMA: she had a windbreaker and a walkie-talkie, which was sort of their uniform. She practically sprinted across the floor of the basketball court.

"What's up, John?" she asked. "What now?" She sounded a little exasperated.

"This girl is Bill Shepard's daughter."

She was one of those organized and petite little women we sometimes call soccer moms, even if they're not really moms. She had short blond hair that was cropped into a lid that looked kind of like a helmet, and even with her baggy windbreaker and khaki pants I could tell she was super fit. Her eyes were intense when she looked at me. She was only a little bit taller than I was.

"What's your name? Mine is Libby. Libby Dunbar."

"Emily."

"Your dad is Bill Shepard?"

I nodded.

"And your mom is Mira?"

"Yes."

She took a deep breath. I knew that suddenly people were watching us. Watching me. She put one of her hands on my shoulder and started guiding me away from the men with their diagram of the power plant and toward a door that led into one of the high school corridors.

"How did you get here, sweetie?" she asked as we walked. But I didn't answer because I heard what people were murmuring or saying around us. Somehow everyone knew that this sopping wet, filthy, shell-shocked teenager was Bill and Mira's kid. Here the fucking sky was falling—really, radioactive fallout is about as close as you can get, I think, to the sky literally falling—and these grown-ups had stopped what they were doing as we went by.

"Have you had any iodide?" she asked when I didn't answer her question, and this time I nodded. Meanwhile, all around us people were whispering or telling each other things like: *That's Bill's kid. My God, that's the Shepard kid. They'll want to talk to her—find out how drunk he was when he left home. Shit—that poor girl. Does she know about her dad—about both her parents? We don't know it was his fault. Yeah, we do. We do.*

And, out of the blue, I started shivering. I wasn't cold. I mean, I was wet, of course, but I hadn't even been that cold when I'd been riding on the back of the fire engine: this was mid-June, so it wasn't like the rain was freezing or anything. And the truck never went that fast. But there I was, shaking, as we walked through the gym and then down the hallway. My teeth were actually chattering. And the hallways were crowded, too, with people running back and forth and trying to talk on their cell phones or running back and forth and cursing about how bad the cell reception was inside the school building.

Finally Libby brought me inside the assistant principal's office, which—unlike most of the rooms we passed—hadn't been taken over by FEMA or, based on the signs people were sticking to the cement-block walls, the NRC. It was quiet, and she shut the door behind her. She sat me down in the nice leather chair behind the desk.

I guess because I was shaking, she took off her FEMA jacket and draped it around my shoulders like a shawl. "What you really need is a towel," she muttered. Then she leaned over the desk. "So, Emily. A lot's happened this morning. But you know that. How did you get here? Who brought you?"

I guess a normal girl whose teeth wouldn't stop chattering would have figured out that the best thing to do was to stay cool and answer the questions and get some help. Clearly I was fucked and was going to need all the help I could get. But, in hindsight, I was never going to win the Normal Girl award.

Instead I asked, "Where are my parents? Where's my dad?"

She gave me that stare again, and I couldn't meet her eyes. But I also wouldn't look away, so I focused on her little ski slope of a nose. Someone called her on her walkie-talkie, but without turning away from me she reached down and pushed some button that silenced it.

"Your dad and your mom are currently . . . missing. They are . . . unaccounted for."

I knew what that meant, and there was nothing I hated more than when my parents would beat around the bush or try and find euphemisms—especially euphemisms for my bad behavior or theirs. I knew what "missing" meant. I knew what "unaccounted for" meant.

And so I said—or, I guess, I tried to say, because the words came out in hiccups, like I was choking or gasping for air—"Are you telling me they're dead?"

"No, we don't know that," she said.

But I did. I knew that. She was trying to ease into this, to break the bad news slowly. She leaned in toward me to hug me and I wanted to push her away, but now I really was having trouble breathing. I was practically hyperventilating and I thought I was going to be sick. She rubbed my back and whispered, "We don't know, Emily, we really don't know much of anything just yet." I don't know how long we were like that—maybe two or three minutes. I remember thinking that it must be hurting Libby's back to be leaning over like that, which was—if you were to read the notes one of my first therapists kept about me—uncharacteristically empathetic. Finally my breathing started to settle, but I was still shaking. So I pushed her away, but I wasn't rude about it. I just wanted her to know that I was going to keep it together.

"How many people are unaccounted for or missing?" I asked,

trying not to sound sarcastic or emphasize the words "unaccounted for" and "missing."

"Seventeen," she answered. "At least seventeen."

"Is it still on fire?"

We both knew what *it* was. The reactor.

"Yes. It's still on fire."

"Does anybody know what happened?"

"Not yet."

But they already had their suspicions.

"I have a dog . . ." I wasn't sure what I was going to say, so I just stopped talking.

"What's its name?"

"Maggie."

She nodded. She felt bad for me, and she felt bad for my dog. But the last thing she could do anything about was my poor nine-year-old Maggie.

In the end, there would be nineteen people "unaccounted for" or "missing." And now I am being sarcastic and emphasizing those words when I say them. In the end, there would be nineteen people dead.

. . . .

I had a fourth-grade teacher who told me I didn't always have to be right. I had one in seventh grade—my French teacher—who told me that, too.

. . . .

The problem with always having to be right is that sometimes you're not. And so, if you're like me, those times when you're not, you try and save face—especially after you've seriously fucked up. You make one bad decision and then another, trying to fix that very first fuck-up.

. . . .

A lot of my fights with my parents were over things that were incredibly stupid. We were all very stubborn, which was part of the problem. The serious fights started when I was, I guess, in fifth or sixth grade. Part of it was brain chemistry, of course, but we didn't know that then. (Yeah, I know I blame a lot on "brain chemistry." I worry it's starting to sound like I'm trying not to take responsibility for my bad choices. Don't worry. I am. I do. I'm just trying to explain.)

Also, it's not like my entire adolescence was a complete disaster or that people thought I was a total train wreck. Sure, my parents and I fought and I burned some bridges, and there were moments when I was the definition of a hot mess. But I saw girls in the shelter who were much crazier than I was and made much worse decisions on a daily basis. The truth is, I got pretty good grades, especially in English. I was actually kind of a superstar in English. Ms. Gagne—Cecile—thought I had serious promise as a writer. Every year in May, Middlebury College brings two or three teenage writers from a boatload of high schools—and not just ones in Vermont—to Bread Loaf for something they call their "Young Writers' Conference." The students get to hang out for four days with professional writers and get their poetry or their fiction workshopped. The Reddington Academy English Department was willing to send me there both my sophomore and junior years. I only went my sophomore year, however, because I was being disciplined that May when I was a junior. (I was in a car that a boy I knew—not Ethan—had "borrowed" from his uncle. Unfortunately, he didn't tell his uncle that he was borrowing it, and he only had a learner's permit—not a real driver's license. Also, when the local Newport cop shined his flashlight into the car, we each had an open bottle of beer in our hands. Contrary to the rumors that were flying around the school that month, the beer bottle was the only thing long and slender I had in my hands when we were caught.) I know lots of people at the Academy (and my parents) were frustrated with me because I hadn't spent enough time my junior year freaking out about college—you know, taking AP classes, doing things after school, starting a save-the-world recycling club—but I wasn't ready to admit either that they were right or my decisions were wrong.

And, the truth is, I hid when I had to behind Emily Dickinson. ("Maybe you should start a poetry club," my guidance counselor suggested. Yeah, right. Like that was going to happen.) The irony here is that Emily Dickinson was nothing if not under control. At least that's what people who don't know any better think. Me? Sometimes, I was completely out of control.

. . . .

The leaves don't fall one by one. They fall in drapes. There's a breeze or a gust and a thousand break off at once.

The foliage the autumn after Reactor One exploded was phantasmagorically beautiful. The maples were crimson and cherry and red, the birches an almost neon yellow, and the ash a purple more flamboyant than the Magic Markers I'd used as a kid. We noticed that even in Burlington and the Champlain Valley.

What everyone understands but no one thinks about is that the leaves are spectacular because they're dying. The tree is preparing for winter, and so it wants to shed all those dainty leaves. How does it evict them? It produces a layer of cells at the base of the leaves, so fluids can't reach them. Meanwhile, the leaves themselves stop producing chlorophyll, which is the chemical they need for photosynthesis—the way a leaf uses sunlight to generate food. Without the deep, heady green of all that chlorophyll, the colors in the other chemicals finally get their day in the sun. That beautiful red leaf, in other words, is slowly starving to death.

Incidentally, I did not learn any of this in biology in ninth grade. I learned it in middle school in sixth grade. Foliage season is a big money maker in Vermont, and so we learn about leaves young here. We use a thesaurus to find words to describe it: words like the one I just used, "phantasmagoric." Or—another favorite word of mine—"luminescent."

In any case, the adults seemed to be talking a lot that autumn about the effect of nuclear fallout on the fall foliage season. Supposedly, the leaves inside the Exclusion Zone were as colorful as the tropical fish that nose around the world's most exotic coral reefs. I don't know if that's true or not. It wouldn't be until the following year, long after Poacher and the posse and Andrea and Cameron, that I'd go back—that I'd go home.

And, by then, the prettiest color was rust.

Chapter 6

Libby Dunbar had way more important things to do than to watch over me. And so when she decided—kind of mistakenly, in hindsight—that I was cool, she concluded that she had to do two things: She had to find someone else to look out for me. And she had to get me moved far away from the meltdown zone. She sure as hell had to get me out of the staging area. So she told me to wait where I was and she'd be right back. Honestly, I have no idea what she thought she was going to do, but she left me alone while she tried to solve the little problem that was . . . me. Here is basically our conversation just before she left. (As you can see, I didn't help matters by lying.)

LIBBY: And you have no idea where the rest of the students from Reddington Academy have been taken?
ME: No.
LIBBY: You just didn't get on any of the buses when they came to your school.
ME: I wanted to find my mom and dad.
LIBBY: I understand. And you said your grandmother has Alzheimer's and your grandfather lives in Phoenix.
ME: Yup.
LIBBY: And you have no aunts or uncles.
ME: Nope.
LIBBY: Which I guess means you have no cousins.
ME: I guess.

LIBBY: Your friend—this Lisa Current—
ME: Curran.
LIBBY: Right. Curran. You're friends with the whole family?
ME: Uh-huh.
LIBBY: Okay. Let me see if I can find Lisa's mom and dad.

Given that she was pretty sure my parents were dead (God, that's an awful thing to write), it was pretty clear that she had no plans to have me sent wherever the rest of Reddington Academy was holed up. It really made no sense to just drop me into a sea of high school students who were already wigging out. But I wasn't wild about the idea of spending the rest of the day alone in an assistant principal's office while she tried to find Lisa Curran's mom. I felt that I had to *do* something. Anything. I couldn't just sit there.

So I left. According to one of my therapists, this was "a manifestation of a kindling PTSD." (I thought that was kind of poetic when I read it.) It "presented" with "an exaggerated fight/flight mentality." Apparently, I chose "flight."

Still, I remember when I stood up to leave, I told myself that I was only going to see if she had any tampons in her purse (which she did) and go to the bathroom. Then I might walk from the office to the end of the hallway and peek back into the gym. That's all. Watch the madness there for a moment or two. I actually thought to myself, *You need to be back here when Libby returns.* But when I got to the gym and saw all that chaos, I gave myself permission to go to those double doors that opened out onto the parking lot and the athletic fields. And then, when I saw it had stopped raining, I had to walk out there. When was the last time any of us had stood outside and not gotten wet? It had been days. Seriously, it had been raining practically nonstop for days! So I did, fallout be damned. I went outside. I mean, it wasn't as crazy as it sounds. There were other people out there. Granted, they were trying to cover themselves with anything they could find, using newspapers and trash bags if necessary. But still: they were out there.

I have absolutely no sense of direction, and so I had no idea which way was north: the direction of the power plant and my home. My house. My dog. Maybe if it had been sunny I could have figured it out, but, really, even that wouldn't have helped all that much. As you might have guessed, I was a pretty lousy Brownie and never spent even a second of my life as a Girl Scout. Besides, it wasn't sunny. And so I just started walking across the parking lot, past the cruisers and fire engines and camo-colored National Guard trucks. I was midway to the entrance to the school when I overheard a group of the guardsmen talking under a tent. I stopped and listened, which looking back was a big mistake. There were four of them and they were wearing hazmat suits, but they had pulled off the hoods and were drinking bottled water. They were covered in sweat and looked pretty beaten.

"It's like pilot error," one of the guys was saying. "Operator error is the term. Whatever his name—Shepard—fucked up."

"His wife is the spokesperson for the plant, you know," someone else said. "Pretty despicable, right? Whole family: fucking despicable."

"There'll be a cover-up."

"You can't cover up a fucking meltdown."

"Melt-through."

"We don't know that."

"Besides, the energy company will want this to be human error. If it's human error, then nuclear power doesn't look so bad. The industry doesn't look so bad. And they're both dead by now. There's not a lot of collateral damage when you have dead people you can blame."

"Even his wife? She's dead, too?"

"The side of the container was gone! Just gone! The surrounding building was, like, rubble. You saw the size of the blast."

"Someone was saying he was drunk. That true?"

"Yup. I hear they had a daughter. You watch, they'll make her testify or something. Talk about what an alcoholic her dad was. Make it clear this was all the fault of one idiot drunk."

"Wow. Where did you hear that?"

I knew I didn't want to hear any more. I'd heard enough. I started to run, and it was at the edge of the parking lot that I saw a bike leaning up against the side of a fire truck from the village of Barton. So I took it. I just took it—and I was off.

. . . .

I'm not going to pretend I understand even half of the poems that Emily Dickinson wrote. But when I get them, I get them. I get the rhythms and I get the point:

Life, and Death, and Giants

There's a lot more, but let's start with that first line. How can you not love it? How could anyone not love it? Read it aloud:

Life (slight pause) and Death (slight pause) and Giants. I love that capital G.

Or this:

REMEMBRANCE has a rear and front,—

It really does, doesn't it? Again, that's just the first line. She goes on to compare remembrance to a house with a garret, and God knows I could use a garret to squirrel away a lot of my crazy mental shit—my crazy mental demons. Actually, I need way more than a garret. I need a self-store garage bay. You know, the ones that always seem to end up having a dead body in them? I practically need a warehouse.

And while I have pretty shamelessly thrown my brain under the bus and blamed it for some of the seriously bad choices I've made, I understand that it has its assets, too. It has its moments.

The brain is wider than the sky,
  For, put them side by side,

The one the other will include
  With ease, and you beside.

I love it when therapists talk about boundaries. I really could have used some, right? But how can you fence in a brain? How can you ask a person to rein in something that really is wider than the sky?

. . . .

Andrea often looked like she'd been sleeping in eyeliner—which sometimes was the case, especially when we crashed after bingeing on OxyContin. But the look kind of worked on her. Even when goth was kind of passé, she could pull it off—I think because it always seemed like she was secretly so vulnerable.

When I look back on my days with the posse, I see in my head all of us who crashed at one time or another at Poacher's. It was not really a wild crowd—it's not like we were having raucous parties. Mostly we were just trying to survive, and the sex and the drugs and the robberies were not the product of some rager or keg party gone crazy. It was just how we kept a roof over our heads and tried to stay warm until, finally, we just hated ourselves so much—which was a very high bar, trust me—that either we left or we OD'd. The regulars, in addition to Andrea and me, included Missy, who was nineteen and was from Concord, Massachusetts, and came from unbelievable buckets of money. She had a pink sports car when I first moved in—not kidding—a Miata convertible. But one day her dad and mom appeared out of the blue to bring her home, and when she refused, one of them drove home in her car, so we lost that set of wheels. They couldn't believe what a rat hole their daughter was living in. We couldn't believe that they found her. She once told me that her house in Concord had six bedrooms and four fireplaces. She did cocaine for a while, which most of us didn't, because she had the wallet to make cocaine happen. Poacher loved her for that. But it also wasn't going to last. She claimed her older brothers used to abuse her, which was why she was so fucked up. I never quite believed her. I think, like a lot of us, she was just a head case and made stuff up.

On the other hand, I do believe that Lida, another girl, really had been abused by her stepfather. I don't think she could have made up the crap she told me. She was my age. After her mom and dad divorced, her mom remarried, and her stepfather turned out to be a total pig. He used to make her suck him off for her allowance, usually in the car after he'd picked her up after softball or field hockey. He got her to do it the first time partly by scaring the shit out of her and partly by seducing her. Of course, the "how" doesn't really matter. As a kid, once you do something like that, you're kind of stuck. You feel ashamed and you feel violated and you feel like the worst daughter on the planet. She was eleven years old that first time. She would do it for four more years before she would finally hit the wall and go to her mom. And her mom—who was spineless and pathetic and clearly freaking terrified of her second husband—accused her of lying. Yup, took her husband's side over her daughter's. Claimed that Lida was making the whole thing up. As they say, the River Denial is wide. Anyway, once you put some- thing like that out there, you've pretty much torched any chance of a relationship with your mom, at least if your mom claims she doesn't believe you. So Lida ran away.

Poacher's boys tended to come and go a lot more. Trevor. Joseph. PJ (for Poacher Junior). Trevor and Joseph were older than I was, but PJ was younger. Maybe fourteen. We called him Poacher Junior because his eyes became the same slits as Poacher's when he was stoned, and his arms got as wobbly as those Styrofoam tubes little kids play with in swimming pools. It was like he had a garden hose for bones. The boys—and they really were like boys; some- times it was like us girls were their babysitters—could sit around playing Poacher's Xbox for days. They really could. I think they were as beyond help as the girls, but they didn't show it. Not really.

Teen boys are often more chill than teen girls, but inside they can be just as fucked up.

The big difference is that most of the time the boys could only bring in money by stealing, especially once the teen shelter wouldn't let them back into the life skills classes. But we girls could actually earn cash. We could earn our keep and our drugs because we had something we could sell. (I know now that boys can do what we did, but back then I didn't realize there was a market for underage male hookers. In some ways, I guess I was weirdly naïve.)

But once in a while we did break-ins with the boys, which brings me back to Andrea and sleeping in eyeliner and the robbery. *The* robbery, the one where we all almost got ourselves killed. We're talking a Bonnie and Clyde kind of cataclysm, minus the guns, because only the police had guns. But it was pretty bad. You get my point.

As I said, Andrea didn't sleep in eyeliner because she wanted that zombie smudge look. Usually she did it because she just crashed. Boom. Wilted. Out. And the downside to sleeping in eyeliner, aside from the fact that you look like you just got dumped at the prom by your boyfriend and have been sobbing for hours in the bathroom—See? Sometimes I can come up with analogies that are "age appropriate" and not batshit crazy—is that you can get eye infections. And eye infections just suck.

The plan was to break into Missy's aunt and uncle's house in Shelburne. Shelburne is a very swanky suburb just south of Burlington. When Missy first left Concord, she was supposed to live with them. That's how she wound up in Vermont in the first place. The family thought that a change of place might straighten Missy out. (There was another girl like that at the shelter. Like Missy, she needed a lot more than a change of place and a different roof over her head.) The house where her aunt and uncle lived was kind of like mine back in Reddington: unapologetic meadow mansion. It was on a hill that looked out at Lake Champlain and the Adirondack Mountains, and it had these awesome ports for iPods on a wall in almost every single room. It was two years old, but it still smelled brand-new. The floors were a beige wood and still shiny as glass. There were white throw rugs and blue throw rugs and huge black-and-white photographs of leaves over the couches and beside the fireplace.

And there was an alarm system, but Missy knew the code to turn it off.

At least she did once.

Or at least she did when she wasn't high as a kite on Percocet and beer.

You can probably see where this is going.

There were five of us squeezed into Missy's convertible: Missy and Andrea and Trevor and PJ and me. Ridiculous, I know. I honestly don't know why Andrea and I were there. I don't know why PJ was there. It really just should have been Missy and Trevor—or even just Missy, if she was willing to take a few trips.

Even though Missy hadn't really lived there for two months, the plan was to steal some of her shit, too, so that she could throw a hissy fit and insist that she had had nothing to do with the robbery. We were going to steal a lot of silver and her aunt's jewelry that we could pawn at a few places in Montreal, and whatever electronics we could fit in the Miata—which, given our brain-dead decision to cram five of us into a car meant for four people, two of whom were clearly supposed to be dwarfs, wasn't very much.

We went there on a Friday night in October when her aunt and uncle would be at some gala in Burlington for the hospital, where her uncle was a heart surgeon. Her cousins were both away at college, so the house would be empty. We would just drive in, open the front door with Missy's key, turn off the alarm, and start piling shit into the car. We didn't even bother to park with the front of the car facing away from the house—you know, in the "getaway" position. We figured the worst that would happen would be Missy's aunt and uncle not believing her when she said she had nothing to do with the robbery, but we figured they weren't the type to tell the police they thought their niece was involved.

The alarm system was idiotproof, but we were less than idiots. It was the kind of system that has little boxes on the windows and doors to tell you if one has been opened, and a couple of motion detectors on the ceilings on the first and second floors. When you unlock the door when the system is on, you simply go to a keypad and punch in some numbers, and it turns itself off. You have, like, a minute to punch in the numbers.

The night of the robbery, that minute seemed both like a second and an hour. The keypad was in the front hallway, right beside the switch for the porch and the hall lights, and the minute we open the door and kind of tumble inside, we hear this robotic female voice telling us to deactivate the alarm. At first we're all laughing because we really are pretty stoned. The voice is straight out of a bad sci-fi drama on Spike. But then it dawns on us that Missy is trying to press the buttons with her gloves on, and she keeps hitting two buttons at once. (Incidentally, we were all wearing gloves. We'd all watched enough TV dramas with cops to know that we didn't want to have sex on the beds, use the toilets, or leave fingerprints anywhere. We didn't want to drop a bottle of pills or a cigarette pack anywhere. In hindsight, Missy didn't need to wear gloves because her fingerprints were *supposed to be* all over the house because she'd lived there for a while. But, again, nothing about this robbery was very well thought out.) And so she keeps screwing up the code to disarm the system. Then, maybe because she is wearing gloves so her muscle memory is off, she realizes she has forgotten the code. I'm not making that up. She can't remember the numbers or the order or even the word the numbers would spell if she were to use the letters beside the numbers on the keypad.

And that's when the madness really began.

. . . .

In most ways, I didn't look or act like a rebellious teenager. Slacker? I guess. Underachiever? Could have been my middle name. But, for instance, I didn't do a lot of insane shit with my hair. Actually, I didn't do any, unless you count not washing it for days because you're homeless or stoned. But a lot of girls like me really make a statement with their hair (and often that statement is somewhere between "I just saw a Tim Burton movie and want to look like Corpse Bride" and "I need serious amounts of help and have no idea how to ask for it"). They shave their heads or they dye their hair or they spike it. They get dreadlocks. They get Mohawks. But that wasn't my way of trying to get people's attention. I mean, I'm not even sure I wanted to get people's attention. I wanted to get my parents to stop drinking. I wanted my parents to be happy. I wanted to figure out why, it seemed to me, my brain didn't work like everyone else's.

But, still, my parents and I found all kinds of reasons to fight and sometimes my parents' behavior completely sucked. Here is one memory that I think about a lot. And, in all fairness, I probably think about it because it was one of the moments when I really hadn't done anything wrong. I have plenty where I'm the culprit, and they haunt me, too. I'll get to some more of them, I promise. But this one? I'm just a kid in the wrong place at the wrong time.

It was a Friday night and I was thirteen. I was in eighth grade and it was sometime in March. I had been at my friend Lisa Curran's home, watching videos on YouTube (tons of movie previews, which for some reason we could watch for hours) with her and her mom and another friend of ours, a girl named Claire, and baking cookies. Lisa's mom loved to bake. We didn't always do such incredibly wholesome stuff as bake cookies, but we happened to that night. About eleven o'clock, Claire's dad came to pick her up. I figured my dad was right behind him. When he'd dropped me off, I'd said, Please pick me up at eleven. But eleven became eleven-fifteen, and eleven-fifteen became eleven-thirty. I knew Lisa's mom wanted to go to bed, so this was getting seriously awkward. So, I called my house and my mom answered the phone, which surprised me because usually she was out like a light by eleven-thirty. But I recognized the tone of her voice instantly: it was this low, controlled, throaty voice she used when she was trying not to appear drunk. I asked if she or Dad could come and pick me up, and she said she would be right over. She said she thought Claire's dad was bringing me home, which was a total lie.

The Currans had a pretty short driveway. They lived about four miles from us in an old farmhouse that Lisa's dad, the airline pilot, had restored when he was younger. But like a lot of farmhouses, it was pretty close to the road. And so we saw the brights of Mom's Subaru as she was speeding down the road and then heard the brakes as she must have squashed the pedal to the floor and tried to make the turn into the driveway. She made it, barely. But she sideswiped the Currans' metal mailbox, ripping it off the wooden post. It would be a few years before I'd key Philip's mom's Beemer, but I'd seen other cars keyed by then, and the passenger side of our car looked like some kid had keyed it in a parking lot somewhere. I wouldn't see the full extent of the damage until the next day, but even at night we knew it was scratched and had a pretty impressive dent.

And we sure as hell all heard the brief, acidic metal-on-metal grunt of her hitting the mailbox in the first place. "Sounds like a robot just farted," Lisa said, which was pretty funny—and pretty accurate.

Of course, Lisa's mom didn't think it was funny. She was worried and ran outside. My mom didn't even have time to get out of the car before the three of us had sort of surrounded it: the Currans on the driver's side and me on the passenger side. We were all wearing blue jeans and sweaters—actually, Lisa was wearing a Bruins hoodie—but my mom was in her nightgown. When I opened the passenger door to get in, the light went on and we could all see not only that my mom was wearing this ivory Lanz tent with little blue flowers on it, but that it was covered in red wine. I don't know why we all knew instantly it was wine and not blood. I guess this would be a more dramatic memory if I pretended we thought it was blood. But none of us did. And I know that because Lisa and I would talk about this later. We knew it was wine.

But that still was pretty disturbing.

When I was that age, I had never talked to Lisa or her mom about the way my parents could drink and the way they would fight. I was embarrassed, ashamed, the whole deal. There had been nights when I would try and water down the vodka or the Scotch, pouring half an inch or an inch of alcohol down the sink and adding exactly that much water. I would study the label carefully to get a mark: a kilt, a ship, the letter *S*. A couple of the times after I did that, it made no real difference because my mom and dad had already figured out that they were drinking too much and told themselves they'd only drink wine for a while. But that didn't improve things a whole lot, because then they would simply drink chardonnays or malbecs like the wines were different flavors of Gatorade. My mom leaned toward the white wines and my dad toward the reds. They were in one of their wine phases the night my mom came to get me at the Currans'. The fact her nightgown was sopping wet with red wine was a bad sign, because it was seriously unlikely she had been drinking red and spilled the glass on herself. In my mind, I saw my dad throwing a glass of his malbec on her like she was a campfire he was trying to douse.

"Mira, you okay?" Lisa's mom asked my mom, tapping on the window on the driver's-side door. Lisa was jogging to the end of the driveway, seeing if she could find the mailbox. She did, even in the dark. There was a moon, so it really wasn't that hard. I was standing with the passenger door open, unsure whether I should be getting in to go home or helping my friend retrieve whatever was left of her family's mailbox. It was pretty uncomfortable.

My mom lowered her window and looked at Lisa's mom. Her expression was vacant; it was like she was looking at a stack of junk mail. No remorse that she had just trashed the mailbox and dinged the car. No anger at herself. No awareness even that she was a pretty pathetic sight—and not just because the car smelled like a winery and her nightgown looked like she was trying to dress up as one of the "Walking Dead" for Halloween.

"Mira?" Lisa's mom said again.

From the end of the driveway we heard Lisa yell, "Holy cow! The mailbox looks like a truck ran over it! It's by the lilacs!"

"Why don't I drive you and Emily home?" Lisa's mom suggested. "Let me get my keys—"

There's this joke in the Northeast Kingdom about the weather: "If you don't like the weather, wait a minute." The point is that it can change fast here. Temperatures fall like stones in the lake some days in January. Thunderstorms roll in out of nowhere in July. That's how my mom's temper was. She never hit me—not once. My dad didn't either. But the two of them sometimes went at it like prizefighters, usually because one or the other had touched exactly the wrong nerve: it was like they had stepped on a land mine. *You're making no effort, that's why you have no friends!* One minute, calm. The next? A shit-storm. *I could do this fucking job in my sleep. Besides, I've only had a couple, so lay the fuck off.* And when Lisa's mom offered to drive my mom and me home, she hit one of those nerves.

"I'm fine!" my mom snapped, and now her expression was anything but vacant. She was pissed, one of those psycho chimpanzees that will claw your face off. And, of course, she was drunk. Now she wasn't even going to try and pretend that she wasn't. There would be none of those little shrugs where you innocently say, *Oh, this little bit of wine on my nightgown? I'm such a klutz! Spilled a glass when I went for the phone. Silly me.* "Don't you judge me, Sally! Don't even think of judging me!" she hissed at Lisa's mom, and she grabbed the handle and was about to open the door and get out. I was already sliding into the car and pulling the seat belt across my chest, but I tried to dial down the madness.

"Let's go, Mom," I said. "I'm pretty tired."

I was probably doomed to fail, but it didn't help that right about then Lisa appeared outside the car window with the crushed mailbox in her hands. She didn't say anything, but her mom did.

"Look, this isn't a big deal, but you're in no condition to drive, Mira—"

My mom shoved the door open, slamming it so hard into Lisa's mom that she sent the woman stumbling backward onto the asphalt.

"Mom!" Lisa screamed, dropping the mailbox onto the driveway, where it bounced into the door. My mom nearly tripped over it when she staggered to her feet.

"I'm fine, honey," Lisa's mom said, but she was stunned and looking at the palm of her left hand like she didn't recognize it. (The next day she would have a piece of gauze taped to it, but she insisted the cuts weren't that big a deal.) Then she gazed up at my mom, who was looking down at her. Everything about my mom's body language said, *Get up and I will beat the living crap out of you.* "If you want, Emily can spend the night here," she said to my mom. But I knew how well that idea would go over. And so I said, "Let's go, Mom. Please, I just want to go home." I was crying, but I was hoping she couldn't tell from my voice.

And here's what I mean about my mom and the weather. Something in my tone really did reach her. Something inside her head clicked when she heard that quaver in my voice; suddenly, she saw what she was doing. She saw outside herself.

She knelt on the ground and actually hugged Lisa's mom. She murmured over and over, "I'm so sorry. I'm so, so sorry," and Lisa's mom patted her shoulders and said to come inside for a cup of coffee.

Which my mom did. Lisa and I ate cookies and watched an episode of *Gossip Girl*.

Then my mom and I left.

Incidentally, the ride home really wasn't all that terrifying. My mom drove like seventeen miles an hour.

. . . .

It was a real shocker for me the first time Poacher had Andrea and me steal big bottles of Tide. That's right: Tide. The laundry detergent. He wanted us to walk into the supermarkets all around town—the Grand Unions and the Price Choppers and the Hannafords and even the Walmart out in Williston—and then just stroll out with one or two of those humongous 150-ounce jugs of the stuff. He said no cashier was going to bother us at the supermarkets. And at Walmart, one of us should simply talk up the geriatric greeter while the other one of us left the store with the Tide.

I figured the soap was going to be an ingredient in some kind of drug that either he or someone he knew was going to cook. So I said, "You want the powder, right?" But he said no, the liquid was fine. All that mattered was that we come home with the biggest jugs we could carry.

Altogether, we ended up lifting thirty-two of them, or nearly $600 worth of detergent. He was absolutely right; no one stopped us.

And he was telling me the truth when he said the detergent really wasn't an ingredient in some new kind of meth. He resold all that Tide to these two little groceries in the North End and one on the way out to Malletts Bay for ten bucks a jug—or a net profit of $320.

"People just love their Tide," he said to Andrea and me. "It's the damnedest thing." And that night we didn't have to fuck anyone we didn't want to fuck. It was all good and I didn't cry myself to sleep or need any chemical interventions.

Chapter 7

The worst cold was the night in the igloo when it was twenty-seven degrees below zero and the wind coming off the lake seemed as loud as a chain saw. But I had stolen a bunch of those disposable hand warmers and toe warmers from the ski shop on Main Street that afternoon. Each one lasts an hour or two once you expose it to air, and I just kept handing them to Cameron or—after he fell asleep—pushing them into his mummy bag. I would only let him put his head outside the igloo when he wore his wool mask. It covered everything but his eyes and his mouth, and that's important when it's that cold out. It's essential to cover every bit of your skin that you can.

The next day, I stole a small folding Sterno stove, but that didn't do all that much to keep us warm. Maybe it would have been great if we felt like cooking, but it was too cold outside to cook. Mostly we ate energy bars and fruit and cheese sticks, which are all easy to steal. I wanted to be sure that Cameron got plenty of calcium and fruit.

There were times when I was a totally unfit guardian (I almost wrote "big sister"), but not those nights. I was homesick and sad—and you don't know homesick until you think you will never, ever see your home again. But sometimes I think I was at my best when the world seemed to be at its worst.

. . . .

When I left the staging area, my plan was to bike north on Route 5 through Coventry and try to get home. Even if my parents were dead, there was still my dog. And I wanted her. I was afraid for her. And so I was going to return to Reddington to rescue Maggie.

In hindsight, this plan was completely bonkers. But I wasn't thinking straight. (As a matter of fact, I was *so* not thinking straight that I was fantasizing I would run into my mom and dad on the road in Mom's Subaru. I really was. There they would be, driving the other way and trying to catch up with the kids from the Academy, and Maggie would be in the backseat. I was actually scanning the roads for our car. How is that for crazy?) I was no more than two miles from the staging area when I got to the very first checkpoint. There was a pair of guardsmen in those hazmat suits standing there, and there was a line of orange traffic cones in the right lane. One of the guardsmen was windmilling his arm so the vehicles leaving the Kingdom would keep moving, while the other stood before all those cones with his rifle slung over his shoulder like a sentry. I would describe the dudes for you, but mostly I would be making it up. You don't get a lot of detail through the mask of a hazmat suit. But I had the sense they were young and tough and pumped up by the importance of their work. I guess if you're an adrenaline junkie stuck in Vermont, it doesn't get much better than a nuclear meltdown.

"Whoa, other way, young lady!" the one with the gun told me when I reached him and stepped off the pedals of the bike. You don't sound like Darth Vader through those masks, but your voice does sound muffled. He had to shout and his breath would fog up the visor.

I started out pretty calm when I answered him. I was trying to be super reasonable. "I'm really sorry," I began. "I'll be fast. My dog is at home and I think my parents are gone. I need to rescue her."

"Not happening," he said. "No one's allowed through."

"I understand," I said. "I will be really fast. I know the danger. That's why—"

"Look, you need to turn around, little girl. That's an order!"

It was probably the word "order" that set me off. As most of the counselors and therapists I've had over the years have been only too happy to tell anyone who asks, I don't respond well to commands. And so I snapped at him. "Just forget it!" I said. "Okay? Fine! Let my dog die back there!" And then I stood up on the bike like I was going to do what he said, but instead of turning around, I tried to ride past him and continue on my way home. What was he going to do, shoot me?

Well, he didn't shoot me. But he was fast, and he grabbed the back of my shirt before I had pedaled more than six feet and gotten going. And when he pulled back on the cotton, he spun me around and I wiped out. He stumbled, too, but he didn't wind up on the shoulder of the road the way I did.

"What the hell, girl!" he said, looking down at me. "I said you can't go back there! Have you lost your mind?"

"No! I just want—"

"I know, you just want your dog, I get it," he said. "But no one's allowed back in there. God, everyone's trying to get out!"

I remember I started to say something about Maggie, and just verbalizing her name suddenly had me weeping. I was bawling that I wanted my dog and I wanted my parents and I wanted to go home.

"What's your name?" he asked me. "Where do you think your mom and dad are?"

Before I could answer, that other dude, the one who had been directing traffic, shouted, "We don't have time for this, Rick! Put her in a car going south—any goddamn car—right now!"

This Rick guy's eyes and mine met for a split second, and then he dropped his rifle and started trying to lift me up. He was using his hands like a forklift, jamming them under my arms, and it hurt like hell. It was partly a reflex against the pain, but I lashed out and kind of karate-chopped him in the elbows. Maybe he was afraid I was going to reach for his gun, which hadn't crossed my mind, but he crabbed his way over to it. And I used that moment to lift my bike and take off. I knew I wouldn't get far if I tried to pedal north, back toward my home in Reddington, so I went south. I figured they were too busy to bother chasing me if I was heading away from the meltdown like everyone else—which was the case. They didn't go after me.

I told myself I would find another way back in, another road, I would rescue my Maggie. But I knew in my heart that wasn't going to happen. There was no way back in. I was leaving Maggie behind and there was nothing I could do. I was leaving like everyone else. And so I pedaled and cried and pedaled and cried and kept saying out loud, as if she could hear me, *I am sorry, Maggie, I am so, so sorry.*

....

Maybe because I'd stolen the bike, I parked it just outside the front door to this convenience store five or six miles away from the checkpoint so I could keep an eye on it while I went inside. People were kind of desperate, and I didn't want someone else to steal it from me. The store owners were closing because they were supposed to evacuate, too. But they were torn between safety and greed. I wasn't the only person hoping to buy something quick. There were five of us in line when the sheriff came in, and all of the others had what looked to be the last of the store's water and Gatorade in their arms. I had, I discovered, two bucks on me, which was just enough for a Tiger's Milk bar.

The sheriff was a paunchy guy, and he was wearing a breathing mask. The rest of us, of course, were just sucking in plain old radiation air. But he pulled the mask down so it was hanging around his neck when he said to the man and woman behind the counter, "You need to close up shop now. Let these people buy what they want, but no one else comes in. I want this place locked and you folks on your way in two minutes."

They nodded and the woman, who I guess owned the place

with her husband, said to me, "What's your name?" when I was handing her my two dollars. She was in her fifties and just trying to be maternal.

"Emily Shepard," I said. It was a reflex.

"Shepard. I just heard that name on the radio," the man beside her told me, trying to recall the context. He snapped his fingers and went on, "Your father—your parents—" And then abruptly he stopped. Just shut up mid-sentence.

The person behind me in line, a tall, thin dude in his late twenties with a green John Deere ball cap who was already seriously agitated, took my shoulder and spun me around to look at me. "It was your dad who did this?" he said, part question and part statement. For a second no one said a thing. Then, suddenly, everyone in line was screaming at once, at me and at each other. It was madness. This couple behind him, a man and a woman who were old enough to be my parents but were unbelievably skanky, each grabbed one of my arms, and the woman kind of leaned into me and said with the worst beer breath ever, "We've lost our house! Because of your fucking father, we've lost our house! What have you done?"

Instinctively I wriggled free and looked at the sheriff, who was already trying to get between me and these two screwballs. He was pissed, I could tell, and at first I was relieved because I thought he was going to give these lunatics a piece of his mind. Nope. He was actually pissed at me. "Young lady, we're going to need to talk to you. You're going to have to come with me right now."

"I didn't do anything!"

"I didn't say you did. But we need to know what happened. We need to know what you know. Come with me."

"Are you arresting me?"

"Have you done something wrong?"

Looking back, he was probably just being sarcastic, like, *Why would we arrest you? It's not like you've done something wrong.* But the people in line were staring and yelling about how people were dead and more were going to die and they'd all lost their homes, and all I could hear were words like "cancer" and "ruined" and "melt-down." Words like "your father." These people didn't know me or my father, but they hated us both. They hated me. And I thought about what I had overheard back at the staging area.

Whole family: fucking despicable.

There'll be a cover-up. Blame the dead people.

They had a daughter. They'll make her testify. Talk about what an alcoholic her dad was.

"No," I answered the sheriff, "I haven't done anything." But I don't know if what I said even registered with him, because the people behind him wanted to lynch me, and other people were streaming into the store to try and buy last-minute provisions and hoping there might be some water and bread left. The sheriff screamed at the owners, "I want these people gone now! And I want that door locked! Do you hear me?"

And that's when I ran. I took that second to escape. I didn't know what was in store for me, but it was clear that everyone loathed me and everyone loathed my dad, and even if they didn't arrest me, they were going to make me say horrible things about my family. When the sheriff tried to herd the mob away from me and get the owners to lock the door, I bolted. I didn't look back when they were yelling at me to stop, and I didn't dare turn around because even a millisecond might be all they'd need to catch me. I hopped on the seat of my bike and pedaled as hard and as fast as I could, weaving like a crazy person through the traffic jams. And I mean this: I didn't look back until I had gone at least a couple of miles.

. . . .

Like I said, the biking was hard, especially when the adrenaline from my escape was gone. I knew a few boys at school who were serious bicyclists: they clipped into their pedals with those special shoes and wore yellow bike jerseys. Their bikes weighed as much as a fat cat or a small dog.

The bike I stole wasn't like that. It was a mountain bike. And I figured out pretty quickly that a mountain bike actually sucks if you are trying to bike up a mountain. They should only call them off-road bikes. Or, maybe, really flat-road bikes. But it had lots of gears and that helped. And when even in a granny gear I couldn't muscle my way up a hill, I would just get off the bike and walk the damn thing. I tried to be happy that at least it wasn't raining.

Besides, there were some stretches during the first two hours when I couldn't go very fast anyway. The roads were still packed with people trying to get away. It was so sad. Just these long lines of Vermonters who were terrified of the radiation or terrified that they were about to lose every single thing they owned. Sometimes people who were better bicyclists than I was would pass me, and sometimes people on motorcycles would pass me. Sometimes I would pass walkers. We would all just kind of grunt at each other. No one with a vehicle offered to give me a lift because often I was making better time than they were—which, as I said, still wasn't all that fast. I would peek into the cars and trucks, and people's faces said it all: numbness and horror and shock. I would glance at the things they thought were important and had chosen to bring: the computers—laptops and desktops—the paintings, the photo albums, the pillows, the quilts, the brown bags of groceries. The gallon jugs of water. Water and computers: it fascinated me. Lots of the people who weren't driving were staring at their iPads and tablets for news.

And then there were all those animals, and every one of them made me think of my Maggie.

It was like we were all trying to reach some seashore with an ark before everything fell completely apart.

When I thought about anything other than my family or running away myself, I thought of how I had stolen the bike I was on. I'd never stolen anything before. I wasn't even the kind of kid who would pocket a tube of Bubble Yum from the general store in Reddington. I guess the bike was the start of my whooshing down the slippery slope that eventually would have me stealing pretty much whatever I needed to survive.

Was I more scared than everyone in those cars and trucks? I guess in some ways. I mean, unlike all of them I was positive that my parents had just died. And I was convinced that somehow my dad was responsible for this nightmare. Or at least partly responsible. And, yeah, I felt like a marked person. I felt like people were after me, too. Does that excuse my stealing a bike? Probably not. But it explains it. I really was on the edge of delirious. I may have looked like just another refugee on a bike, but I was close to the kind of emotional meltdown that would have made my outburst at the checkpoint look downright mild.

Eventually, of course, the traffic opened up. While a lot of us were going west, we would hit different roads going south and cars would peel off. There was always a steady stream and it was always going in one direction (away, away), but it started to move. By now it was late afternoon, but this was June and so the sun wasn't going to set for hours. There was a part of me that was beginning to wonder what I was going to do after dark: Should I stop? Should I sleep? Should I just keep going? And if I did stop, where? I had no idea if I was still getting dumped on by radiation, so I decided I would just forge ahead. Like everyone else, now I just wanted to get as far away from the Kingdom as I could.

When I reached another hill at about five-thirty, I got off my bike again and started pushing it up the shoulder. I had gone maybe half a mile when a bread truck pulled up beside me and stopped. I didn't really have the antennae for bad shit then that I do now, but fortunately it didn't matter. The fellow driving it was wearing a brown jacket with both his name and the bakery's on it. His name was Sandy and he looked about fifty-five or sixty, but he had thick white hair and the sort of deeply lined hands I always associated with the dairy farmers I knew.

"Need a lift?" he asked me.

I paused and he must have sensed my hesitation.

"I don't bite," he said. "I understand if you don't want to get in. But I have three granddaughters and a pair of grandsons. Some are in Jeffersonville and some are in Essex Junction. I promise you, I'm harmless."

Suddenly I was exhausted. All the air went out of me like a popped balloon. I was tired and hungry and thirsty. Unbelievably thirsty. It had been hours since I'd had even a sip of water. I nodded. "Yes. Thanks," I muttered, my voice beaten and hoarse.

He pulled off the road a few feet ahead of me so the cars behind him could pass and turned off the ignition. He jumped out, opened the back doors, and then lifted the bike into the back, leaning it between the racks of bread and English muffins and hamburger buns. When I got in the front of the truck beside him, he must have sensed that I was in a bad way. Without asking me what I wanted, he reached into a little red Igloo cooler and pulled out a bottle of water for me. Then he reached behind him and grabbed a loaf of bread off the nearest rack. He unspooled the twist tie and handed me a couple of slices.

"Obviously we're not supposed to do this," he said, and then he took a piece for himself. "But I don't think today anyone's going to care."

. . . .

So, the robbery—the one where we almost wound up like Bonnie and Clyde's gang in that very scary black-and-white photograph. It's the one where a gang member is sitting in this field in his underwear with half his head shot off, but he's still alive, and his wife is being dragged away from him by a guy in a necktie and another policeman. There are policemen everywhere in the photo, but Bonnie and Clyde have gotten away. I saw it on a special about the Clyde Barrow Gang I watched one afternoon with Ethan on the History Channel. How weird is that? There was actually a time in my life when I was watching the History Channel after school.

Anyway, Missy pulled off her gloves with her teeth and was

about to start trying to punch in the code to disarm the alarm at her aunt and uncle's house with her fingers, but Trevor stopped her.

"No!" he hollered at her, and batted her arm down. "Fingerprints!"

She screamed that the code was gone, just gone, meaning gone from her head, but by then it was too late anyway. It went off, a car alarm but it seemed a lot louder: the horn was on the front porch, so it was practically over our heads. It was deafening and I know I screamed. Andrea did, too.

And, of course, this also meant that right that second the local police were being notified automatically.

Trevor picked up Missy's gloves off the floor of the hallway and then dragged us all into the kitchen. I expected we would run back to the Miata, but I guess his instinct was only to escape that screeching bleat, which meant running in the opposite direction. In the kitchen the sound was muffled, but still plenty loud. We all still had to yell to be heard.

"Look, we should get out of here," PJ was saying, and I remember I was nodding like crazy.

But Trevor shook his head and said, "We still have a few minutes before the police get here, right? We give ourselves sixty seconds and grab all we can and then—"

And then the phone rang, and it was on the wall right beside me and I jumped. Trevor looked at the number and name on the screen and saw that it was the alarm system company.

"I guess they call to see if we set off the alarm by accident," Missy said, sniffling and wiping at her nose. It suddenly dawned on me that we hadn't broken any law. I wondered what would happen if Missy answered the phone and told the company that she had come home to get something and just forgotten the code. Merely a false alarm, no biggie. Then we could all drive back to Poacher's, get stoned, and try some other house some other night.

But the answering machine picked up before I could say a word, and the company didn't bother to leave a message. There was no turning back now.

"Okay, people, let's do it: sixty seconds!" Trevor said, and I followed Andrea into the dining room so we could steal the silver, and Missy ran upstairs to grab as much of her aunt's jewelry as she could find (and, supposedly, her aunt had some serious ice). Trevor and PJ started pulling the plugs from the Blu-ray player and the flat-screen TV in the living room, though how the hell they thought they were going to fit a TV almost the size of a pool table into the back of a Miata was beyond me. But they were male, and so they had to at least try, right? (Me? I would have just unplugged the Xbox and called it a day.)

Andrea and I had these cloth laundry bags with string ties, and we just started throwing candlesticks and silverware and these oil lamps that were probably pewter and not silver into them. It was hard to focus with that off-the-hook-crazy alarm coming at us, but it's not like what we were doing was brain surgery. We had been at it maybe half a minute, shoveling knives and forks and spoons from this sideboard into our bags, when suddenly Andrea dropped her bag and swore.

"Shit!" she said. "My eye!" Then she ran into the bathroom on the first floor beside the stairs. I followed her.

"Something's wrong with my eye! It's like there's glass in there!" she was saying, and while she had turned on the water, she was staring at her eye in the mirror. It was her left eye, and I could see it was vampire red. And I could see something that looked like a dollop of green goo at the edge near her nose when she turned to face me. "What the fuck?" she shrieked. "It hurts so fucking much!"

I heard Missy pounding her way down the stairs, and she paused when she saw me standing in the doorway to the bathroom. "What happened?" she asked.

"My eye!" Andrea wailed. "Something's gone wrong with my eye! It hurts and I can't see out of it!"

"You can't see out of your eye?" Missy said.

And before Andrea answered, Trevor and PJ came up behind Missy and me. "Let's roll," Trevor said. "Done and done." He was holding a coffee table and PJ had a vase. I guess they had given up on the TV and felt they had to steal something to earn their keep. Still, that coffee table had as much chance of making it into the Miata as the TV.

"I can't see!" Andrea screamed at all of us. "Don't you fuckers get it? I can't see! Something's happened!"

I knew Andrea was capable of losing it; I'd witnessed one of her tantrums the day we had met at the shelter. (Let's face it: All of us, as our therapists liked to say, were a little too impulsive and a little too emotional for our own good. We ratcheted up the drama. We talked some serious shit.) But this was bad, and it didn't help when first Missy chastised Andrea, saying, "I told you, you can't sleep with your eyeliner on!" and then Trevor yelled at her for taking her gloves off. He pushed between Missy and me and turned off the faucet and started wiping down the sink with his gloved hands.

But Andrea just turned it on again and stamped her foot and then collapsed on the tile floor against the toilet. She curled up her legs against her chest and wrapped her arms around her knees. She was sobbing and repeating over and over that she was in agony and she was going blind and no one cared. I leaned over, half hugging her and half trying to get her on her feet. But I really didn't accomplish either. Andrea was taller than me and seriously stubborn when she wanted. We're talking unmovable object.

"Andrea, we need to go," I begged and my mind was racing as I tried to think of what to say. It didn't help that the family's asinine alarm was flipping all our brains sideways. "We'll take you to the emergency room," I added, which at the time I thought was inspired. In hindsight, of course, it really wasn't all that brilliant. It was only what a normal person would have suggested, right? "We have to get you to the hospital."

She looked at me—and her eyeball, I saw, really was disgusting—and I could tell that I had gotten through to her. Something had clicked. She put one hand on the floor and one on the toilet and pushed herself to her feet.

"Okay, let's get out of here," Trevor said, and we all raced through the house and piled into the Miata. I grabbed Andrea's sack, so I was carrying two, and Missy had hers, but we left that ridiculous coffee table behind on the front steps. PJ was clinging to that vase like a little kid with a teddy bear. He really did look like a five-year-old.

Missy was driving because it was her car, and Trevor was in the seat beside her. Once again, Andrea and PJ and I were wedged into the backseat, which was fine with me, even though I wound up in the middle. I held Andrea's hand and told her she was going to be fine, she was going to be okay, but in the back of my mind I was thinking, *Well, that's why God gave us two eyes. So if we sleep in our eyeliner and go blind in one, we have a backup.* But I didn't say that.

Missy had just put the car in reverse when we saw the flashing blue lights racing down the road and turning toward the driveway. The driveway was maybe a hundred yards long, and it was lined on both sides with pine trees six and seven feet tall. This was a pretty new meadow mansion. So what kind of a badass was Missy? Without saying a word to any of us, she turned off the headlights and gunned the car straight ahead and off the driveway, roaring into the side yard and then racing over the patch of ground where her aunt had what she called an Italian garden in the summer. Tomatoes, basil, peppers. Stuff like that. But there were still those wire tomato cages, empty now like pieces of broken chain-link fencing, and Missy plowed right through them. In the moonlight they made me think of the debris in some postapocalyptic zombie movie, which then made me think of Cape Abenaki, and what it must have been like those days inside the Exclusion Zone.

Meanwhile, Trevor and PJ were whooping like rodeo cowboys. They thought this was hilarious. The Great Escape and all. Then Missy drove through the next-door neighbor's yard, dinging some little kid's metal swing set. It wasn't that late, and so there were still lights on at that house—and at the next one. But even if it had been two in the morning, I have to believe the burglar alarm would have gotten the neighbors out of bed. (Further proof that Missy could have been one heck of a serious criminal, if she'd wanted:

she had the instincts to keep the headlights off as we raced across people's property.) We must have rock-and-rolled through half a dozen yards, and some were obstacle courses. Think *The Amazing Race*. In addition to the gardens and that swing set, there were long piles of logs and prefabricated metal tool sheds and lawn tractors and birdbaths and a picnic table with those attached benches. There were Adirondack chairs. There was a plastic playhouse. There was a gazebo. We dinged that, too, because we were trying not to run over a sandbox Missy saw in the dark at the very last second.

But then we reached someone's driveway, and she turned the car hard to the left and for a second it felt like we were only on two wheels and were going to flip over—which would have really put a damper on the evening, because none of us were wearing seat belts and the convertible top was, of course, down. I think we were probably only going forty or fifty miles an hour, but that's fast if you're driving at night without headlights through the backyards of rich people's meadow mansions.

I remember breathing a sigh of relief when we were back on the road. Missy punched on her headlights and slowed way down. She wasn't sure what the speed limit was, but she guessed it was thirty-five. By now the flashing lights were long gone, as was the sound of that house alarm. I looked at Andrea and her head was bowed and her hands were over her eyes. I wondered if crying was going to make her eye better or worse, and I told myself it was only going to help because the tears might wash away some of the gunk.

We drove until we got to this little elementary school and Missy pulled into the parking lot. I wasn't sure why—I guess none of us were—and so she told us. "I'm going to cut across the playground. I want to be sure we're on Dorset Street before the police," she explained.

And that might have been the end of our night, but Missy decided to press her luck. She accelerated off the pavement onto the grass, and we banged hard into a railroad tie for some little raised garden bed. And we hit it in just the right way that we kept going and didn't even get a flat tire, but PJ went flying from the car, still clutching that lame vase. Missy jammed on the brakes and stopped, and we all jumped out after him. Even Andrea.

When we got to him, he was curled up on his side in a ball. He looked up at us, winced, and then closed his eyes. "I am so fucked," he grunted, his voice almost inaudible. Right about then we saw the blood starting to stain the side and the shoulder of his gray hoodie. There were big and small shards of the vase all around him.

"One hell of a face plant there, PJ," Trevor said, and I think he was trying to lessen the tension. "Can you get up?"

PJ didn't answer, so Trevor squatted beside him and repeated the question. This time PJ shook his head. "Give me a minute," he groaned.

"Okay, then. Good to know," Trevor murmured, mostly to himself, and he went back and turned off the car lights. About then Andrea remembered that she was supposed to be going blind—which, for all I knew at the time, she really was. "I still can't see!" she wailed hysterically, "I can't see and none of you care!" Then she fell to her knees beside PJ. Trevor and Missy and I stood there for maybe half a minute, trying to figure out what the hell we were supposed to do. I was terrified for PJ. I was terrified for Andrea. I mean, I cared about these people, as fucked up as they were. They were my friends.

That's the moment in my mind that feels just like that image from the documentary about Bonnie and Clyde. A bunch of wounded criminals sitting in a field, one of them maybe dying and the other going blind.

....

It was after that cluster fuck of a robbery that Missy's parents came to get her and bring her home, leaving instead with only the Miata. They must have known that we were the ones who had broken into Missy's aunt and uncle's home, but no one ever pressed charges. We made a little over a thousand dollars from the stuff we sold, but that wasn't nearly as much as we had hoped we would. And it was a lot of work and had involved a lot of risk. We were flirting with way more legal trouble if we'd been caught than when, for instance, we were walking out of the Grand Unions and Walmarts with big jugs of Tide. That would have been just a misdemeanor if we'd been caught. But that nightmarish moronathon at Missy's aunt and uncle's would have been a felony.

Later that night we would bring Andrea and PJ to the hospital, but just in case we drove almost an hour south to Porter Hospital in Middlebury. The doctor and the nurse who took care of them were cool, but the receptionist was a total bitch. It was like it was our fault that we didn't have insurance. (Okay, it was. But, really, did we have to be lectured about it right that moment?) Andrea was fine. In the emergency room, they numbed her eye and then touched it with a little strip that left behind this orange dye. She screamed like she had just been impaled in a slasher movie and then yelled at the doctor for having coffee breath, but he just nodded and said they should both try and breathe through their noses, and kept right on examining her. (That's what I mean about how cool he was.) He was middle-aged but still seemed pretty buff, and when he was in her face it was like they should have kissed. It was very intimate. But, of course, that didn't happen and she finally chilled and became an okay patient. He flushed out Andrea's eye with saline solution and gave her some antibiotic ointment. He told her not to share her mascara brush with me.

PJ's situation was more complicated because he needed stitches for the two huge gashes on his arm and his side. And he had broken a couple of ribs. The vase and that fall had done a real number on him. He had to spend the night in the hospital.

The next day when we went to bring him home, he was gone. He just up and left in the middle of the night without telling anyone. We texted and called him for days, but he didn't respond. Finally we gave up. We never did see him again.

Chapter 8

This is not the most important thing I am going to tell you, but it may be the most interesting: Did you know that a lot of Emily Dickinson's poems can be sung to the theme from *Gilligan's Island*? Not kidding, this is totally legit. When my English teacher, Ms. Gagne, first told me that, I had never heard of *Gilligan's Island*. But she explained to me it was an old sitcom, so I looked it up and watched it on YouTube. It's from the really early days of TV: the 1960s. The first year, they didn't even use color film, which makes it look prehistoric. And the show is ridiculous. As lots of people before me have pointed out, they're stranded on this island after a shipwreck and seem to build whatever they want out of coconuts and bamboo . . . but for some reason they can't fix their boat. Still, the starting music has a catchy tune, and you can learn it pretty quickly. I bet most of you know it, especially if you're from my parents' and grandparents' generations. So, try it.

> *Because I could not stop for Death,*
> *He kindly stopped for me;*
> *The carriage held but just ourselves*
> *And Immortality.*

> *We slowly drove, he knew no haste,*
> *And I had put away*
> *My labor, and my leisure too,*
> *For his civility.*

See what I mean? Pick another of her poems at random and see what happens. Most of the time, it works. I don't know what this says about Emily Dickinson's writing or American sitcoms of a certain era, but it sure was helpful when I started trying to memorize some of my favorite poems.

You can also sing "Because I could not stop for Death" to a sort of disturbing folk song called "The Yellow Rose of Texas." You probably know that tune, too. Go ahead: try singing the poem to that song. What's really interesting to me is that "The Yellow Rose of Texas," supposedly, was written about a Galveston, Texas, girl named . . . Emily.

Sometimes, it seems that everything is connected, doesn't it?

Someday I will put together a list of Interesting People Named Emily. They won't have to be famous. Just interesting.

. . . .

Sandy, the guy who delivered bread for that bakery, wasn't on his rounds by the time he picked me up that afternoon. Like everyone else, he was either trying to get away or get to family—or both. He was on his way to Jeffersonville, where his daughter and son-in-law and two of his grandchildren lived. He was meeting his wife there.

"Why don't you wait at my daughter's house for someone from Burlington to pick you up?" he said. "It'll be dark soon."

I had told him that I was a boarding student at Reddington Academy, not a local, and I had grandparents who lived in Burlington. He seemed so nice that I almost confessed to him who my parents were, but after what had occurred at the convenience store and what I'd overheard back at the staging area, I was worried about the reaction I'd get. So I said—as I would a lot that year—that I was from Briarcliff. And when we got to the house, I was very glad that I hadn't told him who I really was. The TV was on, and his wife and his daughter and his son-in-law were watching the endless stream of news from Cape Abenaki. And every few minutes, I would hear my dad's name and it was never good. There was film, shot from Canada, I guess, of just billows and billows of smoke roiling up from the reactor. In front of the plant was Lake Memphremagog, and the water was calm and dark and seemed to stretch forever. It had always seemed to me to be a very long lake. But after the rain and the flood? It seemed massive, much wider than usual—because it *was* much wider than usual. I could see how high the water was against the first row of cooling towers. And there were talking heads debating the severity of the explosion and explaining maps and diagrams on the screen and (of course) offering their opinion as to the cause. It had stopped raining, and some of them seemed to think that everything would have been okay if it had stopped a day or even half a day sooner.

And, they hinted, everything might still have been okay if my dad had been sober. But then someone would say that no one knew for sure if he had been drunk or if alcohol had figured in the disaster. But everyone agreed that operator error was involved. Something about an isolation condenser. Someone, most likely my dad, had turned it off and then—for some reason—could not get it restarted. There were witnesses among the survivors—people who had fled the building before the explosion. My dad was dead, and so he was the perfect choice for the fall guy.

Sandy's daughter had married a guy named Walter Thomas, and the Thomas family home was small but very cozy. It was a yellow and green ranch house, and everyone clearly enjoyed snowmobiling. They had two massive machines and two little ones for the kids—who were younger than me—and a whole room dedicated to clothing and gear and the trophies the kids had won at junior snowmobile competitions. The girl was named Melissa and she was scary smart. Kind of a jock, too, based on the ribbons and medals and photos that hung on the walls along the stairway. Clearly she was going to be an all-American something someday. She was eleven. Her brother was nine and much quieter. I was too numb to have a strong opinion about either of them, but Melissa didn't seem to mind that I was going to sleep that night on an inflatable mattress on the floor of her bedroom. I guess that was enough for me to like her.

And, thankfully, they had two cats and no dog. I think I would have lost it completely if they had had a dog.

So, I took a shower and then ate dinner with the family. I was too sad and scared and tired to say much, but I lied shamelessly and impressively about my situation when they asked me questions. At one point, I went into another room and pretended to talk to my parents and my fictional grandparents on my cell phone—which was long gone by then—and I even made a pretend call to Lisa Curran. I must admit, after that one, I considered lying again and saying my cell was now out of juice and I needed to use their landline. Then I would call Lisa's cell and beg for help. But I would have had to make that call in front of the family, because the landline phones seemed to be in the living room and the kitchen, and that would have meant toppling the whole house of cards I had built from my lies. And I couldn't bring myself to do that. Not yet, anyway. I didn't want them to see what a liar I was or who my dad was.

Sandy's daughter was named Bridget, and she was a hairdresser—but she was probably the least glamorous hairdresser on the planet. Bridget Thomas said she mostly did blue hairs, which did not mean eccentric, attention-starved teens: it meant old ladies. Like her dad (like everyone in the family), she was very nice. She was going to bring me to my fictional grandparents in Burlington the next morning, because I'd said they both had pretty bad eyesight and didn't drive much. I was okay with this plan, but I wasn't wild about it. It meant that I would have to come up with a boatload more lies when we got to the city. I'd have to make up some address or pick some random house and hope no one was home. Then I'd have to come up with a reason why no one was home that was so logical that Bridget wouldn't feel any reason to wait. When Melissa and I turned out the light in her bedroom around ten, I hadn't come up with one yet.

"Are you scared?" she asked me suddenly as we lay there awake in the dark.

Incidentally, I almost wrote "as we lied there awake in the dark," but I know the difference between "lay" and "lie." I had a seventh-grade English teacher who taught me the difference. We were working from a textbook, and he read this sentence from it aloud: "Father is laying tile on the kitchen floor." Then he looked up at all of us and said, pretending to be confused, "Tile. What an interesting name for Mother." I never forgot that. Of course, given how much I was lying in the days after Reactor One melted down, it would, in fact, have been correct if I had written, "as I lied there awake in the dark." I told Melissa some serious whoppers that night as we talked before she finally fell asleep.

But I also admitted to the girl that I was scared.

"Me, too," she said. "But I'm not sure why. They say the radiation won't come this far."

"It won't," I said. "You'll be okay. We'll be okay." But I didn't believe that. I was just trying to make her feel better. If I'd been honest, I would have told her that she was scared because what *they* said didn't matter. *They* didn't know what they were doing. And, on some level, she had figured that out. I also understood, but didn't know how to explain at the time, that even the people who weren't totally fucked—everyone, in other words, who did not live or work near Cape Abenaki—were scared of the unknown. None of us knew what this was going to mean for our food or our water or our air. None of us knew if the electricity would suddenly go out and ATMs would stop working. None of us knew anything.

That night all I understood was what I felt. And what I felt was dread.

....

The inflatable mattress was comfortable enough, but I still slept pretty restlessly. I woke up about five in the morning, just before the sun was going to rise, but the sky was already growing light outside one of Melissa's bedroom windows. Because I had never fallen into a very deep sleep, I didn't have a *Where am I?* moment when I opened my eyes. I knew right where I was. I knew instantly my parents were dead.

And as I watched the light begin to trickle into the room, I realized it was actually going to be a beautiful sunny day—the first in forever. A sunny day in June? Once upon a time that was awesome. It was all it took to make a person smile.

I thought of what it would be like when Bridget asked me for my grandparents' address over breakfast.

ME: Um, I'm not sure. But I know how to get there.
BRIDGET: What's their phone number? I can call them.
ME: I don't know it.
BRIDGET: Would you mind getting it from your mom or dad in that case?
ME: Oh, I can find the house for you. I know right where it is. I just don't know the names of most of the streets in Burlington.

I imagined Sandy offering some solution as well. Pulling a Garmin out of his delivery truck and handing it to his daughter, after I had gotten a street address from my parents.

And so I climbed out from under the light blue sheet on the inflatable, found my clothes, and got dressed. Everyone was still sound asleep. I went to the kitchen as quietly as I could and found a magnetic notepad on the refrigerator where they kept an ongoing grocery list and ripped off the top sheet. I wrote them a thank-you note. I said it was a beautiful day and I thought I would ride my bike into Burlington. It was only about thirty miles away. (*Only*. I was there by early afternoon, but I was toast. My knees ached, my butt was sore, and my back was actually spasming.) At the bottom of the note I wrote my name: Abby.

When I was about two or three miles down the road, I wondered if they would be so worried about me that they would call the police. In my imagination, I saw some missing persons report or AMBER Alert and all of Vermont looking for a teenage girl named Abby Bliss. I wondered who would be the first person to google her and discover that she'd actually been dead for a hundred years.

But they never did call the police. Or, if they did, a teen girl who wanted to ride her bike thirty miles to Burlington was the last thing a state trooper or sheriff was going to worry about the day after Cape Abenaki exploded.

. . . .

Sometimes I think I have talked too much about pills. We did a lot of pills, but we also smoked a lot of dope. Once one of us had come up with a twomp—twenty dollars in Poacher-speak—we would score whatever we could.

Just so you know, I never tried heroin. Poacher said heroin was like "God kissing your cheek," but I felt very small those days and wasn't sure how I would handle something as big as God getting that close. We had a drawer in the kitchen beside the sink with nothing but needles and spoons and cotton swabs. It kind of scared me.

And as for meth? I once watched Trevor and PJ try and shake and bake a batch in a one-liter bottle of Pepsi, and I was terrified. I didn't mind the cold pills. They seemed way more harmless than the painkillers I'd discovered I liked. But peeling batteries? Lighter fluid? That's just insane. When Poacher came home, he nearly blew a gasket. "What the fuck are you two trying to do," he screamed at them, "blow up my apartment?" Apparently, if you don't know precisely what you're doing, it's easy to turn what once was a harmless one-liter bottle of Pepsi into a firebomb. Live and learn.

Nine months later when I had lost everything, including Cameron, and was trying to make my way home to Reddington, I occasionally came across shake-and-bake debris in the high grass by the side of the road: those plastic one-liter bottles filled with brown sludge. Sometimes they'd still have a tube. I was grossed out. But I can remember also feeling like I'd dodged a bullet. By then I didn't think I had much of a future—that was, after all, why I was going home—but at least I was going out on my own terms, not because one of my idiot roommates had blown us up while trying to cook himself a little meth.

....

I used to love to go skiing with my dad. I had a snowboard and I rode pretty well, but usually I skied so I could be with him. We would talk on the chairlift in ways we never spoke elsewhere—in ways we couldn't.

I used to love to watch DVDs of *Friends* with my mom. We would sit on the couch in the den and sip hot chocolate. My mom made very, very good hot chocolate. Sometimes she made it with a sprinkling of coconut and sometimes she made it with a dash of hot chili powder. She never made it from a packet.

I loved how sophisticated and exotic my mom was in some ways. Just think of her name: Mira. I used to love to look at the *New York Times Style Magazine* with her those weekends when it would appear with the Sunday newspaper. Sometimes, she'd show me pictures of the ways she had dressed when she was living in Greenwich Village before she met my dad. It was nothing like how she dressed in Vermont.

I used to love to be read to in bed when I was a toddler and a little girl. My mom and dad would alternate nights, and the rule was that they would read me four books when I was very young and then forty minutes to an hour when I was older. One night when my dad was reading to me from *Sideways Stories from Wayside School*, we got to the scene where we learn that Calvin has a tattoo of a potato on his ankle, and for some reason we wound up laughing hysterically for fifteen minutes. We just couldn't stop.

I loved my bedroom with my stuffed animals and trolls and the chest that still had my dress-up clothes from when I was a little kid.

I loved my bookcases, two of them, both white, which went to the ceiling. I loved my window seat in the sun. I loved my diaries and my journals.

I loved my clothes. I loved my iPod. I loved my phone.

I loved the posters I brought back from the Emily Dickinson Homestead in Amherst when I was fourteen that my mom had gotten framed.

I loved Maggie. I loved the way my dad called her Maggie May and sometimes sang her a line or two from that song when he rubbed her tummy.

I am telling you this so you know that my life wasn't always wall-to-wall suckage. I know I've tried to make that point before, but it's really important to me that you get this. Sure, my parents were not happy in Vermont. They didn't belong here. Sure, they fought in ways that left me scared. They drank—they drank a lot. And, of course, I was starting to screw up well before the melt-down that made me an orphan.

But if I am being as honest as I promised I'd be, you need to know that in some ways I was really a lucky child. I know I brought a lot of my nightmare down upon myself.

. . . .

I'm not sure why I picked Burlington. But I know now that the homeless of all ages from northern Vermont and New Hampshire and upstate New York wind up there. Always have. It's a city, which means it has social services. And drugs. And bars. And people—some of whom want to help you and some of whom just want to exploit you.

And I guess I was following the crowds, that whole stream that was flowing away from the Kingdom. It was amazing the sort of chaos I found in Burlington. Reactor One had exploded little more than twenty-five hours earlier, and already there were tents all over the waterfront and City Hall Park and I heard for the first time the terms "walker" and "downwinder." I've already told you that most of the walkers didn't actually walk to Burlington; like-wise, many of the downwinders didn't technically live downwind of the fallout. Some of us, like me, were from right smack in the middle of the disaster—not downwind of it at all. And others were coming from areas that, in the end, would prove to be safe. Or, I guess, safe enough. But there were lots of pregnant women among the downwinders and lots of young moms with their toddlers and lots of old people. These were people who didn't want to leave anything to chance and just got the hell out.

Sometimes I think we all got used to the word "walker" instead of "downwinder" because it had one less syllable. And it was a lot faster for everyone who gave a damn about Twitter to hashtag, right?

Still, it took me a while to even get those last few miles into the city to see all the madness for myself. Traffic on the roads around Burlington was either at a complete standstill or moving no more than a couple of miles an hour. And I couldn't even really bike around the cars a lot of the time, because what was supposed to be two lanes in each direction had become four lanes in one and one in the other. That's right, five rows of vehicles were wedged into four lanes. And the sidewalks were filled with people who had hitchhiked their way this close or had gotten rides from friends (and, I guess, bread trucks), and so even those of us with bikes finally just got off them and walked them for miles.

But the road into Burlington is filled with fast-food and coffee places like McDonald's and Starbucks and Moe's, and they were all giving us bottles of water and juice until they ran out. It was kind of sweet. The police officers were trying to move the cars along, but it was gridlock at every intersection. People would ask for news, and the news was just depressing. The worst for me? This was the moment when I learned that my dad's engineer friend Eric Cunningham had killed himself. Apparently he had survived the blast, but he felt so bad about whatever had happened—whatever had gone wrong—that he'd shot himself with a hunting rifle later that day. I didn't even know he had one. I mean, he and my dad

played paddle tennis together. Once in a while, they went skiing together. (They never went hunting together. My dad wasn't
a hunter.)

Still, at least it wasn't raining. And when I finally reached the
top of the hill above Burlington, Lake Champlain and the Adirondack Mountains looked like a travel and tourism ad. Really, everything Vermont is supposed to be. As a matter of fact, because the
sun was out, I was kind of sunburned by the time I was finally able
to climb back onto my bike and coast down the shoulder of Main
Street into the city.

Chapter 9

I never did get my driver's license, as you know, but I did have a learner's permit. A couple of days a week, my parents would drive to and from the plant together in my dad's Audi. So I'd just take my mom's Subaru and drive wherever. To Lisa's or Ethan's. One time all the way to Littleton, New Hampshire, where there are actual stores with decent blue jeans and tops. Obviously this was against the law and impressively clueless. I never got caught by the police, but when my parents found out what I was doing, it was kind of like being busted. They screamed at me and I screamed back. And then they took away my phone and grounded me for a week.

. . . .

Poacher was very smart—or, at least, smarter than a person might sometimes think he was. One time when we were all sitting around with a nice little buzz on watching the news on TV, some expert started talking about operator error at Cape Abenaki, and what went wrong and why the fuel rods broke and the uranium pellets fell out and started melting down. It was the eleven o'clock news, so we were all pretty chill.

Poacher sat forward a little bit on the mattress, shaking his head, and said, "Those poor fucks never had a chance."

Trevor, who was in one of those slightly defiant, challenge-the-alpha-male-father-figure modes, said, "I don't know. I think they blew it. Don't you? Just screwed up. I mean, weren't they trained for this sort of bullshit?"

"Oh, sure, they were trained," Poacher answered. "Some might have been very well trained. But there are some folks who have the right stuff and there are some folks who just don't. I saw that all the time in Kuwait. There are some people who will stay cool no matter what's going down, and there are some people who wig out. Or do nothing, when doing anything is better than doing nothing. They just freeze. And those dudes in the control room running Cape Abenaki? This was no drill. This was the real thing. And they're just, like, operators. They *operate* systems. That's what they do. It's all rote. It's all procedure. And think about it: these days, all the procedures are on computers. Sure, they probably had some paper manual explaining what the fuck they were supposed to do. But if it's anything like the systems shit I saw in the army, all the piping and instrument diagrams would have been stored on the computers. And so when the computer network goes down— poof!—a big part of the road map they need is gone. The electronic records just disappear. I mean, I have no idea what kind of light is left when the batteries are failing. Is it dim? Is it, suddenly, pitch-black? Those poor *operator* sons-of-bitches must have been shitting in their pants. Picture it. I don't know, maybe one of them had the right stuff. Maybe not. But all that training? Forgotten in the panic. In the dark. I feel for them. They're just people and it's black or at least almost black and you're in this control room next to a pair of nuclear reactors and you know that at least one of them is about to explode and there's not a thing you can do. Not one fucking thing. Let's face it: When you can't find the valves or the piping or whatever the fuck materials you need? Game over. Game . . . over." And then he made that noise the Pac-Man games make when Blinky, Pinky, or Clyde gobbles up the very last of your Pac-Men, and he spiraled his finger like water was leaving a bathtub.

I was pretty sure he was right. Over the years I'd overheard conversations here and there between my dad and mom or between my dad and other engineers about the emergency procedures. And so now I saw my dad, standing there in the control room in his white PCs—maybe even my mom too. (PC was the term they used for "protective clothing." It has nothing to do with "political correctness." Don't forget, this was a nuclear power plant we're talking about. The last thing a nuclear power plant worries about is political correctness.) I saw him standing there in those little booties they were all required to wear. (In fact, my dad wore booties over his booties. There were very special ways you got in and out of your clothes, even your gloves. There were "change-out" pads and a whole "change-out" protocol.) And suddenly I knew I was going to be sick. I got up off the couch, stepping on PJ's leg on the way—he yelled at me and I ignored him—and ran into the bathroom and started vomiting into the toilet. Andrea was right behind me, holding my hair away from my face and rubbing my back. I was puking and crying and I couldn't stop for, it seemed, forever.

When I was done, I was surprised that no one was in the doorway watching. Asking me if maybe I had swallowed some pills I shouldn't have. Andrea explained that they had come to see what the hell was going on, but she had made them go away and leave me alone. Then she ran some hot water and helped me to wash my face. We were sitting together on the side of the bathtub.

"You didn't take something wacky, right?" she asked.

"No. It was just . . . just those people in the plant."

"That's why you were crying?"

"Uh-huh."

See what I mean about what a great sister Andrea was? Looking back, I wish I had confessed right that moment that I was imagining my parents in the dark in that control room. Maybe if Andrea had known who I was, she would have stayed. Sure, in those days most of Vermont hated anyone who had anything to do with Cape Abenaki, but I don't think Andrea would have cared. I really don't. She was that kind of friend.

....

When I reread what I've written so far, I seem to be crying a lot. I guess I do cry pretty easily. I'm sorry.

But, in all fairness, I was in kind of a bad place. I think it would have been way weirder if I wasn't crying all the time—or, at least, as often as I was.

....

For a while I wandered aimlessly around the tents and blankets on the grass in Burlington's City Hall Park that first afternoon. If you didn't know the world was ending, you might have thought it was a Phish concert, except the crowd had a lot more old people and a lot less dope. The air smelled mostly of fear. Eventually I dropped my bike on the grass beside this little amphitheater garden, and then I collapsed on the ground right beside it. It was early in the afternoon and I had picked a spot between a family of five on these Disney beach towels and two senior citizen grandparents with a little hibachi. Everyone wanted to feed me, and I let them. It was a bit like a picnic, except for the teeny-tiny detail that everyone was still scared to death that the plume was going to come this way, and everyone was cursing the company that ran Cape Abenaki and everyone associated with the nuclear power plant. It was kind of a hate mob mentality.

But we all still had to eat, and I was famished. I ate a couple of these Smucker's Uncrustable prepackaged peanut butter and jelly sandwiches, which a few weeks later would become one of my favorite munchies when I was stoned off my ass, and I ate grilled lamb and onions on wooden skewers. The Uncrustables were courtesy of the younger family, and the lamb was from the older couple.

After we ate, the Disney dad offered to bring me over to the Red Cross tent and see about getting me some help, but I wasn't sure I liked the sound of that plan. The Red Cross would try and get me—Abby Bliss—reconnected with my parents, and no good was going to come from that. Pretty quickly they'd figure out that I had made up this name and then they'd figure out who I was. And I wasn't convinced people would be real excited to meet Bill and Mira Shepard's daughter. Meanwhile, that grandmother— who was actually spreading face cream on her cheeks and offering me sunscreen, like our biggest problems that day were wrinkles and sunburn—was suggesting that I visit the shelter for homeless teens not far from the north end of Church Street. She had read an article about it in the newspaper the day before yesterday. I thought about my options and decided that the shelter strategy seemed a lot more promising, especially because there I could pretend I was just a run-of-the-mill runaway—not a walker who needed to find her mom and dad. I'd have to convince them I was eighteen, but I figured I could make that work for a while. All I was trying to do was buy a little time to figure out what I was going to do in the long run.

And so about six-thirty I showed up at the front door of the shelter.

The weirdest thing that happened my first night there? Someone stole my bike.

. . . .

Here is that list of Interesting People Named Emily I promised. Again, my rule is interesting, not famous—though most of these women are somewhere between sort of and seriously famous.

Emily Dickinson: Poet and recluse. She might, in fact, be the world's most well-known recluse, and it's not easy to be famous and private. That's an impressive accomplishment and makes her *very* interesting.

Emily Watson: Actress. I've seen two of her movies, and she's very good. Plays crazy people and moms. I approve.

Emily Stetson: Claimed to have put stakes through the hearts of twin vampires in a village in Wales in 1905. Was never charged with a crime because there were no missing persons and they never found any bodies. But here's what makes her so interesting: she was thanked by the vicar for digging up two graves in the church cemetery and giving a pair of souls their much-deserved rest. The village loved her. *Loved* her.

Emily Post: Stupendously OCD about manners.

Emily Brontë: Gave us *Wuthering Heights.* 'Nuff said.

Emily Paulsen: First girl to play running back for a high school football team in Vermont. Broke her ribs in ninth grade, her left leg in tenth, and had a concussion in twelfth. But her junior year? She led the state in rushing yards.

Emily Blunt: Another actress—and, like Emily Watson, British. Also like Watson, she's great at playing women about to go mental.

There are also a couple of nineteenth-century women's rights activists named Emily, but I couldn't finish reading the web pages I found about them. Way too boring. They are not (just my opinion) very interesting. Sorry. Maybe they weren't crazy enough for me. Maybe my definition of interesting is "crazy."

. . . .

I slept like a dead person my first night in the shelter. I don't recall a single dream.

My room was slender and not all that long and there was absolutely nothing on the walls. It had a bed and a dresser and a window. It faced out on an alley and a brick building, but I really didn't care about the view. It was on the third floor, and so it was a little steamy in June, but I knew I was lucky to have it, as bare and Spartan as it was. It was, after all, the last room the shelter had left, and I only got it because they had just moved the girl who was in there before me—one of their success stories—into a little apartment of her own. And while a few other kids told me later that they'd been pretty frightened their first night in the shelter, I think I was too exhausted to be scared. Besides, I had no idea of the drama I was in for: the endless, energy-sucking, always-on-the-edge-of-hysteria drama queenitis that was Situation Normal for most of the girls there. And I thought that once upon a time I had been high maintenance? Yeah, right. I didn't know the meaning of the expression "high-maintenance."

Anyway, in the morning I woke up feeling so good that I began to believe my parents might not really be dead and were out there somewhere looking for me. They were worried and desperate—which made me excited and hopeful. And so even before I had showered, I asked the girl in the room across the hall if I could use her phone. (This would, of course, prove to be a gigantic mistake.) Her name was Camille and she was a runaway from Barre, Vermont. Her mom and dad both worked in a company that specialized in caskets for infants. No wonder she was so fucked up: her parents made coffins for babies. But she handed me her phone, and immediately I called my mom and dad and left them both messages. I told them where I was and to please come get me. Then I figured I'd hang out at the shelter until they called.

But, of course, I wasn't allowed to hang out at the shelter. They had told me the night before that I was supposed to be out of there by eight in the morning, but I didn't think they'd really care. They did. So I borrowed Camille's cell a second time and left the number for the shelter's drop-in on my parents' phones and said they could find me there. I said to ask for Abby Bliss, and I'd explain why when we were together.

I became a part of Edie's caseload right after breakfast, and I spent the rest of the morning making up stories for her—and the other therapists and counselors she introduced me to—about this Abby Bliss person. I talked about a high school I never went to and a neighborhood I could only barely envision. A lot of what I was describing I probably didn't really remember: I was building a world from photos I'd seen on my parents' computers or in the photo albums that lined a couple of shelves in a bookcase in our den. (For a while, my mom actually printed out photos and put them in albums. That stopped when I was about nine or ten, I guess. Then the photos just piled up in drawers. Who had time? Besides, by then we were keeping our photos on our phones and Facebook and Tumblr.)

Once Edie had decided that I wasn't homicidal, suicidal, or schizophrenic—I guess that's the big three you want to avoid if you run a teen shelter—she wanted to call my mom or dad. But I kept stalling. I told her I didn't want them to know where I was and, besides, they were on a cruise somewhere in the Caribbean. I begged her to please wait until they were back. I implied there were *serious reasons* why I'd had to leave home. She probably didn't buy any of it, except for the idea that I was eighteen. And since I seemed so freaking well behaved, she was going to let it slide for a few days and see what developed.

So, I went to my first "life skills" class right after lunch, the first step toward my first fifty-buck MasterCard. Then a volunteer who I guess worked for Edie—she went to UVM and was studying to become a social worker—gave me an Old Navy gift card that some shelter "angel" had donated for emergencies like me, and I went and bought some new underwear and a shirt. Then I hung out in the Fletcher Free Library. (Supposedly, everyone used to hang out at Borders, but then Borders went out of business and everyone migrated to the public library. Further proof why we need book-stores: people who work in bookstores are way less likely than people who work in department stores to get in your grill if you're a homeless goth kid with a face tattoo.)

Most of the homeless kids at the library would kill time by surfing the computers or they'd find a *People* or a *Maxim* or a *Rolling Stone* magazine floating around in the periodical room, but I wanted to steer clear of news of any kind. I was doing this thing that I know now is called "magical thinking": if I didn't see or hear some sort of proof that Bill and Mira Shepard were among the dead up at Cape Abenaki, they might still be alive. And I had overheard enough to know that the official list of casualties was now in the news.

Besides, it was packed in the periodical room. Packed. The place was filled with the usual homeless and patrons, but today there were dozens of walkers as well. And I mean dozens. The lines for the computers by the reference desk were freaking ridiculous. It was like the lines outside the movie theater on the opening night of a new *Hunger Games* film. So I went upstairs to the library's poetry and fiction sections. I began thumbing through the collections they had of Emily Dickinson, but I had seen most of them before. I owned two of them. I even owned two of the three biographies on the shelf. So I took a stack of books, including *The Journals of Sylvia Plath*, and I sat on the floor in a corner by a window. I came across one line in her journals that I wrote on my hand with a ballpoint pen: "Kiss me and you will see how important I am." It's not from a poem, but it is poetry. I think it's a better single line than any lyric that Taylor Swift or Katy Perry has written so far, and I like their songs as much as any teen girl. And it reminded me of one of my favorite things that Emily Dickinson wrote:

The Waves grew sleepy—Breath—did not—
The Winds—like Children—lulled—
The Sunrise kissed my Chrysalis—
And I stood up—and lived—

This is from one of the poems that make me wonder if her life had fantastic secrets she never shared. Tell me the woman who wrote "The Sunrise kissed my Chrysalis" didn't at least once—and maybe way more than once—wake up in the arms of a man. How could she not?

And when I came across that Plath line that day at the library, I remember thinking how everything in the world is connected. I wanted to write it all down, all the connections, not just ten words on my hand. I wanted—I needed—my journal.

And, of course, I wanted my parents. I wanted Maggie. I needed them, too.

When I left the library to return to the shelter, I went down some back stairs so I didn't have to pass through the room with the computers and the news and the possibility that I might see Bill and Mira Shepard's names on a screen or on the front page of the *Burlington Free Press*.

Chapter 10

One day at the very end of September, nearly nine months before the meltdown, I came to school drunk. I wasn't as drunk as everyone thought I was, but I was pretty hammered. I'd had a few shots of my parents' Cutty Sark instead of oatmeal for breakfast. Maybe more than a few. Drank from halfway up the ship's sails to down below the words "Scots Whisky." My goal was to get caught, which I did, and make a point to my parents, which I think got lost in all the shouting and the grounding and the embarrassment and my guidance counselor getting all sanctimonious and judgmental.

"You're a junior, Emily," she said to me. "Don't you get it? This is the year that decides, more than any, where you are going to go to college. Why would you do this? Why?"

Well, the answer was pretty simple: so my parents could see what a drag it is to hang around with a drunk. There were probably better ways to convey that message than missing my chair in homeroom when I tried to sit down or crashing into my French teacher in the hallway and sending him into a wall of lockers. I think my breath was flammable.

Just for the record, I meant to fall out of my chair. I did not mean to body-slam Monsieur Poirier into a bunch of metal.

....

The moon was melting down, a waning gibbous of orange.
It wasn't really. It was just the moon. But it was tinged with

red and no longer full. But that was the first line in the last poem I wrote before Reactor One exploded.

> *The moon was melting down,*
> *A waning gibbous of orange.*
> *The horizon was lost to the sea.*

I wrote it in the middle of May. Obviously there's more. Probably too much more. I think it's interesting that I used the verb "melting." I really was thinking nuclear reactor, not ice cream along the sides of a waffle cone. It was a love poem. The problem was that there was no boy I was in love with then, so the poem sort of sucked. It was about this young couple's first kiss. Maybe it would have been better if I'd written about how there was no boy in my life that night who I wanted to kiss, and *that* was the problem. *That* was the sadness. Maybe the poem was meant to be melancholy.

Anyway, when I stood on the street outside the entrance to the teen shelter a couple of nights after I arrived, the moon really was poppy, and it was just on the far side of full. It was, obviously, right about where it had been a month earlier when I'd written that poem. So I remembered those words as I stood there, watching the other kids smoke, and I thought of how pretty the sky was over Burlington. The Northeast Kingdom was a disaster—a Chernobyl-sized disaster—but still the sun rose and the moon waned and the sky was impossibly pretty.

And I wondered how in the name of fuck these kids could afford their cigarettes. A pack of cigarettes at the general store in Reddington cost something like eight and a half dollars. That's roughly forty-two cents a cigarette. You couldn't shoplift cigarettes, because they were always kept behind the counter. But then I saw what they did and I got it: they passed around the cigarettes almost like they were joints. There were five of us, and the other four girls were passing two cigarettes back and forth.

I was still pretty shell-shocked those days. One minute I

was keeping it together and the next I would be in a bathroom somewhere—the shelter, the drop-in, the library, the shopping mall—running the water so no one would hear my pathetic, hiccupping little sobs. There were times when I was practically hyperventilating. I knew by then that my parents were dead. And I knew by then that everyone hated them. I didn't hate them, of course. I probably loved them more now that they were dead than I had when they were alive—which, because I understood this, didn't help my frame of mind a whole lot. I also knew that people were seriously exaggerating what my dad did or didn't do as the plant inched—make that tumbled—toward the precipice; they had to be. By the time my dad went to Cape Abenaki in the middle of the night, it must have been hours since he'd had a drink. It was three in the morning when he went there. He'd gone to bed around eleven. Besides, I don't think either of my parents had drunk very much the night before. It had been a pretty calm evening.

"Take a puff," one of the kids said to me on the street. "Go ahead."

I didn't smoke, but I looked at the tip of her cigarette and it seemed kind of inviting. Besides, I saw no reason not to anymore. I figured I had been exposed to so much radiation that my insides probably glowed in the dark. Lisa's mom sometimes said to us after we did some crazy shit, "You teenagers think you're immortal, that's the problem." Maybe back before Cape Abenaki we did. I did. But now? I was pretty sure I was the exact opposite of immortal. So I accepted the cigarette, held it like a doobie because I couldn't figure out how to hold it like Betty Draper on *Mad Men* or Johnny Depp wherever, and took a puff. I coughed, but not like people do in the movies when they pretend they can smoke. Wasn't a big deal. Then I took a second drag and blew the smoke in front of the moon.

"Our little Abby is growing up," Camille said. "No longer just an art nerd. Getting rid of those airs and finally getting real. Trying to be human. Trying to be one of the gang." She said it with serious condescension and it was edgy and strange. First of all, it was weird to hear her calling me "little Abby." As far as Camille knew, I was only a year younger than she was: I'd been telling everyone I was eighteen. And I was sort of confused as to why she'd call me an art nerd. It's not like I was walking around in my black "Dwell in possibility" T-shirt. (Yeah, I had one.) Finally, I had no idea I had been putting on airs. I was trying to be invisible. I wasn't even around most of the time—which, arguably, might have been part of the problem.

But Camille was the Queen of the Tribe those days. You know that TV show, *Survivor*? Well, I'd been at the shelter a couple of nights by then and had begun to figure out just how tribal the place was. Just how tribal life on the edge of the streets was. A high school bunch of mean girls is nothing compared to a clique of homeless kids or runaways. We're talking pig-head-on-a-stick tribal.

"Little Abby: makes me sound like a comic strip kid," I told Camille. I wasn't sure what to say, but I had to say something, and this sounded pretty harmless. I was even trying to smile a bit as I said it.

"Oh, you are no comic strip kid. You have serious secrets."

"Nah."

"Abby Bliss: What kind of name is that?"

"Scottish," I answered.

"Made-up, I'd say," Camille told me, her tone a little accusing, and the other girls nodded and chuckled, their eyes a little wide. Think of those *National Geographic* or Animal Planet kind of videos: the lion was about to catch and eat the warthog or gazelle.

"Well, Camille sounds pretty made-up, too," I said. "It sounds like you should weigh a thousand pounds and be singing opera somewhere." This was, in hindsight, not the smartest thing I could have said. Why I felt the need that moment to in any way challenge Camille is beyond me. Maybe it was because I had tried to dial it down a moment ago by only reacting to the "little Abby" part, and I thought my comic book line was pretty innocuous. You know, it's like my name was part Li'l Abner and part Little Orphan Annie.

And maybe I was suddenly feeling threatened—that Camille was on to me. (Which, of course, she was.) Maybe I thought I needed to be tough to protect myself. But the problem was that I was still an outsider. I wasn't a part of Camille's tribe because I was always hiding out in the library. I didn't even know the names of all the other girls out there on the street with me. And I wasn't a part of a rival tribe, so I had no one to stand up for me. Still, it's not like I told Camille to go fuck herself or something. Saying her name sounded like a fat opera singer's was pretty lame. Not super toxic. At least that's what I thought. Nope.

"You think I'm fat?" she asked me.

And then one of her girls asked me that too: "You think Camille's fat?"

Camille was big, but she wasn't fat. She had hair that was usually red, but she had bleached it white with peroxide and was moussing it up into a pompadour. She had blue eyes that lots of actresses would have killed for and whole constellations of freckles (which, I gather, she hated) on her cheeks and arms. She was built kind of like some of the girls I knew who started the first-ever girls' rugby team at Reddington: a little burly but really just athletic. You know, solid. Strong. Most of those kids started that team because they thought it would look good on their college applications: It was feminist. It was out of the box. It was funny. "No, of course not," I tried to reassure Camille. "I don't think you're fat."

"But you think I have a fat person's name."

I did, that's true. But that doesn't mean Camille *is* a fat person's name. And I know it probably sounds now like I'm a fatist—you know, that I have something against fat people—but I'm not. It's just that the name Camille sounded to me that night like an opera singer's, and opera singers are often men and women of a certain size, if you get my drift. Besides: we all bring associations to names. We just do. You say Camille, I think opera singer. But maybe you think tiny eighty-pound Olympic gymnast because you once knew a girl named Camille who could rock the parallel bars or do backflips.

"I don't know," I mumbled. "But I think there's a very famous opera singer named Camille." This was somewhere between a lie and a guess.

"You think?"

I shrugged. I looked at the other girls, but none of them was going to be of any help whatsoever. "Look, I'm sorry," I said. "I didn't mean anything."

She glared at me and then dropped the cigarette butt on the sidewalk. "Where do you go during the day? You tell me the library, but no one ever sees you there."

"I am at the library."

"No you're not."

"I am. I'm upstairs. In the fiction section."

"With the made-up shit?"

"I guess."

She seemed to think about this. "You know what I should do?"

I shook my head.

"I should call those numbers you made from my phone. See who picks up. Maybe then we can learn whether Miss Abby Bliss is a lot of made-up shit. Maybe we'll learn if you really have any reason to be so high and mighty."

My stomach lurched when she mentioned the calls I'd made on her phone. I hadn't thought about whether someone might wonder who I was calling and try the numbers. That first morning, I hadn't understood the politics of the shelter—the fact that I was a newbie and needed to fly way under the radar. I guess Camille must have thought I was pretty ballsy when I asked to make those calls on her phone.

"I don't think you're fat. I think you're pretty. And I like the name Camille," I told her. I figured it would be way worse to beg her not to call those numbers—you know, draw attention to it. That might make it absolutely clear that I had something to hide. But I know my voice must have sounded pretty pathetic and beaten and small. Already I was wondering if somehow I could steal her phone for a minute and delete those calls from its history.

"How much do you like *me*?" she asked.

"I like you," I said, not actually answering her question.

"Then kiss me," she said, and she turned the side of her face toward me. She tapped her index finger on a little Rorschach of freckles just below her cheekbone. "Kiss me right here."

I saw the other kids were staring at me pretty intensely. Two were smiling just the tiniest bit. They loved this. It was even better than lion-devours-gazelle because it was right in front of their eyes. So I kissed Camille exactly where her finger had been. It was a pretty dry peck, but it was all she really wanted. This was just about making sure everyone knew I was her bitch. I figured that would be it. Nope. She reached her hand out and began to finger the earring dangling from my right earlobe. Remember that antique necklace I told you about? The Danish one made of moonstones that my mom loved? Well, these earrings weren't antique, but they were made of moonstones and silver and by the same jewelry company. My parents had gotten them for me for my sixteenth birthday. They were kind of valuable and meant a lot to me. I know they were my favorite pair of earrings I'd ever owned.

"I sure do like these earrings," Camille said, trying to hit that perfect tone between seductive and bullying. I knew where this was going, but didn't say anything. I'd been wearing those earrings, except when I showered and slept, since Reactor One had exploded. I put them under my pillow when I went to bed at the shelter, because I knew someone might try to steal them. But I had never imagined that someone might try to take them from me while I was actually wearing them. I mean, who steals your earrings right out of your ears? No one at Reddington Academy, that was for sure.

"I think we can be friends, Abby Bliss. But you need to show me a little love, too," Camille murmured.

I didn't want to give them up, but I also didn't want her to call the numbers I had left on her phone. At the very least, I needed to stall for time so I could try to delete them. (I would expend a *lot* of effort at the shelter stalling for time—especially when I was trying to prevent Edie from calling my pretend parents or the high school in Briarcliff.) So, I didn't even wait for Camille to ask: I pulled the hooks out of my ears and dropped the earrings one at a time into her hand. I didn't cry—I almost did, but I didn't—and I'm very glad about that.

But you know what? When I look back on that moment now, I kind of wish I had gone up to Camille a few days later, when I was on my way out the door of the shelter, and gently touched one of the earrings in one of her lobes and said, "Those earrings, bitch? Pretty fucking radioactive."

. . . .

I got no great insights into life the one time I did windowpane. They—well, Andrea—said most of the time I was just curled up naked on the floor of the shower, super depressed. But I also don't think it messed up my brain any more than it already was.

And I was pretty clean when I was with Cameron. I did a bowl the weekend we finally came in from the cold, but that was it. Let's face it, I had to have my head on straight. I was all that little guy had.

. . . .

I years had been from home,
And now, before the door,
I dared not open, lest a face
I never saw before

Stare vacant into mine

This was one of my favorite poems Emily Dickinson wrote. It's more about memory than it is about returning home and wondering what sort of welcome awaits. It's more about change.

But when, nine months after Reactor One exploded, I struggled back home to Reddington—filled with self-loathing because of what happened to Cameron and having given up on my own life completely—I interpreted it both ways. It felt like years since I'd been there. And I wasn't sure what face would greet me in the mirror in my own bedroom. (I wasn't worried about who would greet me, because I knew the Exclusion Zone was—at least supposedly—deserted.)

Also: I promised you I would be honest. I promised myself I would be honest. If I am not going to be miserly with the truth, I should rewrite a sentence from that last paragraph. Here goes:

But when, nine months after Reactor One exploded, I struggled home to Reddington—filled with self-loathing because of what I had done to Cameron and having given up on my own life completely—I interpreted it both ways.

Sometimes I just wish I could go back in time. God. I so really do.

. . . .

Other times I do this: I try and imagine what's going on in someone else's life at the exact same moment that something is happening to me. Sometimes I focus on how unbelievably monumental shit is going down somewhere, at the same time that the rest of us are just going about our daily lives. I mean, think of all the people who were just grocery shopping in Concord, New Hampshire, or Austin, Texas, when Reactor One exploded. Some woman somewhere is putting a jar of pickles in her metal shopping cart at a Price Chopper at the exact same time that another woman—my mom—is being blown into who knows how many little pieces. (I will never know how many little pieces. But I do know they were all radioactive.) And sometimes it's comparisons that are not quite that extreme.

But here is another one I think about: What was I doing at the precise moment when a seriously nasty dirtball named Bob Rouger took his hammy, middle-aged fist and popped it into a nine-year-old kid's eye?

When I was first thinking I was going to tell you about Cameron's foster dad, I started yet another poem I didn't finish:

The G was hard as in rug,
Not soft as in rouge.

I didn't finish it because suddenly I wasn't sure if "rouge" would be considered a soft *G*. My bad. Anyway, Rouger's name was pronounced "roux" as in something to do with cooking and "grrrrrr" as in batshit-rabid dog.

I ask you: What kind of bastard punches a nine-year-old kid? Seriously: Who does that?

And yet—for ten thousand reasons—Cameron would have been a lot better off if he hadn't run away after his foster dad socked him. I wish he had gone to school the next day with that black eye, because I have to believe that some teacher would have said "Whoa!" and immediately called social services. And while all that would have meant for Cameron was another foster home, it would have meant that someone might have handed Rouger his ass on a plate. Maybe even jail. A girl can hope, right?

So, what was Cameron's crime? He was taking a twenty out of Rouger's wallet so he could go to the Montshire Museum on a class field trip and not have to be, once again, the usual, pathetic foster kid charity case. When he'd asked Dee Rouger, his foster mom, for the scratch, she'd said no, they didn't have it—though, of course, they always had the money to pay for field trips for their three real kids. So, he thought he'd just take a twenty. And he got caught. Not good, I know. But, you have to admit, it has a little moral grayness to it. Besides, things had been pretty nasty all six months that Cameron had been there. Bob Rouger had slugged him before. Dee Rouger had slapped him before. And their real kids? They didn't trust Cameron as far as they could have thrown him—and, according to Cameron, they couldn't have thrown him more than a foot. Two prissy middle school girls and one six-year-old boy.

So, what was I doing the night Bob Rouger was trying to make a nine-year-old kid's eye socket the width of his fist? What was I doing that very moment? Maybe it was the exact second when I was standing outside the Kappa Sig Something fraternity house on Main Street, blowing into my hands and wondering if I looked too skanky to fuck some UVM frat boy who was back on campus so he could drink and ski. It would mean a warm room, and I was freezing. But, in the end, I decided no frat boy who really was from a place like Briarcliff would want anything to do with me. I'd left Poacher's by then and I was kind of a mess.

The Rouger household was Cameron's fourth foster home. After Bob Rouger got medieval on his face, Cameron had had enough. As I said, we didn't see each other later that night, but we were both camped out in that empty coal plant down by the waterfront. I came there from outside the fraternity house, and he came there from the Rougers'. It was the next day that I would see him and learn all about his duct tape art and his precious mummy bag—and realize that for all his swagger, the kid was in at least as much trouble as I was.

. . . .

Cameron was nine and Maggie was nine, but they didn't have the same birthday. Just an observation. And, obviously, Maggie was something like sixty-three years old in dog years.

When I told Cameron that I had a dog his age, I choked on the words and had to tell him that I had a tickle in my throat.

One time when I was in New York City with my mom and dad, we passed a homeless guy with his homeless dog outside St. Patrick's Cathedral. It was a German shepherd and seemed very sweet. Bony, of course, which combined with its very pointy ears made it look like something straight from *The Hobbit*. The guy's little handwritten cardboard sign asking for dough said the dog was named Smokey and they were both very hungry. My dad said they might really be homeless, but they probably made an okay living. My mom wasn't so sure.

I know I've been through a lot, but sometimes I'm not sure I can think of anything sadder than a homeless person with a homeless dog.

Chapter 11

I sometimes hear people talking about how normal things are now, compared to those first weeks after Reactor One exploded. It's true. There is the Exclusion Zone, and it must suck to be a Vermont dairy farmer because no one wants Vermont milk or cheese anymore. But for most of the world—for most of Vermont—the Cape Abenaki meltdown is just another bit of old news. Tsunamis. School shootings. Syria. We watch it, we read about it, and then we move on. As a species, we're either very resilient or super callous. I don't know which.

But those days in late June and early July? The nuclear power plant was pretty much on everyone's mind, even when they weren't talking about it. People tried to do their jobs, but everyone's head was someplace else. I think that was clearly the case with Edie, my counselor at the shelter. Edie knew what she was doing. I think she was a great social worker, I really do. But it was probably a little harder than usual for her to focus. I'm kind of amazed that airplanes weren't falling out of the skies because pilots were thinking about Cape Abenaki when they were supposed to be flying their 787s. I'm a little surprised that anyone survived brain surgery back then.

My point? I think Edie would have been on to me right away if she hadn't been a little preoccupied. I was able to buy time at the shelter because I insisted I was eighteen, which meant that I didn't need my parents' permission to be there. And I got a little more time with the weekend, because schools and agencies were closed. But by day five, I could see things were starting to unravel. In theory, my parents were back from the cruise now, and I could see that Edie was losing patience with my insistence that there was some deep, dark secret why I didn't want them to know where I was.

"Briarcliff High School, right?" she said a little too casually to me on Monday morning, and I knew that she was going to call them and ask about this person named Abby Bliss. And while the school might have been in the chaos of finals or getting ready for graduation, someone there was going to pick up the phone and look up some records and tell this social worker from Vermont that no one named Abby Bliss had ever been enrolled there.

So, to postpone the inevitable, I told Edie that my mom was coming to Vermont on Wednesday and they could actually meet and talk about my situation. The dialogue went pretty much like this:

EDIE: You spoke to her?
ME: Uh-huh.
EDIE: When?
ME: Maybe an hour ago. The boat had just gotten back to land. Fort Lauderdale.
EDIE: So you're telling me you called her.
ME: Yes.
EDIE: I thought you lost your phone.
ME: I borrowed one.

She stared at me pretty intensely, probably trying to figure out if I was lying. My biology teacher once talked about how body language and facial expressions are great ways to see if someone can be trusted, so I tried to look real calm and innocent. I stood as still as I could and tried to meet her eyes, but I was also scanning the room to see who wasn't there. If she asked me whose phone I'd borrowed, I was going to be sure and answer with the name of someone who wasn't around that second, so I could get to them first and tell them to back me up—to be sure and say that I'd used their phone. But Edie never asked. See what I mean about people being off their game?

EDIE: Okay, Abby: here's the thing I began to wonder about this weekend.

I waited.

EDIE: Why did your parents even go on a cruise this week?
ME: They like cruises. They go on them a lot.
EDIE: No, I mean now. You left home, you dropped out of school. I would think most parents would be freaking out. They'd cancel their plans.
ME: I left after they left.
EDIE: So they thought you were home all this time.
ME: That's it.
EDIE: And now they're back in time for your graduation.

I nodded, though there was more than a little sarcasm in her tone.

EDIE: How come you changed your mind about telling them where you were? I thought you didn't want them to know you were here.
ME: I have you.

My saying that was kind of a reflex. It was pretty cheesy. So I added really quickly, "And I have the shelter." But Edie raised a single eyebrow and just watched me, and I thought of this hymn we sang one of the only times my family ever went to church in Reddington when it wasn't Christmas or Easter. There was a line in it, "Let us live transparently," and it became this running joke between my parents. They would tease each other and say, "Yup, I can see right through you." I had the sense that moment that Edie could see right through me. But there was nothing else to do but try and ride this moment out and figure out my Plan B.

....

You know what I wish? I wish I could raise a single eyebrow the way Edie could. I think if I were able to do that, I would have said and done way less stupid shit over the years.

....

And, of course, my need for Plan B came way sooner than I expected. I figured I had until Wednesday or Thursday. Nope.

That Monday my exciting day involved going to a class to learn about staying safe from STDs, and mostly we put rubbers on food: bananas, though one boy who knew what was coming showed up with a cucumber. It was one more step toward a fifty-buck Master-Card. After the class, I thought about walking down to the water-front because it was really pretty outside, but that would mean passing the tents and the walkers and I knew I couldn't bear that. I just couldn't. So I disappeared once more into the second floor of the library. A little later I looked at clothes in the stores on Church Street and in the mall. See what I mean about what a weird time it was? Once you were sixty or seventy miles away from Cape Abenaki, people could sort of forget about it, at least for a few min-utes. Girls were buying underwear and boys were buying caps and grown-ups were buying whatever. Shoes. Chocolate. Blue jeans. In Los Angeles, did people even care that a nuclear plant had blown up in Vermont? Yeah, I overheard people discussing it. Worry-ing about radiation. Complaining about the refugees. Talking shit about my dad. But for a lot of people it was just news. Maybe an inconvenience because their electricity bills might go up, but not the freaking fiasco it was for some of us.

I got back to the shelter about six-thirty and went right upstairs to my room. Camille was already there and she strolled in and sat down on my bed. She was acting pretty casual, but I had the sense right away that I was fucked. She wasn't wearing my earrings and I wondered why: she had been wearing them ever since she had bullied them off my ears. She liked them, but she also knew that it really got under my skin when I saw them dangling from her lobes.

"What do you want?" I asked. Our rooms didn't have chairs and I didn't want to sit down next to her on the bed, so I leaned against the dresser. I knew there was at least one other girl already checked in for the night—the girl who hoarded the free newspapers. But she was kind of a recluse and kind of a mousy: she wasn't going to take my side in whatever was about to go down.

Camille looked away from me, out the window. "Just chillin'," she said. "No need to get all crazy."

"I wasn't."

"I don't know. Your voice sounded a little touchy. I keep telling you: I want us to be friends."

"Okay."

"So," she said. "You hear anything new about the meltdown?"

I shook my head.

"It's awful. They say the fires are out. Of course, those poor fuckers who put the fires out are all going to die. Not today, not tomorrow. But they say they're all going to get cancer someday. They're heroes. But they're all as good as dead."

"Yeah, it's bad," I agreed. Really, what else was I supposed to say?

"Already nineteen people are dead."

"Uh-huh."

"And all because the operators were dopes. You know, the engineers? Totally screwed the pooch. And they killed nineteen people."

"It's bad," I said. An understatement, obviously. I was just trying not to say the wrong thing, whatever that was.

"And, you know, people won't be able to live in the Northeast Kingdom for, like, forever," she said. "I once went to that water park at Jay Peak. You ever hear of Jay Peak where you grew up? That Briar-place outside of New York City?"

"Yeah. I've heard of Jay Peak. Ski resort."

"Before you came here, had you ever heard of the power plant? Cape Abenaki?"

"No."

She reached into the back pocket of her blue jeans and pulled out her phone. She held it out like it was a knife, pointing it at me, and looked up. I tried to meet her eyes, but couldn't.

"Abby," she murmured, but it wasn't like she was starting to say something *to* me. She was just trying out my name on her tongue. Seeing what it sounded like. Then: "I went to the library today. Didn't see you there. But I guess I wouldn't, right, because you're always upstairs with the books?"

"The novels. The poetry. I get it: I'm kind of dorky."

She ignored me and went on: "Me? I was using the computers. You know, looking shit up."

It crossed my mind that second that I should just get the hell out. Walk away. Walk downstairs. I mean, I could see where this was going. But I didn't have my Plan B yet. So I just stood there. It was, looking back, a seriously pathetic choice.

"I was looking up names," she said.

"That's cool."

"Ya think?"

I shrugged, waiting.

She swiped the screen of her phone, turning it on, and gazed down at it. "I like the name Abby. I think I like it way more than you like Camille."

"I like Camille, I told you that."

"Nah. But I'm good with it. I like it, and that's all that matters."

"Right."

"Do you like the name Mira?"

As soon as she asked if I liked my mom's name, I knew it was over. She might not know my name, but she knew I was Bill and Mira Shepard's daughter. Even if I could come up with some remotely plausible reason for why I was calling people named Bill and Mira Shepard—and I couldn't, my mind was toast—she wasn't going to believe it. She wasn't going to believe me.

Still, I said, "Camille, there's a—"

But she cut me off. "Know anyone named Bill Shepard, Abby? Wasn't that the name of the dude who blew up the reactor in Newport? What a coincidence. And who is this Mira Shepard? Seems there was a Mira Shepard who worked there, too. Married to Bill. Was always saying how safe nuclear power was and how safe that plant was. Guess she was wrong. I guess—"

I didn't listen anymore. I couldn't. I did what I should have done the minute she started talking. I left. I didn't even try and empty the few pieces of clothing I had in the drawers or grab my toothbrush and toothpaste. I mean, why bother? I just turned and raced down the stairs, past the dude who was staffing the desk, and out into the summer evening. Camille yelled down the staircase at me, "I pawned the earrings, bitch! I pawned 'em!"

The guy at the desk called after me to stop, but I didn't listen. I was out the door and on the sidewalk. I was running, I was running as fast as I could. I didn't slow down until I had turned the corner onto Church Street, that outdoor pedestrian mall, and the only reason I went from sprinting to jogging was because it was too crowded to run like a crazy person on the bricks. I went past the restaurants and bars where people were eating and drinking like it was just another night at the end of June, but nothing was really registering. I had no idea what I was going to do. But then I thought of Andrea. I remembered the statue of the kids playing leapfrog and figured it would be a miracle if she was actually sitting on the bench beside it at that exact moment, but it was still light out so you never knew. And I didn't have anyplace else to go. So I continued down Church Street and, miracle of miracles, there she was. She was sitting on the bench by the statue and sharing a cigarette with a guy who I'd learn in a couple of minutes was called PJ. Poacher Junior.

I was out of breath, but I nodded at her and said, "Hey."

She looked at me, and for a split second I could tell she wasn't completely sure how she knew me. I wondered if she was stoned. But then it all clicked: "Abby, right? From the shelter?"

"Right," I said. "My name is Abby Bliss." I was about to say something like *The shelter kicked me out* or *I think I need a little help*, but Andrea beat me to it.

"You need a place to crash," she said. "That it?"

I started to cry. (See what I mean about what a basket case I'd become? Eleven months earlier I was keying a Beemer SUV. Now? I'm sobbing because someone is willing to share her very crappy mattress with me.)

"Whoa, now," Andrea said, and she stood up and hugged me. Then she motioned for the dude beside her to get off his ass and wrap his arms around me, too. "Group hug, baby girl," she said to me. "Group hug."

....

For my seventeenth birthday, I bought myself my very own X-Acto knife and a squeeze bottle of Bactine at the drugstore on Cherry Street. I didn't even lift them. Paid cash because these were supposed to be presents. No one in the posse knew it was my birthday. I didn't tell anyone.

It was getting cold now, so people were spending more time than ever inside at Poacher's, which meant there was, like, no privacy. PJ and Missy were gone by then, but other kids had shown up. Kids came and went all the time. So I took my birthday presents to myself and a couple of Andrea's Band-Aids from her kit and went to the mall. I camped out in a stall in the ladies' bathroom and pulled down my pants, and there I tried to cut the numbers 1 and 7 into my thighs. It was just a mess. I was just a mess. I mean it: I was never much of a visual artist.

Different people have tried to explain to me why I cut, but it doesn't take a rocket scientist to explain it. I kind of hated myself. I kind of hated the way I was making so many seriously bad decisions. Maybe if the Red Cross had still had that tent in City Hall Park, I would have gone to them and said to whoever was there, "Hi, my name's Emily Shepard. What's yours?" Sure, I would have wound up in a foster home somewhere, but would that really have been any worse than what I was doing? (When I wrote that sentence just now, I meant it rhetorically. But, in all fairness, it is more complicated than that. Just think of the crap that poor Cameron endured. Then add to that how much people hated my family. And, of course, there was still my fear of what the investigators would want to know about my mom and dad.) But going to the Red Cross wasn't even an option anymore, because by then that tent was long gone.

Just so you know, the only time I actually tried to carve numbers or letters into my skin was the day I turned seventeen. Yup, happy birthday to me.

Chapter 12

Like I said, I do not believe that my dad was drunk the morning of the meltdown.

He might have been hungover, but I honestly don't believe even that was the case. My parents hadn't drunk all that much the night before. And given the amount those two could put away, I have to believe they had a pretty impressive tolerance.

But there had been times in the past when my dad had had alcohol on his breath at the plant and people had noticed—at least once with serious repercussions. It happened not quite two years before the meltdown. He was sent home from work ("escorted off site" was the way they put it). As part of the you-fucked-up-in-a-dangerous-business protocol, he was suspended without pay for a month and forced to see a shrink; he had to pee in a cup whenever they asked for the next twelve months. (And I have a feeling they asked a lot.) In other words, this was way more than a write-up in his personnel file. The plant had been required to rat my dad out to the NRC.

After the meltdown, the newspeople had a field day with this—which made me feel like even more of a loser than usual. Why? Because the day my dad was walked from his office to his car and my mom had to drive him home was the day after I got caught kind of skinny-dipping with boys at the pond behind Hillary Lamb's house. I say "kind of skinny-dipping" because I kept my bottoms on. Hillary did, too. But the other two girls, who were both a year old than us, didn't. And the boys who were there were all butt-naked. (Would I have taken my bottoms off eventually? Probably. But I hadn't yet. And would it have been a big deal if I had? Probably not. It was a big pond and it was nighttime.) There were eight of us, total, and we all got in trouble when Hillary's mom and dad got home about nine-thirty at night. The fact that there were empty beer bottles everywhere and a bonfire we weren't keeping a super close eye on didn't help. I think we would have gotten in even more trouble if it hadn't been August, a month when teenagers are supposed to do stupid shit. But it's not like we were having sex. It's not like we were even planning on having sex. At least I wasn't. This wasn't an orgy or something gross. We were just naked or almost naked teenagers and it was dark out.

I was about to start tenth grade. To be honest, I have no idea what I was thinking. I have no idea what any of us were thinking.

You know that expression "You're driving me to drink"? Who knows? Maybe I really did drive my parents to drink.

. . . .

Sometimes I'm excellent with dates. Other times, not so much.

Turning seventeen—and, I guess, the way I turned seventeen—kind of sent me into a spiral. I was smoking a lot more dope and swallowing a lot more painkillers. Poacher was either awesome or satanic, depending on your perspective. The minute I got home, he would reach into the pocket of that leather vest he loved or his army jacket—which he wore a lot because we kept the heat set at something like refrigerator at his apartment—and open one of his little orange prescription vials.

Anyway, I do not know the exact date of what I'm about to tell you, but it was a few weeks after Thanksgiving. Church Street was beautiful because all the restaurants and stores were decorated with Christmas lights, and the north end of the mall, not all that far from the shelter, had a massive Christmas tree. It was gorgeous. The only tree I'd ever seen that was bigger (and, in all fairness, it was a *lot* bigger) was the one at Rockefeller Center in New York City. Still, the one on Church Street wasn't shabby.

Once I was properly medicated, Poacher said I should take a shower. Taking a shower usually meant money was tight and he needed Andrea and me to work the truckers out by the interstate. I nodded and threw my coat in the corner by the kitchen where we tossed pretty much everything we wore outside. Coats. Sweaters. Boots. Some days, it was a pretty nasty-smelling pile.

"Andrea around?" I asked. Once before I'd gone out to Exit 14 by my lonesome, but I was really uncomfortable and kind of scared. I felt much safer when I had Andrea with me.

"Nope," he answered. That was it. But I had this feeling he had been about to say more and decided to stop himself.

"Will she be back soon?"

"Nope," he said again.

Trevor and Joseph were on the couch machine-gunning zombies on Xbox, but Trevor jumped in. He didn't take his eyes off the TV and stop shooting things, but he said, "Her mom showed up. That chick is long gone."

Poacher glared at Trevor, but he didn't say anything. Sometimes, when I look back, I think Poacher was a little scared of the boys. At some point we all saw right through him—I guess we all live a little transparently—but he did give us a roof and a place where we could crash.

"She went with her mom?" I asked Trevor. I was shocked and a little bewildered. "She hates her mom!"

"She did not leave with her mom," Poacher said, and he said it like he was protective of Andrea and would never have let her leave with her mom. "I warned her that her mom was coming before her mom got here. So Andrea split. She's just not here."

"Never coming back," Trevor said.

"She will," Poacher insisted. "She's just lying low."

"Where is she?" I know I sounded pretty shrill. Pretty manic. But I was suddenly really freaked out that my friend was gone. I was kind of panicked, which was no small accomplishment since

I had just popped a couple of Oxies and the apartment reeked of dope. You'd think the stench alone could mellow you out. "Tell me, where is she?"

"Hey, Abby, no need for that tone," Poacher said, and he put his hands on my upper arms in a way that he probably thought was fatherly. "She's fine."

"But she is gone," Trevor chimed in, clearly relishing Poacher's discomfort and my angst. Meanwhile, all kinds of shit was exploding on the TV screen. I couldn't stand it. So I pulled Poacher's fingers off the sleeves of my shirt and marched over to the couch. As if Trevor's hands and the Xbox controller were a game of Whac-A-Mole, I used my fist to whack the plastic onto the floor. It didn't break, which in hindsight is a good thing, but still Trevor screamed at me.

"What the fuck!" he yelled, and for some reason Joseph started laughing. (Actually, I don't know why I just wrote *for some reason*. The reason is probably that Joseph was stoned.) Still, it was Joseph who bent over and reached down and picked up the controller. He inspected it to make sure it was still working and then handed it to Trevor.

"Why the fuck did you do that?" Trevor ranted. "Why? I'm not the one who peaced out on you! I'm not the one who split!"

He didn't get off his ass on the couch, but he was sitting forward because he'd been scorching zombies and shit. I was standing over him. I wanted to shove him into the cushions in the back of the couch. I didn't. But I might have if Poacher hadn't come up behind me and said, his voice this weird and pathetic attempt to sound paternal, "Abby, what's gotten into you?"

I could feel my face reddening. Suddenly I couldn't stand how greasy my hair was. How filthy Poacher's beard was. How our whole world smelled like weed: vaguely skunky and pungent like field grass. I pushed past him and dug my coat from the pile. I looked back at him and asked, making no attempt at all to speak like a human being rather than the stoner banshee I was, "Did she say where she was going?"

Poacher had decided his *Father Knows Best* gig wasn't going to play and so he just shook his head. He looked pretty disgusted with me. "Nope," he said finally.

So I went back out onto the streets to see if I could find her. I thought it was just perfect that Trevor shouted after me, "She took her shit, Abby, she's gone!" while Poacher was saying, "Young lady, you come back! You come back here right now! You have work to do!"

Yeah, right. Work to do.

I did find Andrea. She was at the bus station, which is actually a part of the Burlington airport. We said good-bye. I'll tell you about it later, but I can't right now. It just makes me too sad.

. . . .

Someday I should rewrite this whole mess. Try to put it in some kind of order.

Someday I should probably do lots of things.

. . . .

Sometimes it was the strangest things that would bring Cape Abenaki back into the news my last weeks at Poacher's. In one case, it was nosebleeds. There were six little kids from the elementary school in Newport who all wound up in the same elementary school in Hanover, New Hampshire. They were in four different grades, but they all traipsed into the nurse's office over the course of three or four school days in the middle of December for the same thing: nosebleeds that just didn't want to stop. When the nurse realized they were all from Newport, she did a little research and figured out in about a nanosecond that a nosebleed was sometimes a sign of radiation sickness. The kids—all the kids from that school up in Newport—had been stuck outside in the rain after the explosion longer than a lot of the evacuees because all the emergency vehicles had created a gigundous traffic jam, and it took forever for their school buses to arrive. Before you knew it, someone had figured out that a whole lot of kids from the Kingdom had "compromised" immune systems. They were always sick, and they were always getting colds. Out of the blue, a lot of New Agers wanted everyone drinking tea made from echinacea, and a lot of doctors wanted everyone on vitamin C and orange juice.

A few days after the nosebleed story broke, I got a nosebleed. I wondered if I had radiation sickness and got a little worried. But I didn't have any other symptoms—which, trust me, are unbelievably gross—and so I decided it was just because the night before Poacher had had me sniff a little white for the first time.

. . . .

"Hoarding and territorial issues. Predictable schism between haves and have-nots. Emily exudes education. Speaks like a have, aura's a have. It probably made her a target in the shelter. Probably why she was bullied onto the street."

I saw that written in one of the notebooks about me the other day. It made me feel bad about myself—like I had been putting on airs back at the shelter and deserved to be kicked out. I wanted to tell my therapist here, "If I'm that kind of a snot, how come everyone in the posse liked me?"

But I took a deep breath and chilled and kept that thought to myself. I was tired of confronting people. I guess I figured I had already caused everyone enough trouble. I guess I figured I had already done enough damage.

. . . .

I left the posse for good on Christmas Day. The juxtaposition of my life that morning and my life on Christmas mornings past was just too fucking awful. A year earlier, I had given my mom and dad a poster I'd had made at the photo store in Newport. I gave the store all these pictures of the three of us on Christmas mornings going all the way back to when I was a little kid in Briarcliff and a couple of stanzas from an Emily Dickinson poem:

> *Before the ice is in the pools,*
> *Before the skaters go,*
> *Or any cheek at nightfall*
> *Is tarnished by the snow,*
>
> *Before the fields have finished,*
> *Before the Christmas tree,*
> *Wonder upon wonder*
> *Will arrive to me!*

A girl who worked at the store created a collage around the poem, and it really looked pretty good. There was one picture of my Maggie as a puppy, and her paw pads were massive, way too big for the rest of her, and the girl had positioned the photo so it looked like Maggie was pointing at the words. Then she edged the collage with gold Christmas foil and put it inside a red frame. There is no way I could have done something like that myself. My mom and dad loved it. I think it was by far their favorite thing I ever gave them.

But when I thought about that present—and, yeah, all the stuff they had given me over the years—I couldn't help but compare it with the sinkhole my life had become. I'm not trying to get your sympathy: I knew that the meltdown had made lots of people's lives suck. Exhibit A? I may have been the only kid to wind up an orphan because of Cape Abenaki, but seventeen grown-ups died in addition to my mom and dad, and twelve of them had children who were still living at home. Altogether, twenty-seven other kids lost a parent in the explosion. And then there were the thousands of people who were suddenly homeless: over thirteen thousand, according to one report.

But how could I not think of where I had been a year earlier and the collage I had given my parents? How could I not think of all the images on the poster from all those other Christmases? Maybe I would have stayed with the posse if Andrea had stuck around. But she was gone. Who knows? Maybe I would have hung around another couple of months if Missy's parents hadn't brought her home to Concord. But they had.

So I left. I was terrified by what I saw in the mirror. I was disgusted by what I'd become.

Looking back, I was waffling between suicide and survival. One minute I was leaving with every intention of giving up somewhere on the streets. Seriously: just giving up. I'd simply freeze to death like that poor guy in all the snow in the Jack London short story. It wasn't the worst way to die—at least it wasn't for that dude. It was better than radiation sickness or cancer, right? But then the next minute I would be thinking how I was going to fuck the world by surviving. Take that, Fate, I'm still here. You thought you could kill me? No way. I am unkillable. It takes more than a nuclear meltdown to plant me six feet under.

I was the first member of the posse to wake up that Christmas morning, and I remember sitting up on my mattress and looking around at the room and thinking how squalid it was. Everything looked way worse simply because it was Christmas. Things are supposed to be special on Christmas, right? But the room was dingy and skanky and smelled kind of like a locker room and kind of like a head shop because we'd been burning incense the night before. After all, the night before was Christmas Eve. We didn't have a tree or lights, but Joseph had lifted a pack of incense from the place in the North End where we always lifted our papers and pipes. (Incidentally, there's no symbolism in the fact that I just used Joseph's name and I'm telling you my Christmas story. Trust me, there's no symbolism in any of this. It's all just what happened.)

My room back in Reddington had always been a colossal mess, too, but it was a different kind of mess. First of all, there's a difference between unclean and messy. My room was messy, but it wasn't gross. There was stuff everywhere, but it was always clean. And—and this is important—it was all my stuff. When I would

sit up in bed (which was, of course, a real bed and not just a mattress) and look at the floor, the carpet was covered by my high
heels and my hoodies and my coat hangers and my earrings and
my blue jeans and my blouses and my dresses and my DVDs and
the snakelike cords for my broken iPods and my old cell phones.
Those were my old *Cosmopolitan* and *Elle* magazines. Those were
my posters I had tacked to the yellow rose wallpaper. That was my
Disney glass unicorn. That was my glass pen with a gold-plated
nib. (I didn't really write with it because this isn't, like, the sixteenth century. But it was very beautiful.) Those were my leather
journals where I wrote my poems and my observations that—to
be honest—always seemed a lot more profound at nighttime than
they did in the morning. Sometimes there was some dog hair on
my things in the spring when Maggie would shed, but, seriously, a
little dog hair was about as dirty as my room ever got.

Sometimes my mom would ask me why I didn't put the clothes
back in my dresser or my closet when I was deciding what to wear
before school. Usually it was just because I was rushed and I figured
I would put the stuff away when I got home from school. At least
that's what I would tell myself at seven thirty-five in the morning,
when I had about five minutes before the school bus arrived to
brush my hair and put on my makeup and find my winter boots
and throw my homework in a backpack that some days weighed
as much as a Mini Cooper. It was crazy how much crap we were
supposed to have with us.

So, Christmas morning at Poacher's was sort of a wake-up call.
I stared at Trevor with his hair in his eyes and a girl named Izzie
who I didn't like much, her head in a knit cap to keep warm, and
Joseph, who I could see had an erection even under the quilt, and
two empty orange vials on the windowsill. And I just wanted out.
So, I pushed off my own quilt and stood up. My footing was a little
funky because I was standing on a pretty soft mattress.

When I tiptoed past Poacher's bedroom, I could see he had
passed out in his army jacket. I knew he kept some of his cash
under his mattress when he was sleeping because he didn't trust

us, but it wasn't all that hard to reach underneath it and steal two twenty-dollar bills. Then I stole two more. He didn't even move.

I got dressed in the bathroom so no one would hear me and made a list in my mind of what I should put in my knapsack. I didn't lift any pills or any of Poacher's stash, but I did take a lighter. I guess I was still thinking of that Jack London short story. I wanted to be damn sure I could start a fire if I had to. The biggest decision, weirdly enough, was my X-Acto. I tried to convince myself that I didn't need it. I wouldn't need it. I would only take my Bactine and some Band-Aids in case I got a cut. But, in the end, I did take the X-Acto. I might need a weapon, right? I remember thinking to myself, *But, Emily, you need to promise yourself that you won't use it as a weapon against yourself.*

Of course, I did. That was just one of my many promises to myself that I broke.

When I unlocked the door it made a ridiculously loud click. Had it always made that much noise? Probably. I'd just never noticed. Then I heard somebody coughing, and I was pretty sure it was Tory, a new girl I did like even if she had the ugliest face tats I'd ever seen in my life, and I slipped through the door.

Outside it was sunny. I could see a dusting of fresh snow on the ground. It was pretty and I watched my breath steam into the air.

I zipped up my parka and pulled tight the hood. I had wedged a lot of clothes into the backpack, but I was wearing a lot, too. I was wearing as much as I could. I wished I had left the posse a note, but I didn't know if it was supposed to be a suicide note or a thank-you note. I guess since I had brought all the clothes that I could and my X-Acto, I was hoping more to live than to die. I'm still here, right? But who knows how my mind works. I sure don't.

I remember I heard a harp in my head and I couldn't figure out why. Then I got it: it was the harp from that Beatles song Poacher liked about the runaway girl. "She's Leaving Home."

Nope, I thought. I am not leaving home. I am just . . . leaving.

A.C.

Chapter 13

I am exactly five feet, two inches tall. I was more than a head taller than Cameron, and supposedly a head is about ten inches long. So I would say that Cameron was just over four feet tall. Four feet and a couple of inches. He had hair the black of a stovepipe and the tiniest little ski jump for a nose. Once I tried to write a poem about what he looked like, but I just got depressed. I ripped the paper into shreds. I still know the first couplet, but I can't bring myself to say it.

His eyes were green.

His mummy bag was red. His mummy bag twine was blue.

. . . .

The first day after Cameron and I met, I tried to turn him in. It was one thing for me to live like a lunatic hobo, but it was another thing for a nine-year-old kid. I explained to him why even with his incredibly awesome mummy bag he couldn't live on the streets, but he was pretty firm. He said he would not go back to a foster home. I told him there were plenty of great foster homes, but he didn't believe me. (In truth, I'm not sure I believed me.) So I decided I would just bring him to the police station on North Avenue. I knew where it was. But he figured out where we were going and took off. I would say he took off like a shot, but that would be a serious exaggeration: he went as fast as he could with a huge black plastic garbage bag in his arms, which was not very fast.

Watching him run was actually kind of comic. Fortunately, I'd cadged some money on Church Street, so after I'd caught up with him I was able to win him back. I brought him with me to Muddy Waters, that hipster coffee joint Andrea had shown me, and bought us both hot chocolates with whipped cream. (Now *that's* living large.) This was when he showed me his robot made of duct tape.

I remember I was kind of afraid that some grown-up would see us and think I was his babysitter and I was the one who had given him his black eye. But no one seemed to care, which is kind of interesting in and of itself.

I still thought I might go to the police station without Cameron and ask whoever was there to keep their eyes out for a nine-year-old boy with a mummy bag. I kept this as an option in the back of my mind.

....

Two days after we met, Cameron told me that he had almost no memories of his mom and none of his dad. He never met his dad. He said he got confused about whether some of the things he remembered were from when he was a toddler and still living with his mom and his grandparents, or whether they were from his days in his first foster home.

We were sitting in the sun down by the lake, which was rock-solid frozen. But the sky was blue like a sapphire, and with the exception of the seagulls, the world felt very still. The seagulls, of course, were crazy. I love seagulls, especially the giant ones that will walk right up to you and practically threaten you into giving them your bread. I also love to watch them fly. Unlike some birds, seagulls always look to me like they enjoy flying. (Not all birds, of course, make flying look like a chore. I think barn swallows are having a blast, too.) Anyway, I used to really enjoy the seagulls. That might just mean that I had nothing better to do a lot of the time that winter, but there are worse ways to kill an hour or two than watching seagulls until it gets too cold, and then going to the library and reading till the place closes for the night.

It sounded like Cameron's mom was rail thin and always pretty strung out. At least based on the way he described her she was strung out. I'm thinking crystal meth. But he never said she was a druggie. I'm just making a guess from a few of his clues. He remembered her as pretty old. Thirties, he thought. She was no teen mom, in other words. He had grandparents in a town south of Burlington called Shoreham, but his grandfather was seriously violent. He was always whaling on Cameron's grandma and mom and Cameron when they were all living together. His grandparents had an apple orchard up a hill from Lake Champlain and Cameron recalled it was huge. Of course, when you're a little kid, everything's huge. For all I know, it was five apple trees in the backyard. When he'd been in the first grade, he confessed, the apple trees had spooked him. He half expected them to come to life in the night and start hurling apples at him. Or they would do things much worse. Unlike the trees in *The Wizard of Oz,* these bad boys could walk. In Cameron's imagination, they stomped from the orchard to the house and smashed in his bedroom window, climbed inside, and stabbed him to death with splintered branches.

I think his mom might have been cooking meth at his grandparents' house, which was probably one of the reasons why his grandpa was beating the crap out of everybody. Meth causes all kinds of trouble. One time the police came to the orchard—at least Cameron thought maybe this happened.

He couldn't tell me how he had wound up in that first foster home or any of the details of why his mom had abandoned him. He had no idea if his mom was alive or dead. Sometimes he would tell me he hoped she was alive and she'd get her act together and find him.

"Want me to find her for you?" I'd ask. I figured I could begin by asking someone at the shelter for grown-ups. It was on the other side of Burlington from the teen shelter. I went to their day station sometimes and was able to get a peanut butter and jelly sandwich. (You have no idea how good a peanut butter and jelly sandwich can taste until you've lived in an igloo made of trash bags.) Like the social workers at the teen shelter, everyone there seemed nice enough. And, of course, I could have gone to the police. But how would I do that without having to confess that I knew where Cameron was? If I had to guess, I would have said that Cameron's mom was in jail: the Chittenden Regional Correctional Facility in South Burlington, maybe. It was right across the street from a great bakery. Yup, razor wire and baguettes. I knew where it was. But Cameron never wanted me to investigate. I think he was worried that he'd just wind up back in another foster home—which, of course, was a risk. It was a risk for him, and it was a risk for me. And there was also the chance that someone would figure out that Abby Bliss was really Emily Shepard and just hate me to death.

But maybe Cameron was also afraid that all we'd find out was that his mom really was dead, and then he'd have nothing to hope for. (Been there, done that.)

Or maybe he just knew what a seriously shitty mother his mom was. After all, she'd deserted him, right? I didn't even know her, and I kind of hated her for peacing out on her kid. That's just nasty. I mean, obviously I wasn't his mom, but already I'd figured out that I had some responsibility for him. And that winter I took that responsibility very seriously. No matter what, I was going to keep him safe. No one, not while I was around, was ever again going to punch that little guy in the face. No one. No, sir. *My* life had stood a loaded gun.

....

I love it when the snowflakes are flying like butterflies.

You probably think that's the start of one of my poems. Nope.

It's something my mom once said. She was standing in the den and looking out the window at our backyard and the edge of the woods in the distance. The forest was mostly pine trees, but there were a few maples, too. (Maples make me recall sugaring and syrup, and someday I have to tell you about the sugarhouse rager. That was kind of a fiasco, too.) My mom's back was to me, but she knew I was there. It was about five in the afternoon, toward the end of February, so the light was just starting to fade. And the flakes were huge and fluttering and seemed to be almost rocking back and forth, back and forth, to the ground. They were falling very slowly.

My mom said unexpectedly beautiful things like "the snow-flakes are flying like butterflies" a lot. Remember, her name was Mira. She could be exotic. Poetic. Surprising.

The snow looked like that to me one day when Cameron and I were standing under the eaves of this theater down by the water-front. It was closed that afternoon, so no one was there and we were safe. I remembered what my mom had said about snowflakes and told Cameron. I thought he would like it. I guess he did. But he said, "Butterflies don't live much longer than snowflakes. Most butterflies only live, like, a week or two."

"How do you know that?" I asked, but I was pretty sure it was true. I just wanted to know where he'd learned this little bit of knowledge. Who tells a little kid that butterflies die in a couple of days?

He shrugged. "A teacher."

"Wow. You had pretty serious teachers."

"I don't know. She wasn't our teacher very long. One night she drank this Windex stuff and got sick. The principal said she thought it was Kool-Aid. They're both blue, right?"

I nodded. The principal had obviously been lying to the kids. No one mistakes Windex for Kool-Aid. "Did she die?"

"No. But she never came back to school."

So, to answer my own question: Who tells a little kid that but-terflies only live for a couple of days? A seriously depressed, suicidal schoolteacher. That's who.

. . . .

I'm sure there are a lot of great foster parents and foster families out there. I really am. Unfortunately, Cameron never got any of them. He got the dad and mom who went to jail for making kiddie porn out of his foster home sisters. He got the mom who pushed her foster kids—all three of them, even Cameron—face-first into dog shit when his six-year-old foster sister had diarrhea and trashed the bedsheets. He got the dad who slugged him so hard that he got that black eye.

And, of course, he had his memories, dim as they were, of his own flesh and blood. His mom. His grandpa.

Is it really any wonder that he wasn't about to trust anyone older than me?

. . . .

One of my doctors here asked me the other day if I worried about trying to find friends for Cameron. Yeah, no. I was worried about trying to find him food. I was worried about trying to keep him warm. I was worried about trying to prevent him from getting stolen or killed by some psycho. The doctor wanted to know how I felt about the idea that I was harboring a runaway and wasn't allowing a child to go to school. I got all defensive because she made me sound like some selfish bitch—like I was some whack-job kidnapper who was treating Cameron like he was a pet.

I defended myself by saying that I brought him with me to the library all the time. We read together all the time. I taught him plenty, I really did. And it's not as if people were lining up outside the igloo to care for him—or me. Finally I said to the doctor, "Sure, he was a runaway. But it's not like anyone was looking for him. It's not like anyone was looking for me."

"People were looking for both of you," she said.

I thought of the hours and hours we spent in the library or near the boathouse by the lake or on the benches on Church Street. "Well, then, no one was looking very hard," I told her.

This wasn't a great thing to say, but I was pissed. And what I did those months? It's all very hard to explain. I was just doing my best.

And given Cameron's total refusal to come with me to the police station and go back into a foster home, sometimes it seemed to me I really had two choices. Either desert him or protect him. I chose to protect him. I knew it wasn't going to be forever. Eventually, I knew, we'd have to come in from the cold. I guess I just thought it would be together.

....

Just for the record, when it got a little warm I did try to find Cameron some friends. I did try to find him some buddies. You'll see.

....

In the middle of January, there was a huge protest march in Burlington against nuclear power. It began at the waterfront, not all that far from our igloo, and went up Main Street to the university, where there was going to be a big student rally and a bunch of speeches inside this massive chapel on the commons. The protesters lucked out: the skies were clear and there was a midwinter thaw. It must have been forty degrees that Saturday, and it felt even warmer because of the sun. Cameron and I watched the parade—the drummers and the people with placards about Cape Abenaki and Fukushima and Chernobyl and Three Mile Island and some place I'd never heard of called Rocky Flats—from just outside Muddy Waters.

"Kind of like closing the barn door," one older guy with white hair in a red check jacket said to us, his arms folded across his chest. I explained to Cameron what that meant—how the expression was kind of a joke about bothering to close a barn door after the horses had left. Then I told Cameron—who knows why—to try and imagine the power of more than a million horses. That was how much power there was in a four-hundred-megawatt plant. (It's just amazing the fun facts that stay with a girl when your mom and dad work for a power company.)

The fellow beside us looked at me and said, "You sure know your stuff."

I shrugged and said, "Science class," and then turned away. I was afraid I had already drawn too much attention to us.

It's funny, but in the years before the Cape Abenaki meltdown, everyone in Vermont was arguing about wind power. People in favor of wind talked about how it would dial down our need for fossil fuel. People opposed said it would ruin the state's natural beauty. Looking back, I bet people on both sides wish today that the state's biggest problem was a couple of fucked-up ridgelines. They wish they could spend boatloads of time complaining about a line of wind turbines on the top of a mountain. It would mean they still had their homes. Me? I actually thought the turbines were kind of pretty in a *Star Wars* distant planet sort of way.

Really, I got almost no shit about nuclear power when my parents were alive. So I guess it's both strange and somehow predictable that now the Shepard name is right up there with Satan.

....

Even when I was with Cameron, I hadn't begun to think of what precisely my "endgame" would be. (I learned that term at a video store in the mall. They were showing a video of a popular TV detective drama, and one of the cops used it. I got right away what it meant. I liked it. It was so fatalistic.) But by late January I had the sense that this was all leading somewhere.

....

One crazy cold night Lexie and some dude I'd never met appeared down by the waterfront. Lexie was a friend of Missy's, and once in a while she would show up at Poacher's in the months I was there. The first time I'd heard her name, I thought it was some joke about Oxies. I imagined her swallowing whole hand-fuls of them—*lots of Oxies*—and somehow "lots of Oxies" was transformed into "Loxie," which eventually became "Lexie." I thought it was a nickname. Nope. Her real name was Alexandra, and, like Missy, she had grown up near Boston and come from serious scratch. She had dropped out of UVM and was older than most of us. But she was very slight. I'm not sure she was five feet tall. A lot of nights—maybe most nights—she crashed with people she still knew at the university. She only came to Poacher's when she needed to flip a little candy and didn't want to wind up passed out underneath three scummy frat boys. (You know you're a hot mess when you go to Poacher's because it's the "safer" alternative.) She seemed nice enough, but I really didn't hang with her. I had Andrea.

But late one midwinter afternoon, there she was trudging along the rock-hard snow and ice along the waterfront. I recognized her right away from this long, black cashmere duster she used to wear, but I wasn't going to call out to her because she was with some dude I didn't recognize. Cameron and I were just coming back from the library and this little sandwich shop on Main Street where it was easy to pocket their premade egg salad sandwiches on white bread. (It's like they knew the sandwiches sucked and would only be eaten by nine-year-old boys, so they were super easy to lift.)

But Lexie called out to me and jogged over. She introduced me to the guy she was with. His name was Neal and she said he had also dropped out of UVM. I didn't believe her for one second. The guy was a little runt who couldn't have been more than fifteen or sixteen. I was older than he was. But he seemed nice enough. He was shy. The two of them had planned to spend another night in that old coal plant, but the night before there had been some violence, and someone had gotten pounded pretty badly, and now they wanted a new place to sleep. There wasn't much wind, but already the temperature was only a degree or two above zero, and there was going to be a full moon. We all knew a full moon meant the lakefront would become a freezer. So I invited them in. It wasn't the best solution, but I didn't want them to die out there. And, to be honest, I was a little proud of the fact that I had built an igloo that could squeeze in four people.

Still, I wasn't sure what I would have done if they had asked to spend a second night. Neal had that funky smell that seems to stick like Gorilla Glue to homeless men and teenage boys, and Lexie was covering her stink with a head shop's worth of patchouli. Together it was kind of like poison gas. Besides, to make room for them and their backpacks, Cameron and I had wound up sleeping with our knees practically at our chests, two unborn twins in my tummy of an igloo. But Lexie and Neal didn't want to stay another day. Or, if they did, they didn't want to impose on us anymore. They got up with the sun and disappeared. We never saw them again.

Another night, we let a girl crash with us. She was in her twenties and a refugee from someplace in Africa. In the morning, she showed me her foot when she woke up. I nearly threw up. I walked her to Battery Street and put her in a cab myself. I told the cabbie to take her to the hospital ER. Even I know that you don't fuck around with gangrene.

And one time I let in some scrawny woman whose snow jacket actually had patches on it from the 1980 Winter Olympics in Lake Placid, New York. It was light blue and it was antique and, it seemed to me, totally worthless against the cold. She was my mom's age, but way too loopy to be maternal. She was a downwinder from Irasburg and seemed to go in and out of denial. One minute she was getting weepy about her cats and her llamas and her dog, all of whom, she worried, were dying of radiation sickness, and the next she was giggling and showing me these unbelievably crinkled and out-of-focus pictures of her little menagerie. It was kind of heartbreaking. I think she would have been way more intrigued by the fact I had a sidekick named Cameron with me if he'd been a tortoiseshell cat instead of a nine-year-old boy. When I told her about Maggie, the two of us practically lost it.

That's what I mean when I say that people came and went. But most of the time it really was just Cameron and me.

. . . .

The bus station was out by the airport, so you had to take a local bus from the downtown to get there. In fact, it was part of the airport. There was a little ticket counter right by the baggage carousels, and a few times a day a Greyhound would pull up right outside a pair of sliding glass doors. Fortunately, Andrea's bus was late—now, there's a surprise—and so she was still sitting on a blue pretend-leather bench inside those doors when I got there. This was back in early December, still a few weeks before I would leave the posse and find Cameron. Her knees were bouncing up and down, and I could see that she was pretty wired on something. She jumped up when she saw me, gave a little shriek, and then we wrapped our arms around each other.

"I didn't know whether I wanted you to come or not," she said, and we both started crying.

"I should fucking hate you for not saying good-bye," I told her.

We pulled apart and wiped at our eyes. She shook her head. "I didn't say good-bye because I knew we would end up like this," she sniffled, and she pointed at the way her mascara was starting to run. Her parka was unzipped, and I saw she had on what we considered the world's ugliest red Christmas sweater. It was a family of reindeer on their hind legs like humans—a mom, a dad, a boy, and a girl—wearing Christmas caps and trimming a tree. The boy is on a ladder and about to string some lights on his dad's antlers. Of course Dad has no idea. Seriously old school and seriously ugly. We both loved it, and I had promised her once that I was going to steal it from her while she was asleep—maybe even, I'd said, in a couple of weeks on Christmas Eve.

"Why don't you stay?" I suggested. "We'll leave Poacher's and find someplace else—someplace better. Someplace where your mom won't find you."

It seemed that to get to New York City by bus you had to go through Boston, and so Andrea had changed her plan. Now she was only going to go as far as Boston. She didn't know anyone in either place, she said, so what difference did it make? A city's a city, right?

"I have a better idea than you sticking around Burlington," she said. "Why don't you come with me to Massachusetts?"

The notion had crossed my mind. But I was afraid. I was afraid that I really would wind up down the rabbit hole in a city like Boston or New York. I'd never get my shit together. I'd wind up OD'd on heroin. I'd wind up some crack-whore orphan. I'd wind up dead. I mean, six months earlier I had been waking up every day in a nice bedroom of my own with a dog that looked like a black Lab on the floor and a Disney glass unicorn on a shelf. I was going to a pretty elite high school. Sure, I'd keyed cars and gone to school drunk and been a part of this notorious rager at a sugar-house. And, yeah, now I was doing truckers at a gas station and some days popping painkillers like they were M&M's. I had this kind of gross habit with an X-Acto knife.

But I also knew in my heart that I wasn't ready for cities as big as Boston or New York.

"What are you going to do?" I asked her.

"I don't know. Something. Get a job at a Dunkin' Donuts, maybe."

"You'll get fat." I was teasing, of course. Weight was the least of Andrea's problems.

"No, I won't."

"I know."

The glass doors slid open and people started ambling inside the airport. Outside, we could hear the low rumble of the idling bus. "I should go," she said.

I wanted to say *No, please stay, I can't lose anyone else!* but I only nodded. She didn't need to hear that. Then, all of a sudden, she took off her parka, let it fall onto the airport floor, and pulled that ridiculous Christmas sweater over her head. She was wearing a denim shirt that once had been Missy's. "Here," she said, handing me the sweater, "take it."

"I can't! It's too fucking stupid. Besides, you love it."

"It *is* too fucking stupid. But you love it, too." She pushed the sweater into my hands and climbed back into her snow jacket. She hoisted her backpack over her shoulders and then hugged me tighter than anyone had ever hugged me in my life. I mean that: no one before and no one since has ever held me like that. Then in a minute she was on the bus. And a minute after that she was gone.

I had that sweater until the day they took it away.

I had Andrea's texts until they took my phone away, too. Because we did text for a while. Even when the phone no longer worked, I held on to it because it had those texts.

I don't know where she is now. And she doesn't know where I am. I guess she's alive, but I could be wrong. People die all the time. Maybe she just disappeared. People do that, too.

I'm going to stop now. The problem with writing all of this down for you? It just makes me tired and sad.

Chapter 14

When I was sleeping rough, I slept much better during the day. I think that's because I felt safer. This was especially the case when I had Cameron with me. You know that expression "sleeping with one eye open?" I sort of did that most nights. Usually it didn't matter, but it did at least twice. The first time was in the third week in January. I would tell you the exact date, because—as you know—I have a freakish memory for some dates. But not dates that January and February. When you live in an igloo made of trash bags, the days kind of run together. You wake up and lie in your quilt (or your mummy bag) until the library or the mall has opened, and then you go to the bathroom at one place or the other and try to make yourself presentable. You brush your teeth and wash yourself as best you can. You give yourself a little slash in the stall with your increasingly dull and useless X-Acto and press on a Band-Aid. You make your little buddy brush his teeth. You actually put on a little lipstick and eyeliner so people don't think you're homeless. You cadge some money if you see someone who looks promising. You lift a few energy bars and some vitamins from the Rite Aid on Cherry Street. You pocket a few muffins from the buffet at the nice hotel on Battery Street. You read and stay warm in a corner of the library. You doze.

Some days the Salvation Army had a pretty awesome lunch for the homeless. So did some of the churches in the downtown and the shelter for adults—that day station I told you about. We ate really well when the Baptists had a potluck. I couldn't risk bringing Cameron inside with me to these places because I just knew people would ask too many questions and he'd be taken away—which neither of us wanted—so he'd hide out in the library or the mall while I filled my pockets with things he liked or with things I insisted he eat. Like, for every brownie he ate, he had to eat a carrot. Things like that. That was sort of our deal.

We took showers at the Y. I could get a pass from the adult shelter some days. I mention that so you don't think we were disgusting. I mean we *were* disgusting, but I'll bet we were never quite as bad as you're imagining.

Anyway, it was a weeknight in the third week in January, and Cameron was out like a light but I was half awake. Thank God. There were three of us who had set up igloos in that corner of the waterfront. (There were, of course, other stretches with other igloos. I'm just talking about my "neighborhood.") One of the igloos belonged to another Iraqi war vet—I say "another" because of Poacher—and one belonged to a couple in their forties who were harmless but completely insane. They had a grocery cart filled with, among other crap, cat toys. Lots and lots of cat toys, including those wires that have teeny tubes of cardboard at the end. Whenever they saw a feral cat, the woman would play with it for hours and talk to it like the cat was a human being. She was, to be fair, kind of amazing: a feral cat whisperer. Her name was Patrice Thabault. Her partner—husband, boyfriend, brother, I could never figure it out—was named Rick. All three of the igloos were, obviously, off the beaten track. The police would have moved us on if we'd built our igloos anyplace where tourists or people who lived near the waterfront might see them. And, to be honest, I wouldn't have blamed them. I really wouldn't have. We were kind of eyesores. There's a reason you don't see garbage-bag igloos in *Better Homes and Gardens*. If I were to guess the time, it was somewhere between midnight and one in the morning. The thaw we'd had the previous weekend, the Saturday of that anti-nuke march, was over. It wasn't the sort of cold that stung your face and made you a little scared you'd freeze to death in your sleep, but it was pretty brisk.

Way below freezing. Outside I heard the sound of someone walking on the icy snow: their boots were cracking through the brittle skin at the surface or crunching where the snow was more solid. I knew it wasn't a deer or a black bear or even a big dog, because we didn't see animals down by the waterfront, except for the birds and the cats. We didn't even see rats. And I was pretty sure it wasn't a cop, but you never knew. It didn't sound like a cop, because the person was moving pretty clumsily. He or she either had a limp or was a little wasted. I hoped it was someone looking for the war vet or the cat whisperer. I told myself it was nothing, but already my gift of fear was pretty well honed. I was getting that street-smart sixth sense.

I had draped an apron I had lifted from a store called Kiss the Cook across the entrance. I folded it over twice and then tucked it in between two of the garbage bags. It was a very nice flap, if I do say so myself. I usually weighted it down at the bottom with Cameron's and my library books. We could crawl in pretty easily, but it kept the worst of the wind and the cold out. When it was new, the apron was yellow like my bedroom wallpaper, which was why I had stolen it from all the choices I had, but now it was that awful sand brown that snow always gets when it sits too long by the side of the road.

I didn't want to wake Cameron or scare him, especially if it was nothing. And I didn't want whoever was out there to know I was awake. But I wanted to get my X-Acto, just in case, and so I had to reach over and with just one hand lift my backpack over him. (It wasn't easy, and from then on I slept with my X-Acto under the headrest from some junked car I was using as a pillow.) I pulled off the cap and held it in my hand the way people in old movies always hold ice picks. Whoever was out there stopped just outside our igloo. He was wheezing, and he crouched or knelt down on just the other side of the apron. I could smell serious alcohol on his breath. And then I waited to see what he'd do.

I don't know how long I waited like that. Half a minute? A minute? Two? I wasn't holding my breath, but I was breathing without making a sound. I couldn't let him know that I was awake because the only thing I had going for me was surprise. Finally, just when I thought he might leave, he poked his right hand through the side of the entrance, pushing aside the apron. So I stabbed him. I stabbed him hard. He wasn't wearing gloves, and I poked the X-Acto straight into the soft spot between his thumb and his forefinger and then pulled it out. He yanked his hand back, bellowing like I had never heard a man bellow. Cameron instantly woke up, but with my left hand I pushed him behind me, back deep against the inside of our igloo and into this grungy Tonka Truck we had found in the trash that he had tricked out with duct tape.

"What the fuck?" the fellow outside started screaming, "What the fuck?" I climbed up onto my toes and squatted like a baseball catcher. I didn't say anything, but I was totally ready to stab him again. I was ready to pounce. "What the fuck! I just wanna get warm!"

My heart was going like bongo drums in my head and I was sweating. I know, that doesn't seem possible, but I swear it's true: I was sweating. I kept seeing his hand in my head and this weird detail that he bit his nails—which was disgusting because his hand was filthy. And I thought about what he had said: *I just wanna get warm.* A part of me started to feel a little guilty, like I had violated some Homeless People of the World doctrine to love one another or keep one another warm. But there really was no such doctrine. There was no such code. Sometimes we helped each other and sometimes we didn't.

But any remorse I was feeling for stabbing the dude evaporated quickly when he barked at me, "I'm gonna blow your goddamn house down! And then I am going to fucking kill you!" I thought of that hand and decided he wasn't that big. His hand was dirty, but it was kind of girlish. Now, maybe when I started to tell you what happened after Cape Abenaki and how I got here, I made it sound like it's easy to build an igloo. But it isn't. It's hard work. And since this guy wasn't that big—at least that's what I told myself—I decided to attack. He was not going to wreck my igloo, he was not going to "fucking" kill me or Cameron. So I dove through the apron screaming back at him.

See what I mean about my impulsiveness? Brain chemistry. It's everything.

I wrapped myself around his legs and started trying to stab his thighs with my X-Acto, but it suddenly seemed really dull: I'm not sure it was even slashing a hole in his blue jeans. A part of my mind had registered that the guy really wasn't much taller than me. He was heavier, but a part of that just might have been his layers of clothes. Still, he probably could have killed me if he'd wanted to or if he'd had the chance. But suddenly I wasn't alone with him: the Iraqi war veteran and Patrice the cat whisperer and Rick were out there, too. Everyone had been woken up by his screaming. The two men were grabbing the guy's arms and lifting him away from me.

"Edgar, have you lost your damn mind?" This was Patrice, and despite her words, her tone was as maternal and kind as it was with the stray cats she played with. I let go of the guy's legs and stood up. I took a step back and saw that Cameron was crawling through the apron and emerging from the igloo. He rubbed his eyes and then came over to me and nestled against me, wrapping his arms around my waist. He wasn't wearing his coat, and he was still warm like a puppy from his mummy bag.

"Where did she bite you?" Patrice asked him, and she looked over at me and smiled the tiniest bit. She slept in very feminine blue pajamas with white silhouettes of cats on them, a man's gray tweed overcoat, and the ski hat with pom-pom ties she wore during the day. I guess I should have expected she slept in that hat and pj's with cats on them.

"I should kill her," he said, and he glared at me and raised his arm for Patrice like he was that lion with a thorn in its paw.

"You stuck your hand in," I told him. "I was defending myself."

"Knock first. Always knock first. In the meantime, you should go sleep this one off at the coal plant," Patrice told him. Then she looked a little closer at his hand. "What did she stick you with?" she asked.

He couldn't have known, so I showed Patrice my X-Acto. I held it up for her to inspect, but I didn't let go of it. The blade was, much to my surprise, bent. I made a mental note to lift some new ones at the art supply store when it was daylight and the shop had opened.

"Edgar, this is Abby and this is Cameron. Abby, this is Edgar. He doesn't belong here, at least not when he's like this."

"I'm bleeding!"

"Of course you're bleeding. What do you expect?"

"I have some Bactine," I said.

All four of the grown-ups looked at me like I was a crazy person—which I guess I was. Cameron and I crawled back into the igloo to get it. When I reemerged, the men had let go of Edgar, and he was sitting down in the snow. After Patrice sprayed some of the antiseptic on his hand, the two men walked him back to the coal plant, and Cameron and I went back to bed. Apparently, Edgar could be violent. He had once gone to jail for knifing another homeless guy behind a bagel place on Church Street. And he wasn't allowed anywhere near the men's shelter because he was always picking fights. But Patrice didn't believe he meant me or Cameron any harm. He was drunk and probably just wanted a place to get warm.

Still, I viewed this as a close call. I realized after that how I always needed to be on my guard.

....

One afternoon at Muddy Waters I ripped a flyer for some UVM garage band off the corkboard and wrote on the back, *You sense the clock is ticking.* I wrote more, some of which I remember, but it's not worth sharing. I mention those six words, however, because I knew I couldn't go on like this. Eventually I was going to run out of time. Or stamina. Or food. Or warmth. Or, pure and simple, the will to live. That carriage was coming.

And while I had no conscious plan to go home to Reddington— God, I had no conscious plans at all—I found myself beginning to wonder what would happen if I did try and sneak back into the Exclusion Zone. That might, in fact, be my endgame. Some mornings, I would wake up so depressed that the only thing that kept me from leaving Burlington and doing exactly that was Cameron.

I found myself trying to imagine where the other Cape Abenaki families had gone. I figured they'd left Vermont and New Hampshire. They knew they weren't wanted here. I thought a lot about where Eric Cunningham's family had wound up. Eric was the engineer who had blown his brains out. I knew he had a wife. I knew he had a couple of kids younger than me.

But what was increasingly clear to me was that something had to give. The air felt weirdly electric, as if it was July and a storm was approaching. Something was coming; something had to change. I only had so much skin I could cut.

. . . .

I remember explaining to Cameron very precisely why people wore camouflage clothes. He understood it pretty much already because two of his foster dads went deer hunting in November— and, of course, because he was a Vermonter. But I added what I knew about hunting blinds and deer stands (which wasn't much) and how I guessed soldiers used camo gear. Camo clothes and camo tents and camo packs. Camo boots.

"I wouldn't wear it to disguise myself," he said.

"No?" I asked.

"No. It's not like there's anybody out there looking for me. And I think I'm pretty invisible anyway."

I knew just what he meant.

. . . .

Over lunch one day when Cameron and I were sitting on a ledge near the waterfront watching the airplanes bank over Lake Champlain and descend toward the airport, I asked him if he missed his friends. He'd told me a few names. There was an immigrant boy from the Sudan named Jean Paul. A kid named Kenny. Another boy named Finn. He said he didn't know any of them all that well because he'd only been in the Burlington elementary school about four months.

"Do you think about them?" I asked.

He shrugged and took a bite of the energy bar. He chewed very carefully, like he wanted everything to last as long as possible. "I guess. Do you think about your friends?"

"Sure. But I'm not going back."

"Me either."

"Briarcliff is a lot farther away. Your friends are, like, right here. If you could see your friends, would you want to?"

"But I can't."

"I don't know. Maybe you could just show up one afternoon at the skate park."

"There was always a grown-up there. I'd get bagged." By "bagged" he meant caught.

"We could say you were going to school in Shelburne now. We could say I was your new nanny," I suggested.

"That like a babysitter?"

"Yup. Exactly."

He seemed to think about this. As he did, I pointed at an Air Wisconsin regional jet in the skies above the western shore of the lake. It was just starting to dip its wing and begin its turn toward Vermont and the airport a few miles to our east. It was really pretty in the midday sun.

"Some keep the Sabbath in Surplice—I, just wear my Wings,"

I said. "I think of those lines sometimes when we watch the planes and the seagulls." Cameron thought it was kind of random the way every once in a while I would just say aloud a line of poetry I liked. He was used to it by then, but he still thought I was insane.

"What's a surplice?" he asked now.

"Honestly? I'm not sure. But I think it's something a minister wears."

"But the poet was just wearing wings."

"Well, clothes, too." I didn't want him to imagine the poet was naked, because that wasn't Emily Dickinson's point.

"She was kind of overconfident."

"You think?"

He finished his energy bar. "If she thought she was an angel, she was."

"So, you want to see your buddies?"

"I don't know. I'd need a skateboard."

And suddenly I wanted him to have a skateboard. I wanted him to have it more than anything. And while there are many things you can lift—such as hand warmers and energy bars—a skateboard is sort of impossible. It's not just the size. Let's face it, I had lifted gallons of detergent the previous autumn. It's the cost. A skateboard is big *and* expensive. That's a tough combination. But I desperately wanted my little buddy to have a skateboard. I desperately wanted him to see his friends. So, that night I convinced Patrice the feral cat whisperer to keep an eye on Cameron, and then I cleaned myself up at the Y and went out to the interstate exit. It had been a while, but I remembered instantly how gross the men were and the weird things they wanted you to say while they were inside you. At one point I had yet another one of those strange out-of-body moments when I looked up at the dude, a thin and gangly and greasy trucker from Rhode Island, but at least this time I didn't wind up weeping in the fetal position. Instead I found myself thinking, what did I need to do to make absolutely sure that Cameron never, ever became . . . this?

But when I got back to the igloo, I had enough money for a

skateboard and some new clothes for us both. And the next day, when I was watching Cameron pick out a pretty sick board at the skate shop—it had a bunch of skeletons rubbing these magic lamps and all kinds of genies rising from them in blue fog and smoke—I was seriously happy because he was seriously happy. Finally he had something he liked as much as that mummy bag! Finally! He was a little apprehensive at first because he couldn't understand why out of the blue I was so flush, and he kept saying we should save the money for food or an emergency or something. But I was pretty adamant: I knew what I wanted.

The next warm day we walked to the skate park, and Cameron did some pretty mad shit on that board. I was impressed. There was a boy he knew there, but not all that well. Still, the two of them had fun together. I stood there for a while chatting with some very nice mom who had recently arrived in Vermont from Syria. Her name was Nairi Shushan Checkosky (think Tchaikovsky) and she was half Armenian. She wanted to know how long I had been an au pair—her term for nanny—and why a smart girl like me wasn't in college. I said I was earning money for college, and clearly she approved. She gave me her business card because she said she knew other families who might need an au pair. She had dark eyes and chestnut hair and was very beautiful. I gather she was a singer—or had been a singer until everything went to hell in Syria. Now she sold real estate. I think she must have spoken a hundred languages.

Cameron and I went back to the skate park maybe five or six times over the next two months. There was more snow and cold, but there were also times when we could feel the days getting longer and the warmth of spring. Some days we walked past crocuses, a flower that in Vermont has to have a death wish. You pop your head up out of the marshy ground, look around at the sun, and then get hammered with a foot and a half of snow.

But on our way back to the waterfront that first time, Cameron and I watched the sun set over the Adirondacks and it was gorgeous. Postcard perfect. It was one of those moments when, somehow, I was at once impossibly happy and unbelievably blue.

Chapter 15

The sugaring season came early that spring. There were sugar runs by the middle of February, and some people were even blaming that on Cape Abenaki. Me? I blamed it on good old-fashioned global climate change. But for a week after Valentine's Day, whenever Cameron and I would go to the library all of the people in the periodical room were chattering on and on about how much less maple syrup Vermont was now going to produce because so many of the sugarhouses were in the Exclusion Zone. Others were insisting that no one was going to buy Vermont maple syrup ever again, just like no one wanted Vermont milk and cheese anymore. This was, in their opinion, just one more reason to hate anyone who had ever had anything at all to do with the nuclear plant.

My family didn't sugar, but I knew people who did. I even knew some people from the plant—including an engineer, as a matter of fact—who loved sugaring precisely because it was so freaking low-tech. And if you're a kid (and he had kids), a sugarhouse is a pretty enchanted place, even if it's actually a decrepit shed so small it can barely fit an evaporator the size of a pool table. It might be thirty-five or forty degrees outside, but chances are the heat from the wood fire and all that steam will make it feel like a sauna inside. There is the mouthwatering aroma of maple. And there is that whole fake fairy-tale vibe: a shack at the edge of the woods with a roaring, medieval fire inside and something magic and strange occurring in the roiling fluid above the flames—a vat of sap that can be stilled in a heartbeat by a dollop of butter or a little drop of cream. Eventually all of that sap will thicken into ambrosia.

Of course, the first thing I thought of then and I think of now when I see a sugarhouse is the rager. Yeah, I was there. Of course. And I got into trouble. The problem wasn't that we were partying in a sugarhouse: it was that we were partying in the Snowman Haverford Sugarhouse. Snowman was the son of James Howard Haverford, the sewing machine bazillionaire who founded the Academy. Snowman wasn't his son's real name, of course. I have no idea anymore what his real first name was. But he was nicknamed Snowman because he used to take photographs of snowflakes at the end of the nineteenth century with a dude from Jericho, Vermont, named Wilson "Snowflake" Bentley. And Snowman had a massive sugarhouse that was now a museum to sugarmaking and to those photos of snowflakes. In the spring they fired up the evaporator, but most of the time it was a destination for elementary school field trips. It wasn't that far from the Academy, and we often saw a line of yellow school buses there with the names of school districts two and three hours away. And why not? They had the whole history of sugarmaking in there, and the kids always went home with samples of maple sugar candies.

Which, to be honest, was the main reason some kids broke in that night. It didn't start out as a party. There were half a dozen Reddington seniors who were pretty stoned and had the munchies. One of them had a dad who was a sugarmaker and volunteer docent at the museum, and he knew where his dad kept the keys. So the plan was to stroll in, grab bags full of the sugar candy, and stroll out. Except that once they were inside, they decided to start a fire in the stove beneath the evaporator and hang out. And smoke some more dope. And once they had the fire going, they started texting friends to join them—and to bring more weed and beer.

Which was how I wound up there. I was with Lisa Curran and we figured, why not? So we got a ride from a senior named Paul. By the time we got to the museum, there were at least thirty or thirty-five kids there, and maybe half were from the Academy and half were from as far away as St. Johnsbury. Someone actually brought a keg. By the time the police showed up, all of the boys had—I am not kidding—peed into the evaporator because someone figured out that there had to be fluid in the evaporator. A couple of the girls had pulled up their sweaters and were allowing the boys to lick maple syrup off their stomachs.

Lisa and I were only sophomores then and this was the wildest, grossest thing either of us had ever been part of. The two of us didn't get in trouble for breaking and entering or criminal trespassing or vandalism, the way a couple of kids did. But we were punished by our parents and the school and, yup, the law. We were among the students whose parents had to pay for all the damage we did. (This resulted in a scream-fest between my parents and me that I'm really not proud of at all.) And Lisa's and my "legal" punishment? We were among the twenty-four minors who had to go to special after-school seminars for a week on the "important" work of Snowman Haverford. It seems when Snowman wasn't taking pictures of snowflakes and making maple syrup, he was a poet. He might even have been the world's worst poet. But the Academy didn't think so.

Or maybe they did. Maybe they figured out that ten hours of after-school "tutelage" in his accomplishments and work—his tree-tapping innovations, his pictures, his poems—would make sure we never again broke into a sugarhouse to party.

This was one more black mark against me in the eyes of a lot of people at the Academy: further proof that I was the smartest loser they'd ever had to teach—the absolute Queen of the Underachievers.

. . . .

When I think of the word "homesick," I think of kids the first week at a sleepaway summer camp who are missing their moms and dads and their house. I think of some of the boarders when they first arrived at the Academy. Not a super big deal. If they're summer camp kids, they're going to go home in a week or a month. If they're Reddington boarders, they'll blend in soon enough and get over it. They'll outgrow it.

As for me: after the meltdown, I was always and I was never homesick. Never, because—remember—I thought I was never going to see my home again. Never, because I knew for a fact that I would never see my parents again.

So, homesickness becomes merely wistfulness if home has become uninhabitable. It's more like a phantom pain than the kind you can gift yourself with an X-Acto.

On the other hand, I never stopped missing what I had. What I was. What was home.

. . . .

Not always, but often I kept an eye out for Camille or some of the other kids from the shelter. I was especially careful when I was getting Cameron and me food at the Salvation Army or we were using day passes at the Y. And sometimes I did see people—shelter kids as well as the counselors—and either I was able to steer clear of them or they didn't recognize me. The thing is, most of the teens at the shelter would eventually move on: either the shelter would help them figure it all out and they'd go to college or get jobs and decent apartments, or they'd fall off the map and wind up at places like Poacher's. Sometimes they'd disappear completely, heading south to New York or Boston (like Andrea) or even west to L.A. And sometimes their parents would come and get them and maybe over time they would get their acts together. I'm sure Missy's okay. The pendulum could swing either way.

My point? I was totally unprepared when Camille surprised me one day in February. I had seen her from a distance two or three times, but I'd managed to avoid her so we hadn't spoken in almost eight months.

"Hey, you want a cigarette?" Those were the first words out of her mouth.

Cameron and I were sitting downstairs in the food court in the mall downtown. It was, just so you know, the most depressing food court in any mall anywhere in the world. It was belowground and had no windows. No plants. Nothing but the smell of crap Chinese food. But it was warm and it was private because no one ever went there. Everyone ate at the nice places on Church Street or the Starbucks on the floor above the food court. I recognized the voice instantly and looked up. I was reading a three-month-old *Cosmopolitan* magazine I'd found in a blue recycling bin (it was a little too much about Christmas by then, but what the hell), and Cameron was reading one of those classic novels that have been turned into a comic book. I used to pick them up cheap for him at the comic book store. This one was *A Tale of Two Cities.* The pictures of the guillotine and the nobles who were about to be beheaded were seriously cool and, given my frame of mind, a lot more interesting to me than glossy photos of stiletto heels and tips on how to drive a man wild in bed.

So, there was Camille standing over us. She looked great, she really did. I knew instantly she was one of the shelter alumni who were rocking it. She was wearing a very cheerful, robin's-egg blue peacoat, khaki slacks, and a scarf that fell like waterfalls down her front. She was no longer using peroxide on her hair and it was growing out. It was mostly red now.

"No," I said, "I really don't smoke."

She put the pack in the pocket of her coat and smiled. "We're not supposed to smoke in here anyway. Not that anyone cares in this sad little corner." Then she nodded at Cameron, who was looking up at her warily, and asked, "What's your name?"

He turned to me, unsure whether this was someone who would give us our space or someone who might rat us out. I couldn't tell myself. Still, I answered for him. "This is Cameron," I said. To try and turn the attention away from us I told her that I liked her coat and I thought she looked really good.

"I'm at CCV now," she said, referring to the community college. "And I'm a waitress at Leunig's."

"Where are you living?"

"I have an apartment on South Union Street with another girl. It's small—one bedroom. But it's nice. My parents are helping out with the rent."

"Seriously?"

"Seriously. And you? What's your deal?"

"Just hanging out."

"And Cameron is your . . ."

"He's my nephew."

She seemed to think about this and then decided I was lying. I could tell. "I'm working tonight," she volunteered. "My shift starts at five. Why don't you two come by? The food's good."

"I don't know." There was no way I could afford Leunig's.

"Don't sweat it. I'll take care of you. The manager tonight is pretty excellent—the kind of dude who plays Santa Claus when they light the tree on Church Street. Come by early—before it gets crowded."

"Okay. Maybe we will."

"Hey: Wanna know something?"

I waited. "Sure," I said finally.

"I got a new phone."

I waited. She was grinning and I couldn't read her expression at all. I wasn't sure where this was going. Suddenly I was afraid she was going to out me. I feared at the very least she was going to call me "Emily," and I had no idea how I would explain that to Cameron.

"Yup," she continued. "But I made sure that all the numbers and calls were deleted from the old one before I got rid of it—even the calls made by other people to, I don't know, the Northeast Kingdom. I made sure I had wiped it clean."

"Thank you."

"No biggie." She reached into her purse and got out a pad of pink Post-it notes shaped like hearts. She scribbled her phone number on the top sheet and handed it to me. "You never know," she mumbled, patting me awkwardly on the shoulder. "See ya."

"See ya," I said.

Then she turned and left us alone. She probably figured that
Cameron and I would never call her or make it to Leunig's. Still, it
was nice of her to offer. She was right: you never did know.

. . . . , ...

I never thought I was going to live forever—even before Reactor One exploded—and I sure don't think so anymore. One time
for an English class I made this chart of when all these important
people in Emily Dickinson's life died. Her dad in 1874. Samuel
Bowles in 1878. Charles Wadsworth in the spring of 1882; her
mom in the autumn that year. Her nephew in 1883.

She herself suffered from something called Bright's disease, a
kidney disorder, the last two years of her life. Some of the symptoms of Bright's disease and radiation sickness are the same. Vomiting. Fever. Weakness. Of course, those are also the symptoms of
practically everything, so maybe I shouldn't read too much into
that.

Still, I really want to be sure you know that I was never one of
those teens who thought she was going to live forever. It's okay. It
really is.

. . . .

The only good thing about March in Vermont is the sugaring
season. Everything else about the month sucks. I know that makes
me sound like a surly teen, but even the adults who live here know
that the month is a total train wreck. It rains or it sleets or it snows.
Then you get this day where it's fifty-five degrees and sunny and
you think spring is coming . . . and then the next day it snows. The
dirt roads become car-sucking swamps. Somehow, there's mud
everywhere. It used to make my mom bonkers. (I mean it: she and
my dad were just never meant to live here. They just weren't.) Plus,
the school breaks are always in February and April, so you can't

even get away from here on a vacation with your family. Seriously, the whole month is one long buzzkill.

And that year, March came in February. We had those sugar runs that I told you about just after Valentine's Day. We had March mud in February. And we had March warmth in February.

And if you're living in an igloo, March warmth in February totally sucks. It is, quite literally, a home wrecker. The long thaw we had in the third week of February completely wrecked Cameron's and my igloo. The igloo could survive one or two warm days in the middle of winter just fine—like the day of the anti-nuke rally and march up the hill. But I saw quickly that two warm days in a row was the max. The ice was the glue. The igloo would start to sag and buckle on day three. I tried to prop it up with tree branches and a couple of ski poles I found in a dumpster, but they were no help. Cameron tried to duct tape it together, but everything was just too wet. I tried to make a structural skeleton beneath the trash bags with a grungy piece of plywood and this crappy card table—it only had two legs and the plastic covering on the top had big gashes like a serial killer had taken a knife to it—but then the bags just slid down the sides instead of collapsing in the center. What it needed was an architect or a builder and an expense account at the building supply store down on Pine Street. It was a goner.

And it was pretty clear that my neighbors were going to be absolutely no help. They were great if someone started screaming *I'm going to blow your house down and fucking kill you!* in the middle of the night, wrecking their sleep, but otherwise they didn't have a whole lot of interest in being my surrogate parents. Maybe if Cameron and I were cats Patrice would have wanted to look out for us. But these were not what you might call nurturing people. They were, like me, kind of fucked up. I mean, they were grown-ups living in trash bag igloos in the middle of winter, right? What does that tell you?

When I realized that my igloo was going to collapse, I did go to them to see if they had any miracle solutions. But while I was struggling with my ski poles and card table, the war vet had split. Just packed his things and peaced out, leaving behind what looked like nothing more than a pile of moldy-looking garbage bags stuffed with leaves. Patrice and Rick were still there, but they were about to leave, too. Their shopping cart was already filled.

"Oh, Abby, you don't want to come with us," Patrice said when I asked where they were going.

"No, probably not," I agreed, though in fact I kind of did. I really wasn't sure what was next. "But where are you going?"

Rick looked at me and then looked at Patrice. And then he shook his head. (It dawned on me that in all the weeks we had been together down by the waterfront, I'd heard his voice maybe six times. Not a big talker, that Rick.)

"Really, even we're not sure," she said, and it was obvious she was lying. She gave me this halfhearted sort of hug, and I must admit I was kind of glad it was halfhearted because Patrice always smelled sort of like cat urine and sort of like your basic homelessness. Then, because the ground was becoming mush, she and Rick lifted their grocery cart and carried it the two hundred or so yards to the sidewalk that ran near the lake. I almost screamed something nasty at them because inside I was totally bitchcakes that everyone was leaving and no one was going to help. I know I would have popped a couple of Oxies if I'd had any. And I had an incredible desire to take my X-Acto and just start whaling on my thighs. But I didn't say a word because I felt Cameron taking my hand. I looked down and he was just watching the two of them carry away their cart. Then he pointed out a jet high in the sky over the water. This one was climbing and about to bank to the south. Neither of us said a word. I think he wanted me to see it because he was hoping it might cheer me up.

. . . .

Life on the streets is fucking exhausting. It really is. There's nothing harder.

Obviously I found a new place for Cameron and me to crash.

But the change in the weather was kind of a pain in the ass and both Cameron and I got sick. I didn't think it was the flu because, believe it or not, I had gotten Cameron and me flu shots at the Rite Aid one day in January. But now we were both wobbly and weak and our noses were running like glaciers. The problem—and I guess this was the beginning of the end—was that only I seemed to be getting better.

Chapter 16

Sometimes I felt like I had disappeared without a trace. Sometimes I wondered if either of my grandparents was still alive. Obviously my grandma with Alzheimer's would have been in absolutely no condition to lead some kind of search for me. Was she even aware that Cape Abenaki had exploded and her daughter was dead? I had no idea, but I doubted it. On the other hand, my grandpa in Phoenix probably knew of the meltdown and the fact that his son had been killed. He probably knew that Bill Shepard was the guy the nuclear power industry had decided should take the fall, and so now the whole world kind of detested that little boy he'd raised years ago in Arizona. But given how badly my parents always said my grandpa was doing adjusting to the colostomy, he might have died by now, too. Maybe the simple pain of watching his son's memory get abused day after day on CNN and Fox News had broken his heart and killed him back in the summer.

But sometimes I wondered whether Lisa's librarian mom was going all Nancy Drew on her computer or talking to the police. Or maybe Ms. Gagne, my old English teacher. Or maybe even Edie from the shelter. Edie had struck me as very smart; maybe she'd figured out who Abby Bliss really was.

And I was positive that people somewhere had to be looking for Cameron. A lost nine-year-old foster kid? Someone in the state's DCF—Department for Children and Families—must have been getting smothered in whole mountains of shit over that little debacle.

Still, even seven and eight months after Cape Abenaki, it seemed like everyone had way better things to do than worry about what the hell had happened to Emily Shepard. For all I knew, everyone assumed I'd just killed myself and my body would be found when all of the snow finally melted. Or maybe they figured I'd killed myself and my body was decomposing somewhere in that actual no-man's-land called the Exclusion Zone. With so many people relocated, lots of people were still unaccounted for.

And, the truth is, I really might have killed myself if it hadn't been for Cameron. I'm not kidding. But as long as I was responsible for that little guy, I was going to keep putting one foot after another and see what happened.

One of the therapists here said she thought I didn't want to be found because I had issues with my self-image. I didn't say anything back, but I remember thinking, *People pay you for this?* Seriously: file that little observation in your manila folder where you keep the Unbelievably Obvious.

Eventually my curiosity did get the best of me, and I went to a vacant computer kiosk at the library and looked myself up. It was a few days before the igloo would collapse. I googled my family and I googled Eric Cunningham and I even looked at the pages for some of my friends on Facebook before it got too much. And it got too much pretty damn fast. After a few clicks, I thought my head was going to explode. In some ways, it was worse than I'd thought. There were lawsuits and criminal prosecutions: people my dad and mom worked with, people I knew, were going to be defendants in a court case later that year. Criminal negligence. And it looked like whole boatloads of people were suing the power company. As for my dad? As for my mom and dad? It didn't matter that they were dead. They were like war criminals. I was nauseated by the things I was reading about them, the stories ranging from pure snark and lies to "responsible" time lines that claimed to show my father's "habitual" incompetence. His "apparent" alcoholism. The power company's failure to discharge him.

And as for little old me? I had, it seems, run away months ago.

But based on the fact that there hadn't been a single mention of me in any newspaper since July, no one seemed to care. I really had managed to disappear.

When I rejoined Cameron in a second-floor corner of the library, I must have looked a little pale because he asked me if I was all right. I said I was and sat back against a bookcase with a novel in my lap, but I was unable to read a word for the rest of the day. It would be a long, long time before I would open up a computer browser again.

. . . .

I considered my options once Patrice and Rick were gone, including just pretending that my legs were cooked spaghetti and collapsing into the melting snow or falling back into the trash bags that had been my home. But, apparently, I really am weirdly maternal. I couldn't let Cameron down. He was still holding my hand. He had his skateboard in the other. He was, I am happy to report, still wearing the gloves I had lifted for him at the Outdoor Gear Exchange.

So I forced myself to get my act together. I took a couple of slow, deep breaths and then I looked down at him. I shrugged and tried to offer him a little smile. "You ever heard the term 'Plan B'?" I asked.

He shook his head.

"Well, it means finding a new plan when the first one doesn't work. So, give me a minute and I will figure out our Plan B— where we're going to go next."

"I don't want another foster home," he said, and he motioned up toward his eye with the tip of his skateboard. It was healed by now, but obviously I knew what he was referring to. "I'll just run away again."

"I know. But we're not that desperate. Not yet, anyway."

It seemed to me that we had at least two options: I could eat some crow and return to Poacher's. I didn't believe he would turn

Cameron in, if only because it would mean drawing attention to himself. But I had spent enough time with Poacher to know that Cameron was going to be a deal breaker long-term. A missing nine-year-old foster kid? A minor? Not good. You get serious jail time for that kind of shit. Remember, Poacher thought I was eighteen. But I thought he would let us spend a night there, assuming he had room. And maybe while we were there I could find a lead on another posse or a person my age with a little crash pad where we could chill for a while.

Our other option? There were a couple of cheap motels on a strip a few miles from the downtown. They still wanted fifty or sixty bucks a night, but I guessed I could become a regular at the gas stations by the interstate. Or I could for a couple of days, anyway, just until I really did find that Plan B.

But, I must admit, as crazy as it seems I am and as bad as my judgment really is sometimes, I wasn't ready to go that route yet. It was one thing when I was with Andrea and it was one thing when it was kind of a once-in-a-while thing to get Cameron a skateboard. But it was another to make hand jobs and blow jobs the only line items on my résumé. I guessed that might happen eventually, but I wasn't all in yet to become a full-time prostitot.

So I gave Cameron a kind of abridged, PG-version of what Poacher's was like and who might be there. I probably made it sound more like MTV's *Real World* than the putrid rats' nest that it really was. But it was a place where I figured we could get some rest. So he packed up his mummy bag and we filled our backpacks. (He was no longer using a trash bag as a suitcase, thank God.) I decided to leave behind the skuzzy and moldy quilt I'd used to keep warm in those long winter nights. Not a great loss: it was buried somewhere beneath the remains of the igloo. Then we said good-bye to the waterfront and started up the hill to the North End.

. . . .

But, of course, Poacher was gone. Perfect, I thought. This is just perfect.

The front door to the apartment was unlocked, the way it usually was, but I didn't recognize anything inside the place. Oh, it was still disgusting: there was a sticky layer of floor juice across the linoleum in the kitchen, and the windows were shadowed with dots of black grime. But the bedroom where the posse had crashed when we weren't sardining in the living room actually had a bed instead of mattresses pressed side to side on the floor. It was a crap bed—a queen, like my parents'—with a headboard that was nicked and chipped, but it was still a bed. And the other bedroom had a desk and an okay-looking Mac and printer on it. There was different furniture in the living room, too, and some of it I could tell was brand-new from the unfinished furniture store in the North End. It had that new wood smell and was still waiting to be stained. I saw a Bible on the table that also held a little flat-screen TV on a stand and a cable box.

But if someone lived here now who wasn't a total loser like Poacher, why was the door unlocked? I couldn't figure that out. But then I heard footsteps on the stairs below us, and so I grabbed Cameron by the hand and pulled him with me back into the entry-way. I saw a heavyset guy in his late fifties or early sixties trudging up the steps with an empty plastic wastebasket in each hand. He was wearing a blue denim shirt with the sleeves cut away, and he had some serious tats on his arms and his neck: An eagle. Some eagle wings. A motorcycle made out of flames. But he was also wearing tortoiseshell eyeglasses, which made him look kind of like an overweight science teacher from the chin up.

By the time he got to us, he was puffing a bit.

"Can I help you two?" he asked, and then he pushed past us into the apartment.

"We used to live here," I said.

He put down the wastebaskets in his front hallway and rubbed the back of his neck. "I hope not with that drug dealer who lived here before me."

"No. It was a couple years ago," I lied. I had to restrain myself from asking him exactly what had happened to *that drug dealer*, because I really wanted to know. I really wanted to know where everyone was.

"I moved in two days ago. I wanted to scrub the place with Purell—floor to ceiling. You'd think the landlord would have done that. Nope." He shook his head. "I don't know what it was like when you lived here, but it was a pit when I moved in. Only good thing about this place is the rent, which isn't much, and the view, which is actually pretty nice."

"And it's light," I said.

"Yup. It's light." He put out his hand. "My name's Andy."

"Abby," I said. His fingers were kind of moist and clammy, but it had been a long time since anyone had wanted to shake my hand. "This is Cameron—my brother."

He leaned over a little bit and shook Cameron's hand, too. "Hello, little man."

Then the three of us stood there awkwardly for a long moment. He was eyeing our massive backpacks and Cameron's mummy bag. Finally I said, "Well, I guess the place is still here. Thank you."

"I'd invite you in, but somehow I don't think my parole officer would approve."

"Gotcha," I said.

"I kind of figured you would."

I wasn't sure whether I should be insulted or flattered that he figured I was so street-smart I knew the drill about parole officers. But given how Cameron and I must have looked and all the stuff we had with us, it was sort of ridiculous to feel one way or the other. Our deal—who we were, what we were—was pretty clear.

"You need a job?" he asked.

Instantly I took a little step away from him. Looking back, I think it's hilarious that a guy tells me he's a felon and I only say, "Gotcha," like *I understand*. But a guy tells me he has a job for me and immediately I assume he's going to unzip his pants. God, I'm fucked up.

"No."

"Okay. But if you decide you do, stop by Henry's. You know Henry's?"

I did. It was a diner on Bank Street.

"My brother's the manager there. Been there forever. Started as a cook, like, twenty years ago. Now I'm one of his dishwashers. He got me the gig. They always seem to need waitresses there."

Ever since Camille had spotted me at the food court in the mall, it had crossed my mind that maybe, somehow, I could get a real job. A waitress, maybe. Or maybe I could score some hours at a Burger King or Taco Bell. But I had no experience and no references and no ID. Who was going to hire me? And I knew from my days in the posse there was no way in hell that a person could live alone anywhere in Burlington on minimum wage. Rents were crazy. You either needed a good job or you needed subsidies or you had to have roommates.

But now I had Cameron and I'd promised him I'd find us a Plan B.

"If I change my mind, who do I talk to?" I asked.

"Well, you're talking to me for starters. Drop off a résumé at the diner. I'll tell my brother to keep an eye out for it. He does most of the hiring."

"A résumé." Mostly I was just thinking out loud.

"Yup. Piece of paper. Has your experience. Jobs. Where you live." His sentence had started out kind of light and sarcastic, but he'd emphasized the last three words in a way I didn't really like.

"Got it," I said simply. I think it was self-preservation that made me polite. My instinct was to show him just how mental I could be and say something snotty, but I was able to dial it down. "Thank you," I even added.

"Not a biggie," he said. "You gonna be okay?"

"Oh, we're cool," I reassured him. "Maybe I will drop off a résumé." I put my hand on Cameron's back and we hoisted our backpacks off the floor. He cradled his mummy bag the way he liked and I took his skateboard. Then I guided him to the stairs. "Thanks," I said again, and Andy gave me this small salute.

....

When Cameron and I were outside Andy's place and a block and a half away from the building, I realized I had put my hand once again on Cameron's back. It dawned on me that this was precisely the way my dad would guide me through crowds, and the realization made me at once both happy and sad. Suddenly my mind was filled with images that raced past like a Tumblr feed, me at different ages but my dad always looking pretty much the same, and in all of them my dad had his hand on my back and I was feeling either happy or safe or both. There we were in front of Snow White's Scary Adventures smack-dab in the middle of the Magic Kingdom in Disney World, the sky almost the same blue as the Dorothy Gale gingham dress I was wearing. (You know they've closed that Snow White ride now, right? Why would they do that? Crazy and cruel, it seems to me. I get that it was kind of dated, but how could a kid not love that witch? I was terrified of her. I loved it!) That day was the first time I was allowed to go to a ladies' room alone. I was five. My mom couldn't take me because she was standing in line at some other part of the park at some other ride, getting the three of us Fast Passes. My dad later told me that he had waited outside that ladies' room door scared to death that I'd been abducted. Maybe there were two entrances, and some madman was stealing me away and disappearing into the crowds through that other exit. My mom always thought my dad's panic was kind of sweet when he told her about it. Other images I saw behind my eyes of my dad and me with his hand on my back? Walking to the school bus from the edge of our driveway the first day of kindergarten. (Once again, my backpack was way too big for my body.) Walking to a Brownie jamboree. Walking across our backyard with Maggie the puppy in my arms, her leash dangling behind her like her tail.

Genetics, I thought. Genetics. We really can't escape them, can we?

I looked down at Cameron and wondered about the way he would just reach up and take my hand. I didn't imagine a lot of nine-year-old boys would do that. So I asked him, "Did your mom like it when you held her hand?"

I could literally feel him becoming self-conscious and realized this might have been a horrible question to ask him.

And, of course, it turned out it was. We didn't hold hands like that ever again until we were together in the emergency room.

Chapter 17

We went to Leunig's, where Camille had told me she worked. Cameron stood just outside with our stuff while I went in. The place was between lunch and dinner, so except for the bar it was pretty quiet. And even at the bar everyone was drinking cappuccinos and espressos and super-expensive hot chocolates. It really was a very nice restaurant. The bartender said Camille wasn't due for another hour, so I asked if I could leave her a note.

"Yes, sure. But do you mind writing it over there?" he said, and he pointed at the dark corner of the bar near the curtains that went to the bathrooms. I guess I was kind of a check minus in the Project Runway department. I hadn't been able to scare up passes for the Y in two days, and it must have showed. I nodded this was fine and kind of shrunk as much as I could.

"You need a pen?" he asked. He was a pretty handsome dude with a Johnny Depp Vandyke on his chin. Maybe thirty years old and very tall and trim. The uniform at Leunig's was a tight white shirt and a black tie.

"That would be great," I said. "And maybe something to write on."

He nodded and handed me a pen and one of the blank slips they used for bills.

"Need something else?" This was the bartender again. I realized I hadn't written a word yet because I wasn't sure what I wanted to say. If Camille had been there, I was going to ask if Cameron and I could crash on the floor of her and her roommate's place for

a night. That's all I was hoping for: a night. Suddenly I just needed
to sleep and to be inside.

"You know what?" I said to the bartender. He raised his eyebrows and waited. "I'll come back in a couple of hours."

"Cool," he said, and he nodded his head in the direction of the
front door.

....

Next we trudged two blocks to the Kinko's on South Winooski.
It was right by the day station for the homeless, so I knew it well. I
had passed it dozens of times. And there I used six bucks from the
little cash I had left and created a résumé for Andy's brother at the
diner. It was all made up, of course. If the dude chose to call any
of my references, I was fucked. But I hadn't much of a choice. I
dug around inside my backpack, hoping I still had that little pink
Post-it with Camille's number, and fortunately I did. That was the
phone number I was going to have to use as a contact.

When I looked at the résumé after printing it out, I decided
it didn't look half bad. There was a diner I made up in Briarcliff
and a few years babysitting and even an autumn as an after-school
tutor. I mean, I would have hired me. I knew waitressing would
be hard, but I have a good memory for everything but the periodic
table. And I'd eaten at enough diners in my life and seen enough
waitresses "slinging hash" on TV and in the movies that I was
pretty sure I could figure it out. (I've always gotten a charge out of
the expression "slinging hash." It always makes me imagine a food
fight.)

Then the two of us walked back to Leunig's. I considered dropping off the résumé at Henry's Diner first, but given the way the
bartender had viewed me as a sort of stinky mongrel dog, I figured
I should wait a day. I still believed that I—to use another phrase
that always gives me the grins—cleaned up nice. Either I would
shower at Camille's or I would be able to cadge a day pass for

the Y. But I'd be sure I was seriously presentable when I met Andy's brother. After all, I had to for Cameron.

. . . .

Camille was amazing and said of course we could crash at her place for a night—even two or three if we needed to. She said her roommate would be cool. To this day I don't know if Camille changed because she felt guilty for stealing my earrings and sort of running me out of the teen shelter or whether she just grew up and became a really good person—whether the counselors at the shelter got through to her and worked their magic. But she gave me the address and her key because her roommate would be working at Macy's when we got there, and so we walked to the apartment and I went straight to the shower, where I could cut myself senseless and wash my hair. I felt almost human when I got out of the bathroom.

The apartment was in a pretty run-down house a couple of blocks from the Kinko's. It was on the second floor and didn't have a whole lot of furniture, but it was nice and warm and there was this really long table a bit like the one my family had had in our kitchen in Reddington. It was made of the same wood, which I remembered was pumpkin pine. Immediately Cameron unrolled his mummy bag underneath it, and I joined him there in a T-shirt and a pair of ass-billboard sweatpants I'd lifted from Victoria's Secret. We read our books for, like, ten minutes before we both fell sound asleep.

. . . .

Camille's roommate got home about seven-thirty that night. Camille had already texted her that we'd be there. Her name was Dawn, and she was kind of a rarity: she was a girl who, I could tell, had no idea just how pretty she was. Normally, in my experience, a hot girl knows she's hot. Even if they have the brains of a gerbil, beautiful girls usually know this one salient fact: they turn heads. But, I swear, Dawn was totally oblivious.

Now, she wasn't the brightest bulb in the tanning bed. That was clear, too. But pretty or dumb, none of that mattered to me, because here was what she had going for her: she was very nice and she treated Cameron like a puppy. She didn't treat him like a dog, which is an expression that means in reality you treat a person like crap. She treated him like he was the cutest thing she had ever seen—a puppy—and was constantly telling him how sweet he was and how adorable he was and what a buff little dude he'd soon be. Cameron endured it.

And she didn't seem to give a rat's ass that he was a homeless kid who wasn't in school at the moment. A lot of people just might have frowned on that. Not Dawn. Camille wouldn't get home until around eleven that night because she was working until closing, and here was our entire exchange about Cameron's and my sitch while we waited:

DAWN: So he's, like, your nephew?
ME: Uh-huh. Our families lost our homes when the nuclear plant exploded and things kind of fell apart. But next week we're taking the bus to Briarcliff, New York. We have family there who are going to take care of us.
DAWN: God, the plant. That just sucks. The people who ran it? They were the worst, weren't they?
ME: Yup. They were the worst.
DAWN: But Cameron, you are just too cute! This will all be fine, you know. You know that, right? You are just the most adorable little person I've ever seen!

Then she hugged him. Again.

Now, obviously the story I gave Dawn didn't match the story I'd given Camille back in June at the shelter. But since—also obviously—Camille had figured out who I was, it didn't matter. It just didn't.

Still, I had this feeling that I had seen Dawn somewhere before. It wasn't at the shelter and it wasn't at the library and it wasn't at Muddy Waters. It sure as hell wasn't down by the waterfront. But for most of the evening I just couldn't figure out where. She had a beautiful heart-shaped face and very prominent brown eyes, and the only makeup she was wearing was a kind of dull lipstick. She pulled her hair straight back, which gave her a wide, high forehead. That look is hard to rock, but Dawn pulled it off. And then, when she fixed this massive collar on her turtleneck sweater, I got it. I knew instantly where I had seen her before. And I knew why she was so into Cameron.

I'd seen her one day that winter on the street outside of a day care on King Street, when Cameron and I had been walking from the waterfront to the library.

When she'd adjusted the collar on her sweater it was a lot like when she had pulled the collar of her jacket up and over the bottom of her face against the cold. She'd been behind this picket fence they had along the sidewalk to prevent the little kids from running from the playground into the street and getting themselves killed by a car, and she had been absolutely surrounded by rug rats. They were all in snowsuits that made them look like little Michelin men (and women), and I had no idea how they could move as fast as they did. All of the kids had been four and five and maybe six years old, so it's not like Cameron belonged with them. But for some reason it had still made me sad for him. All those kids had each other, and all Cameron had was yours truly.

"You don't just work at Macy's," I said. "You also work at a day care, don't you?"

"Used to work at a day care. No more. How did you know?"

"I once saw you in the yard with a bunch of kids."

"I loved that job," she told me, and her voice got a little sad.

"How come you're not there anymore?"

"I made kind of a bad choice one day, you know?"

I didn't know, so I waited.

"One of the little boys was crazy energetic. Maybe a little mental. And he'd never nap, which was bad for everyone. He'd just keep all the kids in the day care awake. So one afternoon I gave him some cough syrup to knock him out. And maybe I gave him a little too much or maybe it just worked too well. I don't know. But it was really hard to wake him up—the woman who runs the day care almost called 911—and when we finally got him on his feet, he was still super groggy. He was still super groggy when his mom came to pick him up. So, I was kind of fired."

"Cameron is a great sleeper," I told her. It was a reflex. And, fortunately, it was true. Still, I wanted to be sure she understood that he didn't need any help in the shut-eye department. I didn't want to take any chances.

. . . .

You have no idea how amazing it is to sleep on a couch when you have been sleeping burrowed inside a quilt in a trash bag igloo for nearly two months.

Even though I had napped that afternoon with Cameron under the pumpkin pine table, I was out like a light about fifteen minutes after Camille got back from the restaurant and didn't wake up until noon the next day. Dawn had already left for Macy's, but Camille was playing checkers with Cameron. It seems Dawn had made a mad dash to the Salvation Army store as soon as she'd woken up and bought five board games for five bucks. It made me feel a little guilty that I hadn't thought of that—and it made me think a little more highly of Dawn. Maybe she was the Queen of the Antihistamines, but the board games were a good call.

Since Camille and Cameron seemed to be getting along just fine, I went to Henry's and dropped off my résumé. The lunch rush was ending and I met Andy's brother. He was a burly guy, like Andy, and he was pretty curt. All business. But Andy came out from the kitchen and said hello. His brother actually hired me on the spot because I had diner experience and because one of his waitresses had walked out on him that morning, leaving "smack dab" in the middle of the breakfast rush. He wanted me to start the next day. I was supposed to come in at two, when business slowed after lunch, to get trained for a few hours before dinner.

I was pretty jazzed. I spent about an hour on Church Street and panhandled about thirteen bucks before a police officer moved me on, and then I started back to Camille's. I wanted to be sure I was there before she had to leave for work at the restaurant.

Anyway, I was kind of feeling that things were looking up. I really was. You're probably thinking that, too. We couldn't stay at Camille's forever, of course, but just coming in out of the cold and seeing how Camille had turned it around was seriously inspiring. And it had cleared my head. I had to find a place where Cameron and I could live on diner wages and tips—which was not going to be easy—and at some point I was going to have to figure out what to do about my little buddy. He needed to be in school. He needed grown-ups. He needed a real home. That's what I mean about how a night on a couch in a heated apartment had started me focusing again almost like a normal person.

And who knows? Maybe things really would have turned themselves around if I hadn't felt a cold coming on. I felt a tingle in the back of my throat and I started to feel achy. My nose was starting to run. I considered detouring back to the Rite Aid to lift some Airborne or something, but I was only a block from Camille's. I told myself that she or Dawn—God, especially Dawn—might have something I could take. The key was not to get Cameron sick.

. . . .

But, of course, Cameron already was sick. When I got back to Camille's, she was grateful because she was about to leave for work and wasn't wild about the idea of leaving Cameron alone.

"He's been sneezing," she said to me, and pointed under the

pumpkin pine table. The night before he'd taken a bedsheet and draped it over half the table, turning it into a cave. The other half had some notebooks and textbooks from Camille's classes at CCV. But there was still enough light from the undraped side for Cameron to read one of his classic comic book novels. This one, I saw, was *The War of the Worlds*.

I crouched on the floor and peered in. "How are you feeling?" I asked.

"I feel okay," he said, and then wiped at his nose with the back of his hand.

"Getting a cold?"

"Yeah, I guess."

"Let me get you something for your nose," I said. Camille and Dawn didn't have Kleenex, so I took the roll of paper towels off the kitchen counter and tore off a couple of sheets. Then I asked Camille if they had any orange juice. They didn't.

"I'll pick some up," I said. "I want to go to the Laundromat."

"Do you have any money?"

"Not a lot. But I have enough for orange juice and a load of laundry."

"How'd it go at the diner?"

"I got a job. I start tomorrow."

"No shit? That's awesome." She went to hug me, but even though the gesture caught me off guard I was able to stop her before she got too close.

"Whoa," I said, and put out my arm, my hand a wall, like a traffic cop. "I think I'm coming down with a cold."

"You, too?"

"Yup, me too."

Then she went to work, and I emptied out Cameron's and my backpacks and piled all of our laundry onto the floor. Normally Cameron would have come with me to the Laundromat—he liked to sit on the hot dryers—but it was plenty warm at Camille's. Besides, I wanted him to stay inside and rest.

"I wish they had a TV," he said. "Or a computer. It would be cool to watch something. Anything."

Somewhere, I figured, Camille had a laptop. After all, she was taking classes at CCV. But I didn't want to search her and Dawn's bedroom or "borrow" it for Cameron even if I found it. That would have been a pretty crappy betrayal after she had let us chill at her place. "I agree," I said. "Sorry about that."

He sneezed and shrugged, and so I packed up our clothes and left for the Laundromat.

. . . .

The other day I spied this note my therapist had written about me. "Welcomes seclusion. Not precisely antisocial, but reclusive. Aspirationally Dickinson?" Note the question mark she put after "Dickinson," as if she's wondering if I have a girl crush on the Belle of Amherst. Well, duh. If I'd had a pen when I saw that, I think I would have scratched out the hook above the dot and scribbled something like *Watch out, Sigmund Freud.* Honestly, I'm not sure how much of my crush focused on her poetry and how much focused on the mysteriousness of her life. Why did she retreat inside her home—and did she even consider it a retreat? How much of her life was about her daddy issues? Did the child whose father urged her to be "one of the best little girls" in Amherst ever unleash the passion that filled her poetry with one (or more!) of her gentleman friends? There was a novel I read about her in tenth grade that had all kinds of intriguing innuendo. In it she sleeps with a guy with tats. There was one biography that implied she had a wild side.

When I was ten years old, I visited her house for the first time with my grandmother. When I was fourteen years old, I went again with my parents. As I think I told you, I had posters from the Homestead on the walls of my bedroom—framed posters. (My favorite is a painting of her in a long-sleeved white dress looking at herself at the edge of a very still pond.)

I read one essay that suggested Emily Dickinson had a modern-ist approach to poetry as a writer—she had a contemporary sensi-bility. Why? Because elements of her work were short enough to tweet. I remember thinking that was the most ridiculous thing I'd ever read. Just because something is 140 characters or less doesn't mean it's modern. God, think of all the ancient Japanese haiku about cherry blossoms and clouds. Are those modern? No, they're just short.

I don't know, maybe I just wanted to be alone. Maybe I just didn't want to be social because antisocial people have a whole lot less to lose.

Chapter 18

I only ended up working at Henry's Diner for two days. That's it. I got the tips I had earned those two shifts, but I never even got a paycheck. I wasn't able to stick around long enough.

That's what I mean about how, maybe, I was never destined to turn things around.

When I went back to the diner the next day right after lunch to get trained, Andy's brother sent me home. I was, in his opinion, way too sick to work at a restaurant. He was probably right, but I needed to get cash fast because I wasn't sure how long I could impose on Camille and Dawn. (In all fairness, I think I could have imposed on them for a very long time, especially if I was making money and could have helped with the rent. They really didn't seem to mind that I slept on the couch for a couple of nights and Cameron had made a cave out of the one table in their apartment. Who knows? We might have become a new posse—a posse with actual jobs that wasn't breaking into people's houses and mistaking Oxies for vitamins.) So the day after I was sent home I doubled down on the DayQuil dosage: I felt like shit because I really did have one monster of a cold and because doubling down on Day-Quil gets you kind of light-headed and high—and not a good high. But my nose? It was solid. They let me work right up until the place closed for the night, around nine p.m. And I liked the uniform: it had this retro Kat Dennings sort of vibe. I was the youngest girl there; in fact, I was the only waitress you might call a girl. The next youngest waitress was a mom whose name tag said

Shari and who was probably thirty or thirty-five. She wore her hair in this Rosie the Riveter sort of updo and kept it back with a scarf. There was also a really lovely lady named Gail Arnoff with the most incredible hazel eyes; I recognized her from somewhere and wasn't sure where, but then she told me she volunteered at the library when she wasn't working at the diner and I got it.

The platters were heavy and half the time I was terrified that I was going to spill gravy and milk and ice-cream scoops of mashed potatoes, but I never did. The cooks were two old guys who seemed to be barking at me all the time, but I figured out pretty quickly that most of the time they weren't actually mad. As one of my therapists here would put it, they just communicated by yelling. And Andy was (Warning: SAT Word Fast Approaching) avuncular. He sometimes told the cooks to cut me some slack. He chided them about the unfinished food I'd cart back into the kitchen.

When I returned to Camille's, I was exhausted, but I had nearly forty-five dollars in tips in my pocket.

Unfortunately, any happiness that I had earned some real money without begging or sucking some trucker's dick evaporated within seconds of my closing the front door to the apartment. Cameron was way sicker than he had been at lunchtime when I'd left. Way sicker. And he was way sicker than I was. We didn't have a thermometer, but it felt to me like Cameron was burning up. He was rag-doll weak, his head was throbbing, and he said he ached everywhere. His nose was a disaster. So I gave him some NyQuil and convinced him to eat a few spoonfuls of chicken soup–flavored ramen noodles.

My heart hurt for him.

. . . .

That night Camille surprised me. As I was tossing a sheet back on the couch and getting ready to go to sleep, she said she had something for me and handed me a small, square box. It was the perfect size for a pair of earrings.

"Open it," Camille said, when I stared at it for a couple of seconds. "I swear, whatever's in there won't bite. It's not like I hid a scorpion in there or something."

And so I untied the ribbon and opened it. Sure enough, silver earrings with a little blue stone in each. "It's a tanzanite," she said.

I had no idea what a tanzanite was, but that didn't matter. They were pretty.

"I couldn't afford moonstones," Camille went on. "I went back to the pawnshop, but your earrings were long gone. I'm really sorry."

"These are beautiful," I told her, and I meant it. "Thank you." I started to put one on, but discovered the holes in my ears had closed up.

"We'll fix that this week," she said.

I looked at the earring in the palm of my hand. I focused on how vibrant the blue was and nodded. But I didn't say anything because suddenly I was afraid to speak.

. . . .

I went to work the next day, too, as did Camille and Dawn. I felt like the worst mother in the world leaving Cameron in his mummy bag beneath the pumpkin pine table—he'd actually been moaning in his sleep the night before—but what else could I do? When I left, Camille and Dawn were still at the apartment, but I knew they might both be gone by the time Cameron finally woke up.

It was a Saturday and it was beautiful out. It felt like spring. One of the grown-up waitresses at Henry's said she had seen a robin on the way in to work.

I was working all the way through the lunch shift that day because Henry's closed at three o'clock on Saturdays, and so I was back at Camille's by about three-thirty. She had already left for Leunig's and Dawn was at Macy's, so Cameron was alone. He was curled up in a small ball in his mummy bag, asleep, and I didn't wake him. But he was sweating, and when I touched his forehead I was shocked at how warm he still was—and a little worried. I was getting better. He wasn't. It dawned on me that maybe we didn't have the same cold. Maybe he didn't have a cold at all.

. . . .

I hadn't smoked any weed since I'd left Poacher's, but I did that night. Camille and I shared a bowl when she returned from the restaurant. Dawn was seriously DTF—okay, maybe not literally down to fuck, but at least in the mood for a hookup—and had gone to some club on Main Street where she could party and get some. I insisted that Camille and I smoke in her and Dawn's bedroom so Cameron didn't have to breathe any in while he shivered and sweat in his mummy bag on the living room floor. She sat on her little bed and I sat on Dawn's. I hadn't noticed it before, but Camille had this stuffed panda bear the size of a little dog. I thought she was going to use it as a pillow. Instead she sat it on her lap like it was a baby.

"You know," she murmured, "someday you are going to have to bring him to the police."

"He wouldn't go," I said. "He'd just run away again."

"But he's, like, nine."

"He's not *like* nine. He is nine."

She held a lit Bic over the bowl, and I watched the dope glow as she inhaled. It always looked like a night sky with lots of stars to me when someone did that. "You can't do this forever," she said, after she'd exhaled. I knew exactly what she meant by "this." I thought it was pretty interesting that Camille of all people should be trying to get into my head as the voice of reason. "It's more than a little dodgy. The little dude really should be in school. *You* should be in school."

I shrugged. "It's whatever."

"You must have been good in school."

"Never as good as people thought I should be."

"You're an only child?"

"Uh-huh."

She leaned off her bed and passed me the pipe, and I breathed in the smoke and held it. God, it felt good.

"Still. There's something else going on here," she said. "It's not just that he's like this little brother you never had."

"I really like him."

"I get it. I like him, too. Did you see the way he duct taped the checkers pieces? Most colorful checkers set I've ever seen. But there are lots of things I like that I can't have."

"He doesn't have anyone else."

"And neither do you. Is that it?"

When I didn't say anything, she went on: "Have you googled your name? Your real name?"

This was the first time she'd officially acknowledged she knew who I was since she had told me in the food court that she'd deleted the numbers I'd called from her old phone.

"I did. Once. It made me a little sick."

"So you know what's out there—what people are saying?"

"Mostly. But I kind of steer clear of computers and the news."

"There must be people looking for you."

"It seemed to me they stopped a month or so after they started. I didn't see anything about me after July."

"That doesn't mean anything. It just means you weren't in the papers."

"Maybe. But after what they were saying about my dad, I don't want to be found. I don't want to have to testify."

"Because of the shit they're trying to sell about him?"

I must have winced, because her face fell like she had just said the wrong thing. "He wasn't drunk that day," I told her. "Sometimes he drank too much, but he hadn't the night before. And there's no way he was drinking that morning at the plant."

"Even if he was drunk, he's not you. You were never to blame. You're just a kid. It's not like people were ever going to lynch you."

"Those first days, it sure felt like they were. You should have heard the stuff people said to me the day of the meltdown. It was really scary."

"Maybe back then people were a little crazy. They're not anymore. That was a long time ago."

"Nine months."

"Yeah. That's what I mean. That's a long time."

It was, especially now. Even I know that a lot more happens in nine months these days than when my parents were kids. These days, did anyone outside of New England ever even think about Cape Abenaki? Did anyone think about the way only a year ago people were ice-fishing with the reactor a quick skate away? Skiing at Jay Peak? Taking French at Reddington Academy?

I wondered what had been done with whatever was left of my parents' radioactive bodies.

I wondered how my Maggie had died.

I wondered what the fuck I was doing.

It's a good thing I was stoned. It gave me an excuse not to talk.

....

On Sunday morning Cameron was kind of delirious, and I wondered if I was overdosing him on NyQuil by accident. I even had this paranoid thought that Dawn was overdosing him on purpose. Maybe she was secretly psycho. Isn't there some mental illness where moms try and make their kids sick so the moms feel needed and important?

But I don't think I ever really believed that about Dawn.

Still, between the strange ways that Cameron was talking to himself in this half-awake, half-asleep dream state and the fact his body was trembling, I went from worried to scared. I was really glad the diner was closed on Sundays so I didn't have to leave him.

I decided if he wasn't a lot better by dinnertime, I was going to take him to the ER at the hospital up the hill from us and get him some serious meds.

. . . .

Flu shots are a lot like condoms. They're very effective, but apparently they are not 100 percent perfect.

You can just imagine how pissed I was that night when some know-it-all ER resident told me this in his holier-than-thou, I-know-my-shit-and-you-don't tone of voice. "The flu vaccine is very good," he said, "but it's only one of the many things you need to do to stay safe during flu season."

All I had said was "But I got him a flu shot." It's not like I was questioning his "preliminary" diagnosis or even getting all defensive on him. I was, more or less, just speaking aloud. Talking to myself. *But I got him a flu shot.*

And I got this fucking quasi-rebuke. The guy had thick blond hair and perfect skin and rimless eyeglasses. He reminded me of an artsy kind of movie star.

It had still been light out when I'd had a cab bring Cameron and me to the hospital. But there are no windows in the ER so it felt like night anyway. Cameron was lying down on this gurney behind some drapes, and I was standing up beside this crap orange chair with metal armrests.

Looking back, the whole moment shows how surreal and childish my expectations were. I knew I was going to have to lie my ass off about who I was and what our relationship was and why I didn't have a health insurance card, but I was pretty sure I could out-lie and out-bluster anyone there. I honestly expected a doctor or nurse would look at Cameron and say, "Here are some antibiotics, you'll be fine in a day or two." I mean, already I felt much better—practically well—and all I'd been doing was scarfing down DayQuil.

And my lie was pretty simple. I said I was Abby and this was my brother, Alex—two syllables, like Abby, so it was going to be easy for us both to remember—and I had forgotten my phone at home and our parents were in the Adirondacks for some spring skiing, but here was their phone number and it was okay to call them. I said they wouldn't have cell service right now, but they would when they were back at the hotel after dinner that night. And then the number I gave the woman at the front counter was Camille's phone. If anything, the woman who checked us in must have thought that my pretend parents were the assholes; after all, they were the ones who had gone skiing and left their older daughter alone to care for their sick younger son. I said my wallet with my health insurance card was with my phone, but my mom could give them all the information when they reached her.

But two things happened that I hadn't expected.

"Your brother certainly has the symptoms of the flu, but I think there may be a little more going on. When will your parents get here?" Dr. Know-It-All asked me.

"They weren't going to come back until tomorrow."

"Really?"

"Really."

"They should come back now. Right now. We're going to admit your brother."

"For the flu?"

"For encephalitis."

I had never heard of encephalitis, but obviously I didn't like the sound of this. So the first thing that happened that I hadn't antici- pated was that they were going to keep Cameron overnight. And the second? He might be way sicker than I realized.

"What's encephalitis?" I asked, but now there was this ringing in my ears and I was feeling a little dizzy myself. I had to sit down, and so I sort of collapsed into that ugly orange chair and only heard bits and pieces of his answer. The only things that lodged were *inflamed brain tissue, maybe a virus,* and *MRI.* They actually wanted to do an MRI of Cameron's brain.

"So, let's get him admitted," the doctor said when he was done. Then, whether he meant to or not, he put the dagger to me. "I really wish you'd brought him in sooner," he said.

And suddenly someone had stuck an IV into Cameron's arm because he needed fluids and someone else was wheeling his gurney down the corridor and into an elevator. And then, of course, he was gone. Just like that. He was gone.

. . . .

It was the next day that I would learn he was in intensive care. And he was in a coma.

I couldn't see him.

I couldn't even stay at the hospital.

That's how fast it had all gone to hell.

I went there first thing in the morning. This time I went to the main entrance, which was a hell of a lot harder to find than the ER. Seriously. The place was huge and had three stories of glass windows, to give you a sense of just how massive it was. I could see people walking along the corridors two and three floors above me. It was weirdly airy and like the lobby of a nice hotel. I passed the gift shop and coffee kiosks and signs for every kind of outpatient surgery you can think of before I finally detoured, almost by accident, into reception and found a blond girl with a ponytail not much older than I was behind the counter. I told her I was here to visit a patient named Alex Bliss, and she looked him up on her computer and asked me, "Are you related to him?"

"Yup. Sister. What room is he in?"

She paused. "What's your name?"

"Abby Bliss."

She looked intently at her screen and then punched in a few letters. I feared she was typing my name.

"I can find the room, no prob, if you just give me the number," I went on. "I've been here before."

She didn't nod or say anything. She just kept tapping and scrolling her mouse. "Printing me one of those visitor badges?" I asked hopefully.

She ignored me. Didn't even shrug.

And that was when, once more, my gift of fear kicked in.

. . . .

The woman from DCF was my mom's age, but her hair, which was starting to go from mousy brown to gray, was a beach hippie mess. She was wearing a bulky and unbelievably ugly fisherman's cardigan sweater—it had pewter hooks instead of buttons—blue jeans, and Birkenstock sandals with these thick brown socks. (And I thought I was a fashion disaster some days.) But her eyes were a very deep green. She had that going for her. I was pretty sure it was the receptionist who had sounded the alarm, but it was still like this woman had come out of nowhere. One minute I was alone on my side of the counter, and the next there was this person right there beside me.

"You're Abby," she said, and she extended her hand to me. In her other hand was a clipboard. "My name is Mary. Can we talk?"

I didn't nod. I looked behind her to make sure she was alone.

"We can sit right over here," she went on, and used her clipboard like a paddle to funnel me over to a couch. I almost tripped on the coffee table with magazines in front of it.

"So, like I said, my name is Mary," she repeated when we both were seated. "I'm with the DCF—Department for Children and Families."

"Is everything okay with my brother?"

"Alex is in intensive care."

My stomach lurched like I was on a roller coaster and we had just gone straight downhill out of nowhere. "What? Is he dying?"

Clearly I sounded frantic; she put her hand on my leg. "No.

The coma is medically induced. That means the doctors put him into a coma on purpose to prevent his brain from swelling any further."

"His brain is swelling?"

"Yes. There's inflammation."

"Is he going to . . . get better?"

"We hope so," she answered, but she did not sound especially confident. In fact, she didn't sound confident at all.

"But you don't know for sure."

"No. Your little brother is very, very sick."

"Can I see him?"

"You can't. I'm sorry."

"But I can see him when our parents get here from the Adirondacks, right?" I really asked that. Looking back, I don't know whether I was bluffing or becoming a little deluded—like I honestly believed two grown-ups were going to materialize out of nowhere and save my ass.

Mary took a deep breath and then tried to look me in the eye with one of those soulful I'm-here-for-you social worker gazes. (These days, I seem to get them all the time.) "We called that number you gave the hospital last night. It belongs to someone else. Someone named"—and here she looked briefly at her clipboard before staring back at me—"Camille. It does not belong to your parents. Maybe you gave us the wrong number by mistake. It happens. But maybe there's something else going on here. Is there a reason you and your brother are . . . trying to avoid your parents? Tell me the truth, Abby: Is there a reason you two had to leave . . . home? Is your last name really Bliss?"

"I have to go to the bathroom," I said.

"Abby—"

"I really do. I promise, I won't leave."

But, of course, that is precisely what I did.

. . . .

Clearly the DCF was all over this now and I had, much to my utter shame and total regret, gotten Camille involved. She had been walking when I had returned from the hospital the night before, and I still hadn't seen her to tell her what I had done. Now they were calling her phone and it was clear any second they were going to visit the apartment. They still hadn't figured out that Abby was Emily and Alex was Cameron, but they would connect the dots pretty damn soon: as I was leaving the hospital—exiting via this underground parking garage I found so that Mary wouldn't see me running away through those big cheerful windows—I saw a police car rolling in, and somehow I just knew that this had something (everything?) to do with me. Once again, I was shaking. I was as good as outed, and Camille and Dawn might be in trouble for letting Cameron hang there over the weekend.

And I couldn't stop thinking about the fact that Cameron was in a coma and it was my fault. *I really wish you'd brought him in sooner.*

Yeah, me too. Well, fuck you, Dr. Know-It-All.

And, while we're at it, fuck you, Abby Bliss or Emily Shepard or whoever the fuck you are.

As soon as I got to Camille and Dawn's bathroom I threw up and then gouged out so much of my thigh that I wrecked one of Camille's towels when I tried to stop the bleeding. Finally I was able to tape some gauze on the cuts and climb back into my jeans. Then I ran away. I knew I didn't have much time before the police showed up at the apartment, and I wanted to round up as much of Cameron's stuff as I could. My things? Screw it. The only reason I had risked going back to Camille's at all was for the things Cameron would want when—*if*—he woke up.

I was halfway down the block when I saw a police car, its lights flashing but no siren, speeding around a corner. I dove into the bushes, falling on top of Cameron's mummy bag, hoping that they hadn't seen me. Hoping that no one at all had seen me. I lay there for maybe a minute and a half, listening to the car stop outside of Camille's. Listening to the cops exit, not slamming their doors, but shutting them pretty forcefully. Listening to them knocking on the metal storm door and then going inside. Only then did I peek through the bushes . . . and resume my trek up the hill.

. . . .

I tried to take some comfort in the idea that the doctors had "put" Cameron into a coma. But it was still a coma, and I still had no idea if he was even going to live.

You know that expression "a chip off the old block"? Well, I decided, that was me. Just like my dad, I fucked things up. Maybe I should have named myself Apple instead of Abby or any of the hundreds of other choices out there. It wasn't that I had any great love for Gwyneth Paltrow or Chris Martin or thought they were geniuses for naming their little kid Apple. I mean, I liked her movies and his band just fine. That moment I just thought I should be Apple because—to use another cliché—I sure as hell hadn't fallen very far from the tree.

And so that's why I was going back. Going home. Going into the Exclusion Zone that was actually—to use one of those Xbox terms that Trevor and PJ liked so much—a Kill Zone.

Why not?

Fuck the world, I thought. I couldn't do anything right. I didn't belong. I had allowed Cameron to get sick, then I had betrayed him, and now I was deserting him.

I would go back to Reddington to be with my dead parents and my dead dog. I would go home, because home was the place where, when you have done absolutely everything wrong, they have to take you in. I would go home because everyone there was gone, which meant there was no one left I could disappoint or hurt. I could key all the cars I wanted, because now they were all radioactive and no one wanted them. I could get ripped in a sugarhouse museum, because now the maple syrup was radioactive and no one would eat it. I could smash my mom and dad's wineglasses, because now they meant nothing. They were just radioactive crystal.

I dropped off Cameron's skateboard, his mummy bag, and

his duct tape creations—that robot, the horse, a race car—at the hospital on my way out of town. I left them just inside that main entrance with a big note saying they belonged to "Alex/Cameron" in intensive care and to please, please, *please* be sure the little boy had them when he woke up.

And this time I didn't hear any of those "She's Leaving Home" harps when I left—when I left the hospital, when I left Burlington, when I said good-bye to all I had known since Reactor One had blown up. After all, I wasn't leaving home. I was, once and for all, going home.

Chapter 19

It really wasn't all that hard to get inside the Exclusion Zone. I guess I shouldn't have been surprised. Why in the world would a normal person want to go there?

I saw the roadblock up ahead and a pair of National Guardsmen, but I only had to walk a whopping three or four hundred yards around the perimeter before I found a spot in the woods where I could crawl under the fence. It was strung across a muddy channel that spring runoff had carved into the hill and maybe once upon a time the soldiers had filled it in, but now the melting snow and rain had once more scooped out a canal.

I noticed the guards had been wearing masks but not full-on *Star Wars* hazmat suits. Not that I cared.

I estimated I was about five miles from the village of Reddington. Another mile beyond that would be my house. And a few miles beyond that were Newport and the big lake and Cape Abenaki. I'd be home before dark.

I was never much of a hiker. I liked sleeping out in a backyard tent once in a while and I liked skiing and snowboarding, but I'm sure as heck not some kind of back-to-nature dork or, as I think I told you, a Girl Scout. I mention this because I was kind of miserable walking through the muck in the woods. Pretty quickly my feet were soaked, and my blue jeans were covered in mud. The branches were dripping, and I kept getting spray in my hair and on my face. My fingers were freezing because I didn't have any gloves. And I realized how easy it would be to get lost, especially once the sun had set and night fell. So I worked my way back to that road as quickly as I could.

When I got back to the pavement, I discovered that I was no more than a hundred yards behind the roadblock. I'd been in the woods at least an hour and gotten no more than three hundred feet closer to my home. See what I mean about what kind of hiker I am? What kind of backpacker instincts I have? Yeah, none. So I crouched low and walked in the brush along the side of the pavement until the street curved and I could no longer see the guardsmen (and they could no longer see me), and then I returned to the road.

And I saw that already it was falling apart. The spring frost heaves (a term that had given me the giggles one day, because suddenly I imagined the poet hurling into a metal trash can) had wrought havoc on the asphalt everywhere in the Northeast Kingdom, but this was different. Patches of the road were coated in pebbles and dirt from disuse, and some of the edges were collapsing into the embankment. There were downed tree branches and small limbs sometimes smack in the middle of the road, right on top of the double yellow line.

It was desolate and beautiful.

But it also wasn't completely deserted. I had gone maybe a mile, just past a gun store that had always given me the creeps—it was in a small red barn beside the owner's double-wide trailer, and it had padlocks and alarms and wrought-iron grills on the windows— when I noticed a set of tire tracks in one length of dirt on the street. I'm no detective, but I noted they were wide. A National Guard truck, I guessed. Maybe some kind of vehicle involved in some kind of cleanup. I told myself it had nothing to do with a cult of psychotic holdouts living illegally out here, ranging around in some monster pickup with big and stupid tires, but the alarm inside me was triggered. After all, how difficult had it been for me to get inside the Exclusion Zone? Not difficult at all. There could be lunatic survivalists and there could be looters and there could be all kinds of terrifying hybrid mutants. (When you're a girl my age and you're alone and you have brain chemistry issues, the mind travels pretty quickly to AMC and the latest zombie movie. When you're a girl my age and you're alone and you don't have brain chemistry issues, I hope it goes to *Love Actually*.)

I guess it's a healthy sign that I was scared. If I was legit suicidal, I wouldn't have been frightened, right? But maybe I just wanted to die on my own terms—after I got home. After I saw the plant where my parents had died. After I found whatever was left of my dog.

. . . .

Obviously I'd been thinking about Cameron as I had worked my way back to the Kingdom. I walked part of the way, but mostly I hitchhiked. I kept trying to reassure myself that once the swelling in his brain had gone down, the doctors would wake him up from his coma. It would be some real-life fairy-tale magic. Kiss the princess, and she opens her eyes. Pull an IV or whatever out of the little kid's arm, and he sits up in bed. I told myself that everything would work out, and in weeks he'd be in a new home—a good home—and while he might still sleep in that mummy bag, the bag would be on a bed. He would find his friends and he would go to the skate park and he'd show off his crazy mad skills. It had to work out, right?

Of course it didn't have to. I knew that. With every step I took I was reminded that things sure as hell hadn't worked out in the past. Every time I sat myself down in whatever car or truck had picked me up and was taking me farther and farther away from the hospital, an image of Cameron on the emergency room gurney would flash behind my eyes. Sometimes I could blink the image away, but other times it would linger.

I was with people for a lot of the time, because I clocked most of the miles back in somebody's vehicle, but I felt as lonely as I had in my last days in the posse—those days after Andrea had left. I once read a short story about these four guys who've survived a shipwreck and are now in this open boat, and they can see the shore and people on the shore can see them, but the people on the shore don't realize these four dudes are exhausted and in serious trouble because they can't reach the beach. The "inshore rollers" (I loved that phrase because it sounded like the name for a rock band) are too strong. The guys in the boat are in danger of drowning, and the morons on the beach are waving at them. That's sort of how I felt when I would sit beside each person who brought me ten or fifteen miles closer to the Exclusion Zone: I was out at sea in this little boat and probably going to drown, and they had no idea. No idea at all.

Which was fine.

Part of the way there I was in a beige Prius with a very nice old lady who lectured me about the dangers of hitchhiking. Part of the way there I was in a red Subaru with the pastor for a church in Underhill who seemed unbelievably chill and put me at ease by talking about the kind of season he hoped the Red Sox would have. And part of the way there I was with an unbelievably annoying town clerk who drove a PT Cruiser she thought was a trash can. I had to push piles of empty McDonald's bags and gum wrappers and Styrofoam coffee cups off the seat before I could get in, and the floor was a sticky mess from all the soda she'd spilled over time. But she wasn't annoying because she was a car slob. She was annoying because she was volunteering all this stuff about what a cadbury her son was, though of course she didn't use that word. She just said he was a drunk. He had lost his driver's license the week before because of a DUI. Obviously unaware of who I was, she told me about the ways alcohol could ruin your career or your marriage or your reputation. Her son was a newlywed guy who had a silkscreen T-shirt company, and already his wife was pissed at him big-time. So was his partner in their little start-up. "No good comes from drinking too much," she said, shaking her head. "Just look at that engineer from the nuclear plant. Look what he did. Look. What. He. Did."

I saw a convenience store up ahead and said that was where I wanted to get out. She didn't seem happy about this change of plan, but she dealt.

I wondered at one point if I would see Sandy the bread guy. I had liked him and his daughter and the whole Thomas clan. I figured I wouldn't see him, but you never know. One thing I've learned is that six degrees of separation always trumps million-to-one odds. It really does. But he never passed me, and I never even noticed any trucks from his bakery.

. . . .

I saw wisps of green at the tips of the maples. Spring.

. . . .

Halfway between the roadblock and my old school I came across a hillside with nothing but the bones and carcasses of cows. There must have been fifty or sixty of them. Maybe more. On the ridge atop another meadow I saw three living horses with luxurious-looking long winter coats. One was buckskin and two were bay. The bays had white stocking feet. I waved when I saw they were watching me, and then I nickered, hoping they would come to the street. Instead they turned and galloped away. Later I saw barn cats in the window of a hayloft. I saw deer. I saw a pair of mostly—but not entirely—eaten dead moose. And I saw a pack of big dogs that now had gone wild. I wondered if they were the animals that were eating the moose. It was possible. But it might also have been coyotes. I assumed that the cows had died of radiation sickness; they'd drunk from the wrong stream or grazed on contaminated grass. But one of the doctors here said maybe not. Maybe they had just succumbed to the cold or, because they were trapped in that field, run out of pasture and starved to death. I reminded him that they were still dead because of Cape Abenaki.

I remember when I first saw the hill of dead cows I made a mental note that I'd find some bottled water and drink only that.

Or not.

. . . .

The corn had continued to grow throughout the previous summer, but had never been harvested. There were whole fields with acres and acres of dead stalks—tasseled, their ears drooping like a submissive bunny's—that had been bent but not toppled by the snow.

While I was standing before the first of the many fields of dead corn, a helicopter passed overhead.

An hour later, I saw high in the sky the white trails of what I supposed was a passenger jet.

Other than the occasional aircraft, I realized that the Exclusion Zone was going to be very, very quiet.

. . . .

The first place I stopped was the Academy. Someone had locked the doors, but someone else had hurled a concrete block through a first-floor window. After the place had been abandoned last year, weeds had grown through the cracks in the front walkway, and now the long, dead strands lay there like clumps of flat hair. I crawled in through the window and saw that I was in Ms. Francis's office. Ms. Francis was the guidance counselor I was always disappointing. There were still pictures of her two kids and her husband on a credenza and a couple of folders with my classmates' names on her desk. There was a coffee mug with unbelievably disgusting fungus in the bottom.

I figured what the hell and opened a few filing cabinet drawers until I found her folder with my name on it. I brought it to her desk and sat down in her chair. In it I found my PSATs and my SATs and the slips showing all of the times I'd been disciplined. I read my report cards. There was nothing she herself had written about me, and nothing I hadn't seen before. Still, it left me kind of breathless to read all in one place things like "Emily's work has certainly been adequate, but we all know she is capable of much, much more." Or, "It's discouraging to see her utter unwillingness to apply herself. She is coasting. She should be soaring." Or this one: "I'm frustrated. We all are. We all know how gifted Emily is, but so far nothing at all seems to interest her." (That last one caused me to prickle a little bit: Writing interested me. Some teachers knew that. Poetry interested me. Okay, fine, I wasn't into your environmental chemistry class. I'm sorry. Shoot me.)

One teacher asked rhetorically where the little girl had gone who had been such an enthusiastic middle schooler. She hinted that she was worried there might be problems at home, a comment that I remembered had made my mom go ballistic.

Still, when I put the folder back, my eyes were welling up. I shouldn't have looked. It reminded me of what a disappointment I was. It reminded me of the ways I just blew everything apart.

....

My feet echoed along the corridors, and I realized I could really make some noise if I wanted. I considered screaming "Hello!" as if I were at the edge of a long cave and listening to the sound bounce around the walls, but I was actually a little creeped out. There was no electricity and it was already three o'clock, so the sun was falling, which meant there were whole parts of the Academy—such as the bathrooms, which had tiny windows, and the auditorium, which had none—that were almost pitch-black when I opened the doors. I wanted to leave the school by three-thirty so I could be home by five-thirty. That was my plan. I didn't think it would take anywhere near two hours to walk home, because my house was only three miles away, but who knew what might distract me or slow me down along the way. I had usually taken the bus over the years, but I had walked to or from school a couple of times, too, and it had never taken more than an hour and five or ten minutes.

Among the rooms I visited that seemed to be getting the most light that time of day was my old biology classroom. The black microscopes were almost white with dust. So were the rows of textbooks on the shelves and the computer screens on the counters along the rear wall. I hadn't set foot in there in nearly three years now, and I'm not sure what I expected. But I know I hadn't planned on practically vomiting from the smell. This wasn't just some Proustian nightmare—some benign opposite of those tasty little madeleines. This would have made anyone nauseous. The ninth graders had been dissecting crayfish when we were evacuated, and on all of the tables were the trays and the pails and the remains of the animals. The stench was unbearable, and so I slammed shut the door and ran away.

My dad sometimes made jokes about the ways small animals could shut down or nearly shut down a nuclear power plant. One time in Virginia a pelican flew into an overhead power cable and shorted out the connection between the plant and the off-site power grid. A bunch of jellyfish in Florida once blocked the filters at an intake station, nearly cutting off the water the plant had to have. And a few years ago a rat gnawed away the insulation around an electrical cable at a French plant, shorting out the whole cooling system. My dad had other stories. Those are just the ones I remember. His point? It doesn't take a tsunami to raise holy hell.

Later, when I had caught my breath in Ms. Gagne's classroom, I guessed it was the crayfish that made me think of the crazy little wildlife tales my dad sometimes shared.

. . . .

In Ms. Gagne's room, I sat in my chair at my old desk. Then I sat on top of her desk. Then I wandered aimlessly around the room, wiping the dust—which I figured was probably radioactive—off the novels we read and the filing cabinets and the Smart Board. I thought about how, here, the world had just stopped. Everyone had dropped what they were doing and run away as fast as they could. My mind roamed to the rest of Reddington, and I imagined kitchen tables with mice nibbling the toast people had left on their plates. I envisioned washing machines and dryers filled with clothes. I saw shopping carts overflowing with diapers and juice and plastic gallons of milk, now all alone in line at the grocery store registers, and dolls and blocks and little wooden trucks on the floors of the nurseries and day cares.

I wondered where Ms. Gagne—Cecile—was now. I touched the desks where Ethan Gale and Lisa Curran and Dina Ramsey had sat.

Then I went to the old-fashioned blackboard and took a piece of chalk and started writing. Most of what I wrote I erased, but not these five words. This is what I wrote:

Close your eyes, hold hands.

Someday I figured someone would see it. They'd make of it whatever they wanted. Maybe they'd think it was random. Maybe they'd just be confused.

Chapter 20

Our mailbox was still standing when I got to my house. I guess I shouldn't have been surprised. It was white with a red flag, but now that white was more the color of a ratty old T-shirt. The pavement on our driveway was finally fading from asphalt black to a more seasoned salt and pepper. There was that ridiculous stone wall running along the edge of our lawn.

Our house—that meadow mansion that didn't belong—was a yellow clapboard colonial. There was a bay window. There were shutters made of something called "architectural grade" vinyl siding, and they were evergreen. (It mattered to my mother that the vinyl was "architectural grade," because she didn't approve of vinyl siding. But my dad didn't want to have to constantly take down and repaint wooden shutters. Shutters, I gather, are a boatload of work. So when I was in fourth grade, we had the wooden shutters replaced with those vinyl ones.)

Most of the yard was free of snow, but there was a line of small drifts where it had fallen off the eaves on the shady side of the house. The snow was crusted with crap from the roof.

I stared at my bedroom window. At the shade that was half up. At the edge of the curtains.

Neither of my parents was much of a gardener, but this was Vermont so we had flowers along the front walkway and a vegetable garden in the yard on the southern side of our house. We grew lots of tomatoes—mostly cherry and plum tomatoes—and the tomato cages were still upright, but the dead plants draped from the metal like the tentacles on man o' war jellyfish. The tomatoes had grown and ripened after everyone had left and then fallen to the ground and rotted. The flowers along the walkway had died and collapsed under the snow and now were nothing but mounds of decomposing daylilies and sedum and phlox.

For a minute or two I just stood there. Home. I was actually here, I had actually made it. I almost couldn't believe it. Poacher and the posse and the truckers? A different lifetime. The Oxies? Forever ago. All that I'd done and all that I'd lost, all my blistering missteps and mistakes? That was before. This was after.

No, that wasn't quite true. That wasn't true at all. Some regrets can't be undone. There was no "after" Cameron: My letting him get so sick and then leaving him behind? My running away once and for all? Unforgivable.

Still, I would be lying if I did not admit that I stared at the house experiencing all that we bring to one small, simple word: *home.*

Finally I took a deep breath, journeyed up the walkway, and tried the front door.

It was locked.

Of course.

. . . .

The poetry of a nuclear disaster is weirdly beautiful. There is alliteration: rads and roentgens and rems. To a scientist, those are just units of measurement. To a poet? Lions and tigers and bears. Oh, my.

And then there are the "iums." Tellurium. Cesium. Strontium. And—I know this ruins the rule of three, but it is the mother of nuclear iums—plutonium.

Unfortunately, whenever I write those words down I instantly recall the dead cows and the dead moose and the dead birds, and the poems in my head turn to steam.

. . . .

It might have been a schoolteacher who first said, "Close your eyes and hold hands." And it might have been a police officer. It was back in December 2012, right after Adam Lanza had massacred all those little kids and teachers and the principal at the elementary school in Newtown, Connecticut. After Lanza had killed himself, the grown-ups had to walk the surviving kids out of the school building, right past the bodies of their classmates who had been slaughtered. So, to keep the kids from seeing the corpses, either a teacher or one of the police officers instructed the children to close their eyes and hold hands.

I had been thinking of that moment and those words a lot since I had dropped off Cameron's stuff at the hospital in Burlington and started back to the Kingdom. I had thought of it even more since I had passed into the Exclusion Zone. I never quite knew what I was going to see.

It seemed to me that if you didn't know the context of those words, they were kind of pretty. They're like those three *R*'s I just mentioned. *Close your eyes, hold hands* might, if you didn't know the truth, sound life-affirming. I see the words on some dorky note card with the sun setting in the ocean, the sky streaked with red, and a couple on the beach with their backs to the camera holding hands. Maybe the woman has her head on the dude's shoulder. The message, if you think about it this way, is all about taking chances because fate or destiny or God will protect you. Take a risk, have a little faith. It's all about life, not death. It's not about a bunch of small children who've been gunned down with a Bushmaster assault rifle.

Anyway, I recalled those instructions with serious dread in the pit of my stomach as I was walking around the side of my house, past the garden and the stone wall and the white tank with our LP gas that I had thought was a mini-submarine when I was a little kid. My keys to the front door were long gone—I hadn't seen them in months—and so I was going to have to break the windows in the sliding glass doors in the back. But as I was making my way there, it dawned on me: whatever was left of my Maggie was behind those walls. With no one around to let her out, she'd died of hunger or thirst. I had no idea which would have killed her first, but my sense was that either way it was a slow and horrible way to die. In my head I heard her barking for help, but by then everybody was gone and there was no one left to come rescue her.

Still, I couldn't stand outside forever. I was going to have to smash those sliding glass doors to get in—sort of like the way someone before me had broken a window to get into the Academy—because one of the things I had come here to do was to bury my Maggie. She deserved that. And that would mean seeing her corpse.

The problem?

I could close my eyes all I wanted, but I still had no one to hold my hand.

. . . .

So, I lifted a rock the size of a soccer ball from that stone wall, a little impressed that it was finally serving a purpose, and wandered past those disturbing tomato cages with the dead vines clinging to the wire and around the corner of the house. It took both arms to carry the rock, and it was going to take both hands to hurl it through the sliding glass door.

And then I saw something that caused me to stop where I was. I stood perfectly still and stared, my mind racing as I tried to make sense of what I was seeing. I dropped the rock right where I was. The sliding glass door was open. And the screen door had a massive hole ripped in it.

. . . .

Make no mistake, I didn't necessarily believe that Maggie was alive. Still, I couldn't help but get my hopes up that she was. There was absolutely no sign of her anywhere in the house.

Here is what I told myself might have happened. My mom had opened the glass door to let some fresh air in and then, when she went to the plant to be with my dad and see what the hell was really going on, she had left it open for Maggie. Maggie loved to sniff the outside air through the big screen. She would sit up on her dog bed when the glass door was first opened, and her nose would go a little crazy. It was adorable. At some point, either crazed with hunger or boredom or thirst, she had ripped that hole in the screen and gotten out. Thank God. She might be long dead, but at least she hadn't died trapped and alone in the house.

When I couldn't find her or her remains anywhere inside, I went outside and started calling her name. I wondered if the animals thought it was strange to suddenly hear a human voice. It had probably been a long time. I guessed a lot had never heard one. I walked around our yard and the edge of the woods, yelling, "Maggie! C'mon, girl. Maggie, I'm home!" I must have done that for ten minutes, and my voice was growing hoarse.

Finally, when Maggie didn't come racing out of the evergreens, I went back inside and inspected the house a little more carefully. I wanted to see what we had in the way of canned food and bottled water or juice. My plan was to live there. I would write my poems. I would keep my journals. I would become the Belle of Reddington.

I slid shut the glass door so animals wouldn't join me in the night and went upstairs to my bedroom. It was freezing cold, but otherwise exactly as I had left it. There were the jeans on the floor I had chosen not to wear on the morning that Cape Abenaki had melted down, and there was the shirt that I had tossed on my desk when I decided it made my arms look fat. There was the earring I had left on my dresser when I couldn't find its matching partner. There was my armoire, open as always, and there on the top of my bookcase were my journals. The only thing in my room I ever kept neat was the top of the bookcase with my journals. And there they were, lined up between the two brass unicorn bookends.

I was tempted to start reading them right then, but it could wait. I was exhausted. And I figured I had nothing but time.

I took off my clothes, which I realized now were revolting, sponged myself off with water from a Saratoga bottle I found in the pantry, and climbed into my favorite red check pajamas. Dorky beyond belief.

And then I went to sleep in my very own bed. I pulled the quilt over my head and didn't wake up until close to nine-thirty the next morning.

. . . .

The next day I began to clean. Maggie may have gone out through the screen door, but a lot of animals had since used it to come in. I guessed there had been squirrels and raccoons and fisher cats inside the house. The hole wasn't so big that a bear could have wandered in, but the rug in the den and the tile in the kitchen were spotted with mud and animal tracks. The bag with Maggie's dry kibbles, which we kept in a pantry closet, was empty and the heavy paper had been gnawed into little pieces. That might have been Maggie because the pantry door was partway open, but it might also have been wild animals. Also, all of the cereal boxes we'd opened had been destroyed and the wax bags inside them licked clean. Wind had blown rain into the den and the couch was moldy and damp. I found piles of scat in the living room—which, they would tell me later, had probably been seriously radioactive. Lovely, right?

I was never big into vacuuming, but I would have vacuumed now if there had been any electricity. There wasn't. So the first thing I did was drag the couch through the glass doors and out into the sun in the yard. I thought I might dry it out during the day and drag it back inside at night. Maybe in a few days it would be okay. If not, I would leave it in the garage. Both of my parents' cars were gone, parked in the lot at Cape Abenaki, I guessed. So why not store the couch there? Then I got the broom and a dustpan and a bucket and a mop, and I started to clean. I used a little Windex on the glass on the framed poster of my parents and me on the Christmas mornings when I'd been a kid. I went through a whole roll of paper towels as I dusted.

And I ate. Everything in the refrigerator was unbelievably gross, and I just tossed it all into a pair of black garbage bags. The most grotesque thing I found was what I think in another era might have been chicken breasts. I would have poured the liquids that hadn't completely evaporated down the sink, but I didn't have running water, so those cartons and bottles and jars went into the trash bags, too.

But there was still plenty to eat in the pantry. I opened a can of Campbell's cheddar cheese soup, the stuff that was the key ingredient in my mom's mac and cheese, and ate cold spoonfuls of it. I polished off a bottle of Diet Snapple and a can of V-8. (I'm not a big fan of V-8, but I used to drink it because it wasn't hugely caloric and you got some vegetables.) I ate a can of creamed corn.

And when I ran out of the food in my house? I figured I'd wander to our neighbors'. I'd take a walk to the general store in Reddington. I'd throw a rock through the windows of the supermarket in Newport. It seemed to me that I would die years before the Exclusion Zone ran out of food.

. . . .

Every hour or so I would go outside and call for Maggie.

One day I walked to the home of Skylar Furney to steal his bike. Skylar was one of four Furney kids, but I only knew him because he was the one closest to my age. He was a year behind me at the Academy. His two brothers and his sister were even younger; they were all in middle school. But I remembered that Skylar was one of those manic bicyclists, and I figured I might as well use his bike since he wasn't. I wanted to use it to look for Maggie. I wanted to expand my search area.

The tires were flat, but he had a pump hanging on the wall in the garage. See what I mean about what a bike guy he was?

And this was a much nicer bike than the one I had ridden partway to Burlington the previous June. It was very light. It had those clips that fit into the bottom of bike shoes, and at first I feared I was kind of screwed. Obviously I didn't have bike shoes. But then it dawned on me: Skylar did. Duh. If I was going to steal his bike, I might as well steal his shoes. What's that expression? In for a nickel, in for a dime. I wasn't wild about rooting around his bedroom, but I was prepared to. Fortunately, I didn't even have to trudge upstairs: I found his bike shoes in the mudroom right off the garage. And while his feet were bigger than mine, it didn't matter once I clipped in. I was fine.

Well, I was fine after an hour. I fell about sixty times that first hour, and my beginning spills were all on his driveway. It was after about the tenth tumble that it dawned on me: a smart chick would try to learn to ride in clips on the lawn. So that's what I did. If you're going to be a turtle on its back in its shell—that's sort of what it's like to topple over on a bicycle when you're clipped into the pedals—do it on grass, not pavement. There were still patches of snow, but mostly they were in the shade. I even ran over or smashed a few blue and pink crocuses as I practiced.

One of the doctors here asked me, "Weren't you a little grossed out when you were wearing that strange boy's smelly shoes?"

I looked at her. "Really?" I said. "Really?" Over the last year I had been living in an igloo made of trash bags. I had been sexing down truckers in the cabs of their eighteen-wheelers. I had been carving up my thighs with an X-Acto knife. And now she thinks it's going to freak me out to wear some teenage boy's bike shoes? Hello?

You know what? Skylar Furney's male teenage stinkfoot had never even crossed my mind.

. . . .

It was the day after that, when I was passing our little white submarine of LP gas, that it clicked: I could light the stove and heat up my creamed corn and cheddar cheese soup if I wanted—at least until the gas in the tank ran out. I would use one of our fireplace matches the way my mom did whenever we had a blackout in a snowstorm. You just turned the knob and put a lit match near the burner.

The first time I tried it, I was a little tentative: I think I was afraid I was going to blow up the whole house. But it was really kind of idiot-proof. The burner caught instantly.

Son-of-a-bitch, I remember thinking. You can cook. Not shabby.

. . . .

And so I lived like that for three weeks. Maybe three and a half. And then, of course, it all came crashing down. (I know my therapist would quibble with "crashing down." Her spin would be a little different. We would have one of those debates about the "passive voice" and how I need to take responsibility for my actions.)

But until then, I continued to clean and eat canned soups and canned vegetables—sometimes cold, but mostly hot—and polish off all of our jugs of water and bottles of juice. I started to pillage the food at our nearest neighbors' house, the Barbours, figuring when their food was gone I'd simply move on to the next family's. Other than the occasional airplanes and a second helicopter that thwumped overhead on day six or day seven, I was completely alone. I no longer wondered about the wide tire tracks I'd seen soon after returning to the area. I wrote. I wrote poems and I wrote in my journals.

One day I thought I would dress only in white. But then I worried I was getting into a weird area and climbed back into a tan and black dress I had gotten from Free People that I had always liked.

. . . .

My journals went back years. I still had my first Hello Kitty diary. I had my Barbie Rapunzel notebook from second grade. I had my Disney princess pink and purple and yellow notepads, one each for Cinderella and Jasmine and Belle. There were all the salt-and-pepper composition books from my middle school phase. And there were the leather-bound journals I had started to keep in ninth grade. There were six of them, or about two a year. I tended to fill one every six months.

I was fascinated by my penmanship after so long away from them. I had forgotten I had written in only pink gel pens in fourth and fifth grade. I had forgotten I had a phase in ninth grade when I kept trying (and failing) to write villanelles. Nineteen lines. Five tercets and a quatrain. Refrains and repeating rhymes. Supposedly Elizabeth Bishop spent eighteen years on one villanelle before she decided she had gotten it right. Obviously my parents knew about my poems, but few of my friends did. I didn't want people to know. They were . . . mine. How many of Emily Dickinson's poems were published in her lifetime? Ten between 1850 and 1866. One in a book in 1878. That was it. Did she want more? Maybe. Maybe not. But the fact is that most of her work, especially the reams and reams of papers that her sister found after her death, never saw the light of day in her lifetime. In one parent-teacher fiasco that was supposed to be a "conference," my mom revealed that I had all this writing I never shared with anyone. She was trying to argue that I had talent. Mad skills as a writer. I wasn't a total loss. My reaction? Vesuvius. I felt betrayed and kind of wigged out.

When I was reconciled with all my journals that spring, I told myself that cutting had replaced writing, but now that I was home I would write. I threw the X-Acto away.

And, instead, a few days later I simply used a sharp little paring knife that I found in the kitchen. After that I used a pair of nail scissors that turned out to be unexpectedly sharp.

So, now I was cutting and writing.

But, in truth, mostly writing.

My mom and dad had put a beautiful leather journal from Italy in my Easter basket my junior year, and that was the journal I used to begin this story.

I wrote most of the time in my bedroom, just as I had when my parents had been alive, even though I had nothing but privacy. I could have written at the kitchen table, if I'd wanted. I could have written completely naked in the middle of the lawn, if it had been a little warmer. But instead I sat in my window seat, the sun on my back, just as I had a year and two and three years earlier. I would sometimes drape my hand where Maggie had once slept. I would have deep pangs of sadness when I came across a few strands of her fur.

I didn't mind the fact there was no electricity. After half a winter in an igloo, my life felt movie-star luxurious. Besides, I had candles and batteries for a couple of flashlights.

If I had come across a cell phone that still had a charge, I would have called the hospital to make sure that Cameron really had gotten better. I wanted him to awake from his coma. I would have called Camille to see if she and Dawn were okay. But I never found a phone with a charge.

I figured for sure that people were looking for me, but I doubted they'd ever look here.

Besides: the world still had much bigger problems than me. No one was going to look very hard.

....

I got used to a world without music.

....

I got used to a world with dead animals and wild animals and sick animals. I would see a lot of the dead and the wild and the sick as I biked around the Exclusion Zone.

. . . .

I was drawn to my parents' bedroom. Sometimes, I would just stare at the bed, which was still unmade because my mom had rushed out to the plant, and at their nightstands. I made a decision to respect their privacy and vowed I would never, ever go through their closets or drawers. My mom and dad were light-years from perfect, but I believed they had never, ever read my journals.

Still, I spent a lot of time in their room. I curled up on their bed and inhaled the traces of them that remained on their pillowcases and sheets.

. . . .

It wasn't until the day I decided to bike out to Newport and Cape Abenaki that I discovered I was not, in fact, alone. Far from it.

The hill down into Newport had tons of mud on the road, a result of the runoff from thawing snow and the ferocious, icy-cold rains that mark the end of winter in northern Vermont. In the dried mud, I saw more tire tracks—and, clearly, fresh ones—as I sped down the slope. The main street through the center of town had even more tracks, and here I could see they were going in both directions.

When I got to the shore of Lake Memphremagog, it dawned on me what was going on. And right on cue, I heard a third helicopter roaring up from the south and then hovering in the distance. It was just beyond the peninsula, and so while I couldn't see what was beneath it, I knew as well as anyone in the world that below it were the remains of Cape Abenaki. It might take years and it might take decades . . . but they were actually trying to clean up the mess.

Chapter 21

I found a place where I could wait and watch the trucks coming and going without being seen: one of the twin towers of the St. Mary's Star of the Sea Church. It was on a hill overlooking the lake and the city, perfectly situated if I wanted to lurk. (Just so you know, I did not break into the church. I have limits. When everyone had raced away from the meltdown, someone had left one of the side doors unlocked. I was able to walk right in.) The towers allowed me a 360-degree view. I could look out at the peninsula, behind which sat whatever was left of the plant, and I could look down at the city itself and the roads that veered north to Cape Abenaki. Some of the trucks were from the National Guard, but others were from FEMA and the NRC. I could see through the vehicle windows that everyone inside was always wearing hazmat suits, which would have made me uneasy about the radiation around me if I wasn't pretty sure I had already done myself in.

I still had not seen the plant itself because it was shielded by the trees on the peninsula, but every so often I would bike a little bit closer before turning around. And it was clear that soon there were going to be a lot fewer trees: workers were clearing the woods to the south to make room for massive silver and gray storage tanks. And I mean massive; this is not teen-speak hyperbole. They were the size of gymnasiums. At first I couldn't figure out what they were for, but then that part of me that's a nuclear engineer's daughter kicked in and I got it: all that radioactive wastewater had to go somewhere, and those tanks were the destination. It looked like they were making room for hundreds of them.

And always I would call for Maggie when there were no trucks nearby. I had given up hope, but I was seriously into that "magical thinking" routine once again. So long as I kept looking for Maggie, I convinced myself, she might still be alive.

. . . .

I never did break into the supermarket in Newport. There seemed to be too many trucks coming and going through the small city, and I was afraid of being cornered inside there. One time I considered going at night, but for some reason I was afraid. I have no idea why. By now I knew there were no nuclear mutants or AMC zombies walking around. Just wild dogs and turkeys and deer.

. . . .

It was warm now, and maybe that's why my mind went "bear" when I heard the noise outside the sliding glass doors. The bears had come out of hibernation. I was eating a late dinner by candle-light on the floor—the Barbours' vegetable soup and a couple of Luna bars I had found at the Furneys'—when I heard the animal outside. I guessed the flickering candlelight had attracted it, but I didn't know enough about animals to know if that really made any sense. It didn't matter, however, because a second later I heard the animal bark and I nearly tipped over the candles and set the house on fire when I leapt to my feet, because I knew instantly it was Maggie.

I threw open the glass door and what was left of the screen door, and there she was. She jumped at me, her paws almost on my shoulders, and she started licking my face and I was weeping and I think she was, too—at least as much as a dog can weep. But if she was crying, it was, like me, with joy. She was freaky thin and she had nasty sores on her legs and her coat was a disaster: matted and filled with twigs and burrs. But she was alive and a thousand times healthier than I would have guessed. I got her a bottle of water and opened two cans of dog food, and she slept on the window seat in my bedroom that night like nothing in the world had changed.

. . . .

For the next four days, I didn't leave the yard. Maggie didn't either. I didn't want her out of my sight, and I don't think she wanted me tooling around on Skylar's bike. Besides, I didn't need to look for her anymore. Here she was. I brushed out her coat little by little, sponging away the smell of stale swamp, and watched her eat and eat . . . and eat. I figured in a few days I would have to break into the Woodsons' house and steal some of their dog food. But I wasn't worried. Just as there were plenty of cans of creamed corn and vegetable soup in the Exclusion Zone for me, there was probably a lifetime supply of canned dog food for my Maggie. When I would smooth some Bacitracin onto her legs, I would rub some into my thighs, and it seemed as if we both were getting better.

I felt a bit like I had when I had gotten that job at the diner back in Burlington: the future had a little promise. Perhaps I was finally leaving behind the absolute suckage that my life had become.

. . . .

It was a weekday when I finally biked so far that I could see the plant beyond the wastewater storage tanks they were building. Before Maggie had returned I had been inching a little closer on each journey.

I think there were a couple of reasons why I wanted to see it, but the big one was that it was where my mom and dad had died. Where I assumed their bodies still were. It was like visiting their graves. (In a disturbing sort of way, "grave" is the right word. The remains of the Chernobyl reactor are encased in a massive concrete sarcophagus. The Fukushima ruins are, too. So, I figured a part of the cleanup in the Kingdom involved building a sarcophagus atop Reactor One.) A therapist here thinks it may also have had something to do with Cameron: I had tried to be his parent and fallen short, and these visits were about "identification." I was bonding with my mom and dad. Maybe. But mostly I just wanted to say good-bye.

I had to close the sliding glass door at my house when I left because it seemed like otherwise Maggie was going to follow me. But I wanted the house and our yard to be her whole universe from now on, and I think she preferred it that way, too. She only wanted to come with me because she loved me and didn't want to be alone. I couldn't say I blamed her. But I figured nothing would happen to me and she'd be fine here alone.

Obviously, I was wrong. Something, I guess, was bound to happen.

. . . .

I saw the carcass of a massive rubber berm that was supposed to protect Cape Abenaki from the flood. It was in a field between the river and the remains of Reactor One. It looked a little like a giant snake. Around it were hundreds—maybe thousands—of sandbags.

Like everything else, they were radioactive.

. . . .

I guess on some level I understood that the closer I got to the plant, the worse the radiation was going to be. Even a mile away, the folks who were cementing the lake bed wherever Memphremagog met the northern swamps and streams were decked out like astronauts. Their outfits and masks made the hazmat suits I'd seen look like bikinis and swim goggles. I have no idea how they could move. In addition to their masks, they were wearing yellow hard-hats. And while I only watched the concrete mixers and the chutes and the cranes for an hour, I saw a shift change. Maybe that was a coincidence, and maybe they were only allowed to work there for forty-five minutes or an hour at a time. I still don't know.

. . . .

The "containment vehicle"—I've always loved that term—for Reactor One also housed a spent-fuel pool. Delightful. Even from a distance I could see that the roof was demolished. A whole wall was gone, blown away, and in the charred sides I could see rows and rows of rebar spikes. I saw a grid of metal stanchions and scaffolding that looked like it had started to melt—and, in some cases, really had melted. There were three large cranes around the reactor, and I watched a pair of helicopters come and hover above it, and then fly away. While I was there, one of the choppers started to lower something through what I guessed was a hole in the roof, and as it descended I understood what it was: a robot. They were actually lowering robots into whatever was left of the reactor. Something had to clean up all those uranium pellets that had melted down, and it sure as hell wasn't going to be a human something.

I had pulled my bike off to the side of the road, but I was only on the edge of the grass. My bike—well, Skylar's bike—was between my legs. I was at the entrance to the farthest corner of the employee parking lot. I had expected there would still be all the Subarus and pickups and Volvos of the people who once worked at the plant, but all the cars had been towed away or driven off and now were rotting wherever the country housed its radioactive fleet. Instead I saw only a few NRC trucks and a couple of long FEMA trailers. The asphalt had buckled here and there, a combination of frost heaves that no one had bothered to smooth out and the weight from the massive trucks that must have been coming and going since the meltdown.

For a while I gazed at where the offices and the control room had been. Once there had been a building there. It was on the side where the wall of the containment vessel had blown apart. Now it was a gigantic concrete block. That's where my parents had been when they'd died. I rolled around in my mind the idea that if the government had made the effort to get rid of all those cars, they had probably found a way to remove the dead bodies. Maybe the dead were somewhere in the midst of that concrete, but I wasn't sure. I realized now that the dead might have been buried—my parents, of course, among them. And that left me vacillating between emptiness and relief: emptiness because I had wanted to say good-bye and was being denied even that, and relief that their bodies (or whatever was left of their bodies) might have been treated with respect and laid to rest . . . somewhere.

Behind me I heard another of those trucks rumbling down the road, and so I swung my leg over the top tube of the bike so I could carry it with me into the brush about twenty yards away. Instead, however, I tripped. It was one of those completely ridiculous tumbles that just happen, especially if you're not all that practiced at hoisting a bicycle off the ground and trying to hide in the nearby bushes and weeds. So I stood up and started lifting the bike off the grass, but already it was too late. There was this FEMA truck rolling into the lot. The driver jammed on the brakes the moment he saw me.

My instinct was to just run like a madwoman into the brush. I figured that even in bike shoes with clips on the soles I could outrun a couple of middle-aged dudes in hazmat suits and little plastic booties on their feet. But I wanted that bike, and I figured that I could race past them before they could turn their truck around and motor after me.

So I took the bike and ran with it onto the asphalt and clipped in. They were yelling at me to stop, and even though their voices were muffled beneath their masks I got the 411 on what they were screaming. There were two of them and they tried to position themselves between me and the access road to the parking lot, but I was just a hair quicker than they were. They tried to herd me toward each other, like I was a loose kitten or something. One of them almost made a grab for me—looking back, I think he might have if he wasn't worried about ripping his suit if he fell—but he didn't, and I was able to scoot between the two of them. If you didn't know that the whole little world we were in was scarily toxic and nineteen people had died and thousands and thousands more had lost their homes and I was a fucking orphan and cutter, it would have been comic.

Or not.

I don't know. I really don't. As you have no doubt figured out by now, judgment—and what we call *good* judgment—is not topmost in my skill set.

Anyway, I got away. I rode like I was sprinting in the Tour de France, pedaling as fast as I ever had. When I got home, I was exhausted. This was way beyond winded. This was way beyond tired. When I finally collapsed in the den, I discovered that I felt, pure and simple, shitty. I was nauseous and—and I hate to share this detail with you, but I promised I would always tell the truth— I had diarrhea. I was pretty sure I knew the problem: I'd finally gone and pulled an Icarus. I'd flown *way* too close to the sun. The parking lot of the plant? A very bad idea. Seriously radioactive. I told myself that maybe it was just a virus, but I didn't really believe that.

Moreover, it crossed my mind that I had outed myself and the jig might be up. People had spotted me—and no good could come from that. I knew what people thought of my family. And, of course, I knew what I had done. I knew *all* the things that I had done. I thought of my little buddy I had deserted back in Burlington—a boy who, for all I knew, might have died because I'd lacked the common sense to bring him to a doctor. I think I would have been in no-holds-barred panic mode if I had felt even a little bit better.

That evening I curled up with Maggie on the living room rug after dinner and watched a candle burn down in a hurricane lamp that in the old days we'd kept outside on the porch for summer nights. I tried to think through carefully what had occurred. I tried to decide how long it would take for someone to figure out that the girl they had seen on the bike was the missing daughter of a dead Cape Abenaki engineer. Probably not very. Not all the world was filled with morons.

And when someone did make that leap—which really wasn't all that great—then they would come look for me here at my house. It was kind of natural, right?

So, I was seriously pissed at myself. I didn't want to leave my home. This was where I planned to live out my life and, I presumed, die of radiation sickness or cancer. I didn't know if that was five months or five years in the distance. (And, given how I felt that night, I thought it might even be five days.) It's weird, but the greatest desire I had was to outlive Maggie. That's all I wanted that moment. I never again wanted my Maggie to have to fend for herself in the wild.

I would have left that night—*I should have left that night*—but I was just too fucking sick. So I decided that the two of us would leave the next day. Hopefully I hadn't fatally nuked myself and I'd feel better. I wasn't sure where Maggie and I would go, but the hazmat police—or whatever—weren't about to search the whole Exclusion Zone. Who had time for that? And there was nothing but empty houses. I could take my pick of meadow mansions and Victorians and farmhouses and Georgians and colonials. I could live in trailers and double-wides and the grocery store if I wanted. I could go to my home away from home as a kid—Lisa Curran's family's place. Lisa's bedroom would even be packed with clothes I could wear. So, that was in fact what I decided: I'd take my journals and Skylar's bike, and in the morning Maggie and I would leave for the Currans' old place.

But, like a lot of my plans, it didn't quite work out that way. They came for me in the night.

. . . .

There could have been a big chase scene.

It could have been like *E.T.*, with people in hazmat suits pursuing me on my bike, my Maggie running along beside me.

But there was no full moon.

And, in the end, there was no race through the woods.

There was only my shock when I realized that Maggie and I were trapped on the second floor of my house. I had just thrown up into a wastebasket by my bed—I knew not to use the toilet since I couldn't flush it—so I was already awake. I heard the sound of the van and went to the window that faced the driveway and the street. Already they were at the front door. Already I saw someone else stomping like a moonwalker around the side of the house, past those spooky tomato cages, to the back. Maybe we still could have run, but I didn't want that for my Maggie. Maybe I didn't want that for me anymore. I was sick now—whatever it was (and, as I said, I was pretty sure it was radiation) had come on fast—and so maybe I was just done. I'm not even sure I was capable of running. Or, for that matter, biking.

But I also wasn't prepared to face whatever was next. It had been months, but some things, such as the words people said to me in the hours after the meltdown, you never forget:

We've lost our house! Because of your fucking father, we've lost our house! What have you done?

They had a daughter. You watch, they'll make her testify or something. Talk about what an alcoholic her dad was. Make it clear this was all the fault of one idiot drunk.

Young lady, we're going to need to talk to you. You're going to have to come with me right now.

And yet while it looked like there was just nothing I could do—it was over, stick a fork in me—I also knew that someone like Missy would not have gone quietly. In my head I saw her once more racing her Miata in the dark around the swing sets and the gazebo. I saw Cameron throwing his duct tape and pajamas into a garbage bag, his eye black and blue, and leaving the Rougers. And, yes, I saw my mom and dad and the other engineers in the control room at the plant, trying to do what they could to stop a nuclear reactor from exploding. Say what you will about my dad and what he did or didn't do, he fought till the bitter—loud and violent and deadly and bitter—end.

I was shivering, but I didn't know whether it was because I was cornered or sick. I tried to think about where in the house we might hide, places that were big enough for both Maggie and me. I thought of the closets. I thought of the dryer. I thought of the boxes in the attic.

But eventually the hazmat police would go there. The evidence that I was living here was everywhere. It wasn't just my bike. It was everything. It might take them ten minutes and it might take them an hour. But this was a contemporary meadow mansion; there were no secret passageways and walls that spun like revolving doors. There was no back stairway. They would find me. I had run and I had fought as long as I could, but this was it: this was, I realized, my own bitter end. I wrapped my arms around Maggie's neck and allowed myself, one last time, to cry.

. . . .

I got a flashlight, but I didn't turn it on, and I went to the top of the stairs and waited. Maggie, a little curious, stood beside me. Then we both sat down.

They didn't ring the doorbell; they just came in. There were three of them, one entering through the sliding glass doors in the back and two through the front.

I turned on the flashlight so they would know where I was and held my breath like a shadow. Maggie and I were but landscape.

Or, I guess, Landscape.

Then the room was bathed in so much light that I had to squint. Their flashlights were like high beams on a car.

One of the dudes who had come in through the front spoke

to me first. "We don't want to hurt you," he called up to me. His microphone made him sound like a robotic character from an Xbox game.

"Way to ring the doorbell," I said. "Way to knock."

"We're not here to harm you," he reassured me, like I was really such a pinhead that I might have thought that's why they were here.

So I said, "I know." I would have rolled my eyes, but he wouldn't have noticed.

"You need to come with us. We have a suit for you in the truck."

"No, thank you," I said. "I'm fine."

"Little girl—"

"I am so far from being a little girl."

He nodded. "Please come with us."

"Maggie comes with me."

"We thought you were alone. Who's Maggie?"

"This is Maggie," I answered, and I leaned over and scratched her neck where she liked it.

His body language screamed exasperation. Even though I couldn't see his face, I knew he was annoyed. I knew the three of them were irritated as hell. "Your dog?"

"My dog."

"It's Emily, right?"

"Yes."

"The dog is—"

"The dog has a name. I just told you. Her name is Maggie."

"Fine. Maggie can come."

"I want to bring a few things."

"No. Everything here is tainted."

Tainted. I loved it. That was a word I would have expected Emily Dickinson to use, not this guy. He should have used "con-taminated" or "radioactive." I have no idea why he didn't.

"Yes," I said simply.

"Look: your clothes and—"

"My journals. I want to bring my journals and my notebooks. I don't care about my clothes."

He looked at the two other members of his—and please hear the sarcasm in my voice—*rescue party* and one of them seemed to shrug. It suddenly dawned on me that there might be a woman inside there.

"Where are they? We'll get them. You shouldn't be handling them."

I laughed. "Yeah. Right. I'll carry them."

"Does your dog need a leash?"

"No."

"Do you have one?"

"A leash? Somewhere."

So it really wasn't much of a standoff. They let me bring my journals and my dog. That was all I wanted.

. . . .

It was indeed a woman in that suit, and her name was Jeannine. She helped pack me into a hazmat suit of my very own, although mine did not have a mic. Also, it's worth sharing that they didn't dress me in hazmat chic to protect me. I was already burnt toast. They put me into that hazmat suit to protect themselves and their precious van. I have a feeling that if they had bothered to turn their Geiger counters on me, they would have gone off like popcorn kernels in a microwave oven.

At one point I felt a little carsick and so I made sure I knew how to rip my mask and hood off if I thought I was going to vomit again, but it never got that bad. It seemed to me that this was all very barn-door-after-the-horses-have-left, and when I thought of that expression, I was reminded of the protest back in January and explaining what the phrase meant to Cameron. I really didn't care that my suit didn't have a mic, because I didn't want to talk to them anymore. Maggie sat in the backseat with Jeannine and me, more or less content on the floor between us. She had always been a pretty chill dog; she never minded the car. She let them drape a hazmat suit over her like it was a blanket because, like me, she was scarily contaminated.

They told me they were going to take me to a place where I could be scrubbed clean. If I had felt like speaking, I would have made one of my dad's sardonic references to Silkwood showers. I knew what was coming. After that they said they were bringing me to a hospital. If I'd had the emotional energy to open my mouth or give a damn, I would have joked, "Mental or regular?" I figured in my case either would have made sense. But I just sat there. I gazed out the window on my side of the van and I watched the night world go by. "The carriage held but just ourselves . . . ," I thought, and I hummed it in my head to the tune of *Gilligan's Island*. We passed through my neighborhood for the last time and we passed my old school for the last time. We passed the field of dead cows and we passed the gun shop. Then we passed through the checkpoint and the Exclusion Zone was behind us. Behind me. Inside my mask I silently said good-bye.

EPILOGUE

They tell me I will get better. They tell me I am, in fact, getting better. They believe my hair will grow back. We'll see. It seems to be coming back only in patches—in islands and clumps. Even if they hadn't shaved me—all of me, eyebrows and legs and pubes—I gather a lot of it would have fallen out anyway. Gross. One more loss among the many.

For instance, I know I'll never see my phone with Andrea's texts again or get to wear her Christmas sweater. And even if someday I do get around to repiercing my ears, the earrings Camille gave me are gone. They were all taken away from me or I left them behind, which, I guess, is fine. What the hell. I guess they had to take them away; I guess they weren't really worth going back for.

The damnedest thing was the way everyone went ballistic over my cutting. As if that was my biggest problem. Please. I—to use one of their favorite words—used to "manifest" and "act out" in ways that were lights-out crazy compared to a little cutting. I mean, my therapists know about Poacher and the Oxies and my igloo, but I don't bore the dermatologists and gastroenterologists with those little details. I didn't sit down with the oncologists— who mostly just wanted to run tests on me so they have baselines to look at when the inevitable happens someday—and say, "Yes, the food here is kind of a fiasco and I'm not wild about the plastic utensils they want me to use. But it sure beats doing a trucker at a gas station so you can score a crap egg salad sandwich and pay an Iraqi war vet so he'll let you crash on his mattress."

They say I did most of this to myself that day I finally rode all the way out to the plant. I would have gotten sick eventually even if I hadn't, but there were still whole clouds of radioactive dust floating around the parking lot. And—oh, by the way—there was a hot spot pretty close to where I had been standing with my bike. They had bulldozed all kinds of crap under the dirt along that side of the parking lot. My mind started to spin when they were talking about rems and BEIR. (FYI, BEIR is an antonym of beer. We're not talking homonym. Beer is mostly good, unless you're watching your weight. BEIR just sucks. It stands for the biological effects of ionizing radiation. It seems I got walloped by a boatload of rems, which was why we were even having this conversation about BEIR.)

I still don't spend much time on the web these days. I spend a little, but I'm careful. Besides, I don't have the energy. I know if I spent too much time online, I would look up all of the things that I am afraid would set me back emotionally. I would look up my parents and read more about what people had said about them. I would investigate which cancers are most likely to kill me and when the hot particles will lead to hard tumors. ("The bone that has no marrow," Emily Dickinson once wrote, "What ultimate for that?" In my case? Maybe someday leukemia.) I would discover the news stories about me, as well as the ones about me and Cameron that implied I was a complete Looney Tune. And I am not a complete Looney Tune. I am only a quasi–Looney Tune.

And all of that would just depress me. Correction: all of that would just depress me even more.

So, I guess I didn't last very long as the Belle of Reddington. But I have logged some pretty serious time here as the Belle of Ward Six. (No, that's not a cheeky reference to Chekhov. My wing really is called Ward Six by the nurses. Officially it's named for some benefactor, but her name is unpronounceable and very many syllables. So everyone just calls it Ward Six.) And here I get to wear all the white I could ever want, which is only a drag when my nose does that thing where it bleeds like a fire hose or I have one of my coughing jags. Don't ask about what those are like and what comes up. I get squeamish just thinking about it, and I'm a girl who has thighs that look like someone (well, me) got medieval on them. Lines of long puffy scar tissue, some a little pink, some an eggshell white.

In a few days, they said, they would take me out for an airing, if I want. They've offered to show Maggie and me where my parents are buried. You might not think that would be the first place I would want to go, but it kind of is. If I went anywhere, I'd go there. Their bodies are in lead-lined coffins in a special cemetery where all the victims from the disaster have been laid to rest. It's not open to the public.

Maggie is living with the Currans because she can't live here, but they have played fast and loose with the rules and categorized her as a "service dog" so she is allowed inside the hospital. They've done this to be nice. They also shaved her, too. Not kidding. Like me, her hair seems only to be growing back in spots. It looks like doggie hair plugs. We're quite a pair.

Apparently, not everyone hates me just because my last name is Shepard. And while they've asked me lots of questions about my dad, I'm never going to have to testify about anything or get hammered by reporters. They've promised. It seems a lot of people just want to give me some space.

So, Lisa and Lisa's mom bring my Maggie to me almost every day. I know she's well cared for and has a good home. The plan is that I'm also going to live with the Currans when everyone decides I'm not a total basket case. We'll see. Lisa's mom had been looking for me most of those nine months I was hiding, posting things online that I would have seen that day in the Burlington library if I'd spent maybe another five minutes surfing around Facebook or the sites where my name appeared.

These days, I still steer clear of what they call the social networks. It's not that I'm antisocial. I'm just not ready for a reunion—even a digital one. I'm not ready for most of my friends, and I'm not sure they're ready for me. Lisa answers my questions when I ask about Ethan or Dina or Claire. She doesn't tell me much about the other Cape Abenaki families, and I don't inquire. As I suspected, a lot of them have moved far away. Of course, none of the ones who've remained have tried to visit. It's all just too awkward. And they have their own problems, right?

I have not seen Cameron either. They don't put it quite this way, but the implication is that they don't want me to see him. They don't think it would be good for him, and I can tell they're a little afraid I would try and kidnap him or something. Yeah, like that's going to happen. Some days I can barely get out of bed. But he's alive. He's alive and he's healthy. I didn't accidentally kill him. They say that—finally—he is with a seriously awesome foster family, but they won't tell me anything more.

Most days I eat a little and I write a little and I read a little. I watch DVDs of old sitcoms. No TV. No Hulu. No iTunes. My choice. That's too close to what's out there.

And I sleep—I sleep a lot—which I'm going to do right now, thank you very much. They don't know that I stole a steel cutting knife from the kitchen. I don't completely trust myself, but knowing it's there helps. It helps a lot.

So, good night. I'm sorry.

Please know that: I am really, really sorry. I wish I could have stopped even one heart from breaking . . .

But I couldn't. I just couldn't.

Acknowledgments

I want to begin by thanking three people whose work is dramatically more important than anything I do.

First, there is Annie Ramniceanu, associate executive director of Spectrum Youth and Family Services in Burlington, Vermont (www.spectrumvt.org). Annie is not merely an immensely gifted therapist and counselor with Spectrum, working daily with teens battling mental illness and substance abuse; she is also unbelievably patient with novelists asking relentless streams of questions. For half a year she endured my interruptions and helped me to understand the demons that mark Emily Shepard. Her efforts on behalf of young adults in northern Vermont are inspiring.

Second, there is the leadership team at Fairewinds Energy Education, Arnie and Maggie Gundersen. Arnie was an Atomic Energy Commission Fellow and a licensed reactor operator who, as a senior vice president, managed or coordinated projects at seventy nuclear power plants across America. Maggie worked in public information and executive recruitment in the nuclear power industry. Today, through Fairewinds, they strive to educate the public and legislators about the realities of nuclear power—and the issues with aging plants around the world. They volunteered enormous amounts of their time to teach me about the dangers of nuclear power, how a plant works, and what Emily's father's life might have been like. I encourage you to visit the Fairewinds website (www.fairewinds.org), where you can learn more about nuclear power and find an extensive bibliography.

I'm so proud to call these three people—Annie and Arnie and Maggie—friends.

In addition, I want to thank Mimi Dakin, archives specialist at Amherst College—where many of Emily Dickinson's papers are housed—who read an early draft of this novel and graciously shared with me her expertise and insights into the poet. Thanks also to Dr. Mike Kiernan, an emergency room physician at Porter Medical Center in Middlebury, Vermont, for helping me with the scenes at the hospitals in this novel. I also want to send big shout-outs to Rebecca Schinsky for showing me where the work of Emily Dickinson and the theme from *Gilligan's Island* intersect, and to Matthew Furtsch for teaching me about duct tape art. As wiser people than I have observed, you just can't make this stuff up.

There were many books that were helpful. Among them? *Chernobyl's Atomic Legacy: 25 Years After Disaster*, by Jon Glez; *The Day We Bombed Utah: America's Most Lethal Secret*, by John G. Fuller; *Nuclear Power: A Very Short Introduction*, by Maxwell Irvine; *Full Body Burden: Growing Up in the Shadow of Rocky Flats*, by Kristen Iversen; and *Public Meltdown: The Story of the Vermont Yankee Nuclear Power Plant*, by Richard A. Watts. I also want to express my admiration for the remarkable Karen Hesse. Her poignant, powerful, and beautiful novel for young adults, *Phoenix Rising*, chronicles the effects of a fictional nuclear plant accident in southern Vermont. It was published in 1994—a full generation before *Close Your Eyes, Hold Hands*.

My thanks as well to Jane Gelfman and her staff at Gelfman Schneider—Cathy Gleason and Victoria Marini; to Arlynn Greenbaum at Authors Unlimited; and to William Heyward, Todd Doughty, John Fontana, Kelly Gildea, Suzanne Herz, William Heus, Judy Jacoby, Jennifer Marshall, Sonny Mehta, Beth Meister, Anne Messitte, Roz Parr, Russell Perreault, John Pitts, Andrea Robinson, Bill Thomas, and the whole wondrous team at the Knopf Doubleday Publishing Group.

And, once more, I am grateful first and foremost to my extraordinary editor there, Jenny Jackson. I love talking with Jenny about books and (yes) about my books, because, pure and simple, her ideas always make them better. Often they make them a lot better.

I am so fortunate to be married to Victoria Blewer. This is the nineteenth book of mine—seventeen published, two unpublished—that she has read. Usually she is reading the early drafts that no one should have to endure. And, it's worth noting, she reads them for free. That's love.

Finally, I want to express my gratitude to Grace Experience Blewer, Victoria's and my daughter. Grace was nineteen when I was writing this novel, and she was instrumental in the creation of Emily's voice. She was always there to answer my questions about tone, and she taught me a lot—and I mean a lot—of new expressions.

I thank you all so, so much.

BEFORE YOU KNOW KINDNESS

On a balmy July night in New Hampshire, a shot rings out in a garden, and a man falls to the ground, terribly wounded. The wounded man is Spencer McCullough, the shot that hit him was fired—accidentally?—by his adolescent daughter Charlotte. With this shattering moment of violence, Chris Bohjalian launches the best kind of literate page-turner: suspenseful, wryly funny, and humane.

Fiction/Literature

THE BUFFALO SOLDIER

Two years after their twin daughters die in a flash flood, Terry and Laura Sheldon take in a foster child. His name is Alfred; he is ten years old and African American. And he has passed through so many indifferent families that he can't believe his new one will last. In the ensuing months, Terry and Laura will struggle to emerge from their shell of grief only to face an unexpected threat to their marriage. Meanwhile, Alfred cautiously enters the family circle, and befriends an elderly neighbor who inspires him with the story of the buffalo soldiers, the black cavalrymen of the old West. Out of the entwining and enfolding of their lives, *The Buffalo Soldier* creates a suspenseful, moving portrait of a family, infused by Bohjalian's moral complexity and narrative assurance.

Fiction/Literature

THE DOUBLE BIND

When Laurel Estabrook is attacked while riding her bicycle through Vermont's back roads, her life is forever changed. Formerly outgoing, Laurel withdraws into her photography, spending all her free time at a homeless shelter. There she meets Bobbie Crocker, a man with a history of mental illness and a box of photographs that he won't let anyone see. When Bobbie dies, Laurel discovers a deeply hidden secret—a story that leads her far from her old life, and into a cat-and-mouse game with pursuers who claim they want to save her.

Fiction/Literature

THE LAW OF SIMILARS

When one of Carissa Lake's patients falls into an allergy-induced coma, possibly due to her remedy, Leland Fowler's office starts investigating the case. But Leland is also one of Carissa's patients, and he is beginning to realize that he has fallen in love with her. As love and legal obligations collide, Leland comes face-to-face with an ethical dilemma of enormous proportions. Graceful, intelligent, and suspenseful, *The Law of Similars* is a powerful examination of the links between hubris and hope, deception and love.

Fiction/Literature

MIDWIVES

The time is 1981, and Sibyl Danforth has been a dedicated midwife in the rural community of Reddington, Vermont, for fifteen years. But one treacherous winter night, in a house isolated by icy roads and failed telephone lines, Sibyl takes desperate measures to save a baby's life. She performs an emergency Caesarean section on its mother, who appears to have died in labor. But what if—as Sibyl's assistant later charges—the patient wasn't already dead, and it was Sibyl who inadvertently killed her? As recounted by Sibyl's precocious fourteen-year-old daughter, Connie, the ensuing trial bears the earmarks of a witch hunt except for the fact that all its participants are acting from the highest motives—and the defendant increasingly appears to be guilty. As Sibyl faces the antagonism of the law, the hostility of traditional doctors, and the accusations of her own conscience, *Midwives* engages, moves, and transfixes us as only the very best novels ever do.

Fiction/Literature

ALSO AVAILABLE
The Light in the Ruins
Trans-Sister Radio
The Sandcastle Girls

VINTAGE CONTEMPORARIES
Available wherever books are sold.
www.vintagebooks.com